PRAISE FOR *THE DARK TIDE*

★ "A dark, scenic adventure, sensitively written for romantics, Jasinska's debut novel is a fantasy of promises, betrayal, unrequited love, and black magic."

—School Library Journal, Starred Review

★ "*The Dark Tide* demands to be read in one held breath as its tide bears down on all."

—Foreword Reviews, Starred Review

"Jasinska's debut fantasy, a dark fairy tale reminiscent of 'Tam Lin,' but delightfully queer, is thrillingly romantic while exploring the intersections between love, sacrifice, and duty."

—Booklist

"Fans of the enemies-to-lovers trope will be ecstatic with this book... *The Dark Tide* offers an exciting and immersive story with a strong feminist slant that subverts common YA tropes and forges its own original path."

—The Nerd Daily

"Readers will have a hard time putting this one down and, sacrifice or no sacrifice, will wish they could be part of Caldella's festivities and magic."

—Bulletin of the Center for Children's Books

Also by Alicia Jasinska

The Dark Tide

THE MIDNIGHT GIRLS

ALICIA JASINSKA

sourcebooks
fire

Published by Sourcebooks Fire, an imprint of Sourcebooks
P.O. Box 4410, Naperville, Illinois 60567-4410
(630) 961-3900
sourcebooks.com

Library of Congress Cataloging-in-Publication data is on file with the publisher.

Printed and bound in the United States of America.
VP 10 9 8 7 6 5 4 3 2

For Eugeniusz and Mieczysława

Pronunciation Guide

Beata—beh-AH-tah

Jaga—YAH-gah

Józef—YOO-zef

Kajetan—KAI-tahn

Karnawał—kar-NAH-vow

Lechija—leh-HEE-yah

Marynka—mah-RIN-kah

Rusja—RUS-yah

Warszów—VARSH-oof

Zosia—ZOH-shah

The first is my Bright Morning,
the second my Red Sun.
Lastly rides my dearest,
my darkest, Black Midnight.

1.

MARYNKA

THE FIRST TIME THE WITCH asked Marynka to bring her a heart, she was twelve years old.

It was summer. The sun was bright, and whirlwinds were dancing through the kingdom's sea of golden crops. The heat was fierce. Marynka was sweating even before she crash-landed in the wheat field because she hadn't quite mastered the trick yet of changing form and traveling as the wind blows.

The sound of it startled awake a peasant boy who'd fallen asleep amid the grain. He leapt to his feet, face red from sun and shock and even a little fear. "What—" Sweat darkened the blond hair at his temples. He let out a strangled laugh. "Where did you come from? I thought you were a noon wraith. A sun demon, haunting the fields at midday, come to harvest my heart with your iron scythe and iron teeth."

"Maybe I am," Marynka said, struggling to yank a wheat stalk out of the wild tangle of her red-brown hair.

The boy shook his head, fear fading fast as he took her in. His piercing blue eyes lingered on the small scythe she held, her fraying skirt and dusty apron, and finally, the freckles that dotted a band across her nose. "You're just a girl," he said, but with interest now. "Who are you? I've never seen you before."

"I'm visiting," Marynka said. "My family's from Lipówka. The big village with the church." Her gaze drifted over the gilded ears of saffron wheat. "I wanted to see the prince. Is he here?"

Now the boy frowned. "Why would the prince be working in the fields?"

Marynka chewed her lip. "They're his fields, aren't they? Do you know where the castle is?"

The boy scratched his jaw, giving her another curious look. "You didn't see it when you got here? It's hard to miss. But I can walk you there. I'm headed back home for dinner now."

Relief flooded through Marynka, and she quickly fell into step beside him, matching his long strides with two of her own.

"Maciek," he introduced himself, grinning suddenly. "You know there was another girl who wanted to see the prince yesterday. Only it was near sundown then. The bells were ringing for evening prayers. It must be fate meeting both of you. Are you staying long? Do you want to come for dinner? My mother's the best cook."

Marynka shook her head, barely listening as he prattled on. She needed to focus. She couldn't mess this up. This was the first time the witch had given her a task to complete by herself, and she wanted desperately to impress the old woman. Because if she couldn't...

It was simple. Everyone knew if you served Red Jaga well, she would gift you with magic, and if you didn't, if you failed at the tasks she set, well then, she would eat you.

The sun-bleached bones of the girls who had come before Marynka decorated the wooden house in the Midday Forest. There were bone wreaths and skeletal wind chimes, glowing skull lanterns. But that didn't matter. Those other girls were nothing. They had been weak where Marynka was strong. And clever, she reminded herself. She would be the one who survived. Grandmother had saved her, chosen her. She wouldn't let her down.

Hurrying past a little roadside shrine, a cross tied with flowers and pale-blue and white ribbon, Marynka decided she wouldn't tell the witch about her crash landing in the wheat field.

She gripped her scythe, checked the branch she had tucked into her apron tie. Her heart beat faster. She hadn't slept at all last night or eaten anything this morning. Her body hummed with a jittery mix of fear and excitement. Grandmother had shown her how to steal a prince's life; how to blow poppy seed into his eyes and send him to sleep, how to strike his breast with a birch branch three times and open up his chest so she could dig out his heart with her fingers and claws.

Only Marynka had, so far, failed to grow any claws, which was why she had brought the scythe.

"There," Maciek said, scrubbing the sweat from his face with his sleeve and pointing. "Just up ahead. You can see the castle towers through the trees."

They passed a flock of bleating sheep, two cottages with painted window shutters. Somewhere in the distance, someone was shooting in the wood.

Behind her lips, Marynka felt her teeth start to sharpen. The tips of her fingers burned red-hot. She stared at her hands, willing her nails to lengthen.

So intently focused on this was she that she didn't notice the commotion up ahead, the crowd gathering in the dirt road, until she nearly walked into someone's back.

Maciek steadied her.

"What's happening?" Marynka demanded.

Maciek shook his head, frowning. Marynka hopped on her tiptoes, but she was too short to see over anyone's shoulders. Everyone was circled around an old man who was talking very fast and waving his hands. Several people had their own hands pressed to their mouths. A woman was weeping, ignoring a small girl tugging at her skirt.

A boy even shorter and skinnier than Marynka squeezed between the couple blocking her way, popping out in front of her like a cork from a bottle. Maciek immediately grabbed him by the shirt.

"It's the prince!" the boy squeaked in explanation. "He's *dead.*"

"Dead!" Marynka's voice was so loud that more than a few

4

heads turned. But she couldn't help it. The prince was young and healthy. Grandmother hadn't said anything about him being sick.

"What do you mean?" Maciek said.

The smaller boy wriggled out of his grip. He shook a heap of brown hair out of his eyes and favored them both with a grin of gruesome glee. "They're saying a monster got him."

Marynka's grip on her scythe slackened.

"He went to visit a friend yesterday. They were meant to hunt bison, and then the prince would stay the night. But they got word up at the castle that he rode for home in the evening, only he didn't make it back. They've been searching for the past hour. They just found him."

The boy shuffled closer, dropping his voice to a whisper. "Janek said he thought it had to have been a bear at first to have torn the prince into so many pieces. The clearing was red all over with blood. But the wicked thing took his *heart*. Clawed it right out." He grabbed at his own chest to demonstrate. "There was a gaping hole right here."

Maciek crossed himself.

Marynka wasn't breathing. When Maciek nudged her, she jumped and jerked away.

The smaller boy snickered, clearly thinking he'd frightened her with his tale. "You should take your pretty friend home, Maciek. She looks like she's about to faint. And who knows? The monster might still be lurking about."

"Here." Maciek shepherded Marynka away from the crowd.

Marynka let him only because her thoughts were too busy chasing themselves round and round her head. She barely felt her feet moving. What was she supposed to do now? Whose heart would she bring Grandmother? Was there another prince nearby? Lechija had lots of families of princely blood.

But she'd been told to come *here*, to return with the heart of the prince who owned the peasants and fields in the north.

Panic set Marynka's skin alight. Would she be tossed away like the other girls who had been no use to the witch? Would she be eaten? Would Grandmother find herself a new servant? Take back the magic she'd gifted Marynka and…

Wood met her back. Maciek sat her down on a bench set against the side of a cottage in the shade. He crouched in front of her. "Sit here. It's all right. You don't have to be afraid. They'll bring the priest and soldiers to hunt the monster. Try to take a deep breath. Do you want water? I'll go fetch some water."

Marynka's hand lashed out, grabbing his shirtfront, stopping him as he started to straighten up.

It shouldn't have been possible, but Maciek's sunburned face flushed an even deeper red. The tips of his ears were practically glowing. "I know it's frightening," he said softly. "But you shouldn't listen to Staś. He probably made that whole story up."

Marynka could feel his heart pounding through his scrawny chest. A feverish *thump, thump, thump*. She curled her fingers in the fabric of his shirt.

"I promise. It will all be all right."

"Yes," Marynka agreed in a voice equally as soft, reaching into a pocket and bringing out a handful of poppy seed.

Maciek blinked.

Marynka blew the seed into his eyes, and when he slumped unconscious to the ground, she rolled him over quickly and raised her birch branch, beating upon his chest three times.

The magic worked just like it was supposed to, just like she'd been shown. Skin and muscle peeled away, and his rib cage opened with a gruesome crack to reveal a heart richly beating and red.

Grandmother would never know the difference. And now she wouldn't be in trouble and she wouldn't be eaten and she could stay in the forest forever and learn more magic. She only felt a little bad. Her thoughts were already racing ahead.

Marynka pictured the old witch in her embroidered red kerchief waiting, holding out her hands ready to kiss her cheeks and stroke her hair. She could hear her saying, *I knew I was right to have chosen you.*

Congratulating herself on her cleverness, hands sticky red and cradling her prize, Marynka left the village and the unfortunate Maciek behind. She rode the wind again and didn't fall into any fields this time. The journey took hours, but the sun was still shining when she arrived.

It was always shining, here in Red Jaga's forest, where the hour was always midday. On a whim, Marynka picked a handful of crimson poppies, gathering them into a bouquet as an extra gift.

The witch was sadly unimpressed by the offering. She took one look at the flowers and threw them at the stove. One look at Maciek's heart and cuffed Marynka across the cheek.

Blood burst in her mouth. Her vision filled with sparks. Red Jaga's arms were no thicker than broom handles, but she was stronger than she looked, and the blow sent Marynka sprawling to the floor.

She knocked against a wooden chest—the one that always shivered as if something inside of it was trying to climb out. The house was a clutter of strange objects and trinkets, locked chests bulging with holy relics and gold-threaded robes left behind by long-dead princes.

"Only a fool would mistake the heart of a peasant for the heart of a prince. Do you think I am a fool? Do you think I cannot tell the difference? Do you think you can *lie* to me?" Red Jaga's caught Marynka's chin in one hand and jerked her head up to face her. "Oh Marynka, Marynka." The witch's voice softened as she stroked a hand through Marynka's hair.

Heat flared through her at the touch, and she leaned into the rare gesture of affection.

"Do you want me to keep you? If you can't do as I say, you're useless to me. No better than the last girl."

Marynka's gaze skittered over the house's bone-adorned walls.

"It's not my fault," she protested, biting back fear and the tears she knew would only further irritate the old woman. She'd learned early not to let Grandmother see her cry. "The prince was dead. They said his chest was empty, but I knew you'd still need a heart." A witch was only as strong as the number of hearts she'd devoured. "So I—"

"Empty?" Red Jaga's hand stilled against Marynka's temple. Her gold eyes were sharp among the hollows and wrinkles of her sun-browned face. "Did you see who took it?"

"Who—"

"Took his heart," Red Jaga said, impatient. "Did you see another girl? A girl your age? At the castle? In the shadows?"

Marynka shook her head, a panicked tightness building in her chest. "Another girl took his heart for you?"

Red Jaga did not answer at once. She wore a strange expression. "Not for me." The witch released Marynka and moved away, gnarled hands trailing over a sun-bleached skull. "For my eldest sister. She's taken a new servant too. A girl a year or two older than you. She calls her Midnight."

2.

MARYNKA

THE SECOND TIME THE WITCH asked Marynka to bring her a heart, she had just turned thirteen. She was older, wiser—at least she liked to think so—and more than a little obsessed. Almost a full year had passed from the day she'd first lost a heart to Midnight, and the name of the other servant had haunted her ever since.

"Why can't you be more like her?" Grandmother snapped whenever Marynka made a mistake. "You're just not trying. How many more chances do I have to give you? Do I have to find another girl to take your place?"

Marynka bore each scolding in silence. Each punishment only whet her hunger, honed her determination to a point.

It was spring. The world was green. The land rejoicing at the end of a long, harsh winter. Flocks of geese flew over the Midday Forest, and storks returned from warmer countries built their nests alongside cottage chimneys. By the lakesides green-skinned rusałki were busy singing sweetly with the frogs, luring men to watery graves, their voices mixing with the muezzin's call to prayer carrying from the emerald turrets of nearby mosques.

Marynka liked to listen to those songs as she practiced stealing the hearts of the other small creatures lurking in the forest. Every day she was getting better at it, growing stronger. Every day she was becoming a little less human, a little more of a monster. Poppy seed, birch branches, and iron scythes were not her only weapons. She had new magic and she was not afraid to use it.

Grandmother had taught her how to transform herself into a whirlwind, into a fearsome thing, a wraith with eyes like embers and skin that gave off lethal heat. She could summon the sun's fire and drive men to madness with a whisper.

"This time," she promised Beata, digging her fingers into the earth as they lay side by side on their backs in the grass. "This time I'm going to show her. I'm going to beat Midnight to the prize. I'm going to *break* her." She rolled onto her side to better stare at the girl beside her. The girl they called Morning. The third servant of the unholy trio that served the three witches of Lechija. The white to Marynka's red and Midnight's black. Beata served Red Jaga's younger sister and was the closest thing Marynka had to a friend.

"You said that last time," Beata said, sweeping a strand of golden hair behind her ear. "I don't know why you keep trying. She's so much more powerful than us. She doesn't even *talk* to us."

Which was true enough. Midnight only left her dark forest when she was sent out on some new mission specifically designed to make Marynka look bad. She seemed to have been created with the sole purpose of besting Marynka in every possible way. And she seemed to go out of her way to avoid them. Black Jaga visited her sisters, but her servant always stayed behind to guard the house. Marynka didn't even know what she looked like. She'd never seen Midnight's face, though she liked to imagine she was ugly. A pale, ghoulish creature that never saw the sun. A creepy shadow with teeth.

But she'd managed to learn *some* things at least, had committed them to memory, gobbling up the crumbs of gossip the witches let drop when they got together and bragged who had the better servant.

"My Bright Morning has learned to conjure sunlight."

"Ha! My Red Sun can burn a man to ash with a glance."

"Ah, but my Black Midnight can control the shadows now. She can drown a village in endless night. She lured another prince into my forest just the other week."

Even the ordinary people of the kingdom whispered tales of the midnight demon who could summon darkness and cast eternal sleep with a breath.

"She probably thinks she's too good for us," Beata said, lifting a hand to shield her face from the sun. The light fell more softly here in the forest where Beata lived, where it was always morning. The grass was dewy. The trees still half-asleep. The sky was all blushing and dreamy. "She probably doesn't even consider you her competition."

Marynka's nose wrinkled. She ripped a fistful of grass up by the roots. Of course Midnight considered her a rival, as her competition. She *had* to. The thought of the other servant not caring about this as much as she did, as if Marynka weren't worthy of her attention, as if she didn't matter, was simply unbearable. The idea that while Marynka's thoughts were constantly consumed by the other girl, Midnight might not even think of her at all...

"When are you going to give up?" said Beata.

Never.

Marynka ripped up another fistful of grass. "You're so annoying," she informed Beata. She wanted her to be more frustrated. More angry. Beata didn't mind being the weakest servant, which was something Marynka couldn't understand. "If you don't try harder, White Jaga is going to eat you and make your skull into a lantern."

Or maybe she wouldn't. White Jaga was the kindest witch. No bruises ever marred Beata's creamy skin, and from what she'd told Marynka, she didn't get punished when she failed to complete a task, when she didn't return with a heart or forgot to sweep the house or carry a message, when she let dinner burn or a wayward traveler escape the forest, any of the many things Marynka was constantly in trouble for. White Jaga had even given Beata a gift to celebrate her name day: a necklace of glossy amber beads.

She felt a hot stab of envy toward her friend. How had *Beata* ended up with the nice witch? Was it chance or simply luck?

Marynka's own luck had always been fickle. Her life before Grandmother felt like it belonged to a far-off time now, to a fairy tale, and the more of a monster she became, the more she forgot, but some things she remembered.

The only child of a Christian peasant and his Jewish sweetheart, Marynka had been orphaned at an early age. She'd been a restless child. Too loud and too prone to mischief for the aunt and uncle who'd tried to raise her. She couldn't sit still. She didn't listen. She'd picked fights and run off to play in the forest when she was supposed to be doing chores.

It was on a day she'd done just that, whilst racing home with a scrubby handful of poppies that she'd hoped would buy her forgiveness, that she'd rushed out of the trees and run under the hooves of a passing nobleman's horse. She didn't recall much, only the great shadow of the horse and its hooves eclipsing the sun. The vivid red of her own blood and the relief in the man's eyes as he'd looked down, taking in her bare feet, her dirty face, her peasant's clothes. He'd left her there, in the dust, in the middle of the road, and it was there Red Jaga had found her, clinging stubbornly to life.

The witch had saved her. Healed her. Remade her—filling her veins with fire and magic. Heat had devoured Marynka, burning away her past and the girl that she'd once been. She'd awoken in the house in the Midday Forest as something that looked the same on the outside, but on the inside was completely different.

It made her wonder what Midnight's story was, who she'd

been before. Even Beata had yet to share her past, though she likely would have if asked. She was always babbling on about something. It was hard to shut her up. Marynka didn't even have the heart to make her half the time. That was the magic of being Morning. Beata was so unfairly pretty that even Marynka was almost afraid to touch her, let alone cause her hurt. Her violet eyes were bewitching as a spring day's dawn, her hair as gold as linden honey. The sweetest dimples appeared in her fat, rosy cheeks when she smiled. There was the cutest gap between her two front teeth.

"You'll see," Marynka insisted, throwing a handful of grass at Beata's annoyingly pretty face and laughing wickedly when the other girl shrieked and sat up, shaking the green from her braids. "I'll get there first this time. I'll beat Midnight."

And when I do, Grandmother will finally be proud of me.

Her fingertips lit up. Marynka's veins burned red-orange as magic simmered in her blood. Heat hummed beneath her skin, flared through her chest, a sensation that walked the border between pleasure and pain.

"I'll do whatever it takes. This time it will be different. I'm going to grind Midnight's face into ash."

"Can we talk about something else now?" Beata complained, smoothing down her striped apron. "You're always talking about her."

"I don't *always* talk about her."

"She's *all* you ever talk about."

Marynka stuck out her tongue.

"Just so you know. I'm not listening to your whining when you come home empty-handed."

"Yes you will," Marynka said immediately. "No. I mean, you won't have to. Because I won't lose." She rolled to her feet. "You'll see. Just wait."

She set off an hour later in a wild whirl of air and dust, heading for the kingdom's lake district, hunting for a prince named Stanisław.

The wind spun over the land in a whistling column, circling fields and villages and then a castle, until at last it died down to reveal a small girl standing in swirl of crimson skirts.

Marynka tracked her prey to the modest home of a forester where she was, frustratingly, forced to wait. The house was guarded to keep devils and monsters and other wicked creatures like her out. A dead bird had been nailed to the carved lintel over the door, the threshold sprinkled with holy water. The gilded image of a saint sneered disapprovingly at Marynka from behind a window's cloudy pane.

By the time the prince left his friend and started riding down the winding dirt road for home, night was falling unnaturally fast. A darkness dense and cloying shrouded even the moon, snatching the stars from sight.

In moments Marynka was lost within a living, breathing gloom. She could no longer see the path ahead or behind. The night pressed around her horribly, clinging to her like cobweb. She sank her hands into it, felt it slide between her fingers. The dark ate the flames she conjured straight out of her palm, swallowed her panicked curses. It whispered in her ears, planting nightmare visions in her head. And when she finally fought free, free of that mocking black hold, she found the prince...

A crowd had gathered around the crumpled form lying in the middle of the road, around the horse nosing in vain at the man's shoulder. The flames from all their lanterns flickered sadly.

Marynka was so angry she snapped the birch branch she was carrying in two. So angry she didn't hear a voice snap, "Watch out!" and almost crashed into a girl in a black embroidered apron coming the other way.

She sidestepped at the very last second, avoiding a head-on collision. Still seething, she continued walking, steps stomping furiously. She did not look back.

And neither did the girl in the black embroidered apron.

3.

MARYNKA

ANOTHER YEAR PASSED.

And then another, and another. The seasons wore away. Marynka grew intimately familiar with the feeling of her dreams and efforts slipping through her fingers. But she grew stronger still, and taller, though not nearly as tall as she would have liked. She managed to beat Midnight to a heart, and not just once. She acquired a reputation. People spoke of a monster now that liked to hunt princes when the sun was at its highest.

The year she turned seventeen, the kingdom went to war. Troops from neighboring Rusja crossed the border and advanced toward the capital. Lechija's army offered a fierce resistance, but the king chose to surrender. Rumors swirled that he'd been bewitched by Rusja's tsarina, the woman who had given him the crown in the first place. Foreign soldiers were garrisoned in all the largest cities now, and the land where Marynka's parents and grandparents had carved out a life had been given to someone else. Even the land where the Midday Forest stood was declared imperial territory.

Red Jaga told her not to concern herself. "It's not our war. The earth, the trees, the sky, the forest care not who says they rule it. We don't involve ourselves in the lives and squabbles of lesser creatures. You do not belong to that world anymore."

This was a fact for which Marynka was grateful. But there was still the very real threat, the lingering possibility, that she might be tossed *back* into that world if she kept failing to please the witch, and only then if Grandmother didn't just eat her and use her bones to decorate the house.

It was hard to focus, to think, to win, with all of that brewing in her head. She was old enough now to know, deep down, that the witch would never care for her the way she wanted her to, like a real grandmother. But she still couldn't stop herself from trying to prove she was useful, that she was worthy of her love.

"Oh, Bey-*ahht*-kah," Marynka sang under her breath, drawing out each syllable and adding an affectionate twist to the name. "Time to wake up!" She yanked the blankets off the bed.

Beata hissed and groaned and pulled a pillow over her head. "Ugh, why are you here?"

"Did you forget everything? Weren't you listening when they explained?"

"Of course I was listening. I was just hoping I'd dreamed the past two days." Red and White Jaga had agreed to work together for once, sending both of their servants after the same prince, planning to split his heart between them.

"You say that like you don't want to go to Warszów with me," said Marynka.

"I don't want to go to Warszów with you."

"We both know that's a lie." Marynka crawled atop the mattress, rolled onto her back, and let her head fall to rest on Beata's hip. "Aren't you supposed to be a morning person? Come on. Get up, or Janek will hire the sleigh to someone else. There's plenty of people wanting to travel to the city for the Karnawał."

Beata grunted.

Marynka grabbed one of her friend's waist-length braids, twirling the golden rope of hair around her wrist. She stared at the ceiling, at the window. The eaves were toothed with icicles. Outside, the snow was stealing down. Horses dragged a sleigh past the inn, and two dogs chased behind it barking. Somewhere, a group of children were singing hymns in high-pitched voices in return for treats and coins, but worry drowned out the winter merriment.

"I really need this one." She couldn't afford to return home empty-handed. She didn't know if she'd survive Grandmother's wrath if she did. This prince was special. He had been blessed with an uncommonly pure heart.

Over time Marynka had learned that princes' hearts came in all sorts of different flavors, and there were reasons Grandmother desired each kind. There were the sickeningly sweet hearts of the wicked that would extend a witch's life. The salty hearts of the brave that increased her physical strength. Pure hearts, which were by far the rarest, would grow her magic with each bitter bite.

But pure hearts were also the hardest to take because those born with them were beloved and shielded by blessings and protections. Prince Józef was nephew to the king and adored by the people. He was a war hero. A patriot. And supposedly exceedingly handsome. He had fought against Rusja and objected furiously to his uncle's surrender, resigning from the army and handing in his holy saber before going voluntarily into exile in protest.

But he had returned recently, to the royal city of Warszów.

Returned, people whispered, to rouse his countrymen to rebellion against their oppressors, to deliver Lechija from her foreign invaders. The streets seethed with secret hope.

It was a little sad, Marynka supposed, running Beata's braid idly through her fingers, that they were going to snuff *out* that hope. What would become of Lechija with no prince to fight for its freedom? Would other fighters rise to take his place?

Still, such things couldn't be helped. Sacrifices must be made.

Beata was silent a moment longer, then she sighed and rolled off the bed, moving to get dressed—as Marynka had known she would. Beata was the kind of friend who'd pull through for you when it really mattered no matter how loudly she might complain. Whether it was going along with a lie or helping to hide a body, Marynka could always count on Beata in a crisis.

"*You* have to get up too," Beata said, managing to kick Marynka and slip her arms into the sleeves of her kontusik at the same time. Since the war, Lechija's people had discovered a newfound love for their national dress. The silver-threaded outer robe shimmered bright as snow and was trimmed with pale ermine. As always, the servant of Morning was a vision in white. She started to pack away their belongings.

Marynka stretched her arms over her head. Her own kontusik was crimson red and trimmed with fiery fox fur. Its sleeves were slit open from armhole to wrist and trailed behind her when she walked. Her underdress was also red, and her boots—which had once belonged to a prince who had ridden into the Midday Forest and never came back out—were the color of freshly spilled blood.

Marynka was grateful to all the wayward adventurers who wandered into Red Jaga's domain and left their lives and riches behind. It meant she and Beata could easily disguise themselves as two innocent girls from well-off families.

She made a brief attempt to tame her hair, but seconds later gave up, weaving her curls into a fat, messy plait instead, and shoved it under a fur cap tufted with a feather before following Beata downstairs.

The rickety steps creaked underfoot.

"Do you think Midnight will be going after him too?" Beata asked softly.

Marynka's pulse quickened. Midnight. It was always

Midnight. Even in her thoughts, even in her dreams. "God, I hope so." Sometimes they wouldn't clash for months. Sometimes they weren't even sent after the same prince, but the wait, the build-up…

Beata cut her a look. "Sometimes I think you're actually excited to compete with her."

"I have to even the score." Midnight had taken the last four hearts they'd both been sent after. A fact Grandmother wasn't about to let her forget. What was it? What did she lack? What did Midnight have that she didn't?

Some days, the questions were enough to make Marynka wonder why she even still bothered trying. Sometimes she thought maybe she *should* give up, set herself on fire, and let the wind carry away her ashes.

What was the point in trying if she was only going to fail and disappoint again?

They stepped into the inn's spacious foyer. The room was crammed with bodies, people stamping their boots and sipping krupnik—spiced honey vodka served warm—before they set off on their journeys. When the front door swung wide, a biting wind blew in, swirling with flakes of snow that glinted in the sunlight.

The cold air was sharp as a blade in Marynka's throat. She was tempted to burst dramatically into flame the way she did when she lost her temper, but if she set the inn on fire, Beata would probably strangle her for blowing their cover.

She sunk her chin down into her high collar. Maybe it was the temperature, or because she'd been thinking of Midnight, but her gaze was immediately drawn across the room to the blazing hearth and the girl standing by the fire. Her back was turned. Her skirt and kontusik were so deep a blue they verged on black.

But the first thing Marynka noticed was her hair. Her long braid was the icy color of starlight.

Marynka's steps skittered to a stop.

She knew the scent and taste of Midnight's magic—it always lingered, catching like smoke on her clothes and skin. But she still didn't know what her rival servant looked like. Midnight still hadn't lowered herself to associate with them. Marynka had never seen her human face, though she'd caught glimpses of her monstrous one from a distance, flashes of skull-hollow eyes and a mouth full of dagger teeth, the flick and gleam of a pale braid vanishing into the dark.

"It's always the ones with silver hair," Beata muttered under her breath.

"What?" Marynka said. "Did you say something?"

Beata muttered something else about finding Janek, the young man they'd spoken to about hiring a sleigh to take them the rest of the way to the city. It was too risky arriving in Warszów traveling on the wind.

Grandmother had warned Marynka not to attract attention. The witch preferred not to send her hunting for hearts in the large cities. It was safer to prey on princes when they visited their vast country estates. There were too many people in the royal capital and its surrounds, too many priests and soldiers who practiced divine magic, saints who'd mastered the mystic arts through prayer, rabbis who could control golems, and imams who could call down divine wrath upon their enemies. They would destroy a monster like Marynka, burn her with heavenly fire, or worse, bind her into their service—though this final warning Marynka couldn't help thinking a little hypocritical on Grandmother's part.

Only Prince Józef's heart was worth the risk. A pure heart and the power it held. It was too valuable a chance to pass up.

The girl over by the hearth turned. Sharp eyes met Marynka's, and Marynka was so startled to be caught staring she didn't have time to look away. A chill shivered through her head to toe, and she dropped the cloth bag she was holding and had to lunge after it. She could feel those eyes following her, tracking her movements. Her cheeks burned and she cursed herself for getting flustered.

So what if the girl was pretty? She wasn't nearly as beautiful as Beata. She was too pale for one thing—her skin looked like it never saw the sun—and her features were too sharp. If Marynka traced a fingertip along those cheekbones, she'd cut herself.

She shot a glance over her shoulder.

The girl's eyes were still on her.

"You said you could take us as far the city." Beata's voice carried above the clamor in the foyer.

Marynka looked over at her friend. Beata was standing with

Janek. His ruddy face looked testy and he kept rubbing at his sparse mustache. He said something Marynka couldn't hear.

She drifted closer, noting at the same time, that the girl across the room was mirroring her steps.

"My cousin has another sleigh and good horses," Janek was telling Beata. "He's returning from Brzeziny the day after tomorrow. He'll be happy to take you."

"We can't wait two more days," Marynka interrupted, putting two and two together. There were plenty of people traveling for the Karnawał. The two-month long season of wintry balls, glittery costumes, and nightly torch-lit sleigh-parties that stretched from January through February. Color and excitement to carry everyone through the gloom of winter. The festivities lasted right up until Devil's Tuesday, until the moment the church bells rang for midnight, when the Devil himself would stand at the doors and note down the names of those who dared continue their sinful partying.

Someone else had likely spoken to Janek about hiring his sleigh and offered to pay him more than they had. So now he was trying to foist them off on some cousin.

"We need to get to the city as soon as possible," said Beata.

Janek's uncomfortable gaze cut sideways, landing on the girl with the silver braid as she came up beside him. She was taller than Marynka had expected, and she fought down a prickly surge of irritation at just how far she had to crane her neck back in order to meet her gaze.

"I am very sorry." Janek gestured to the girl. "But Panna Zosia is in a hurry. Her uncle—"

"Is unwell," finished the girl called Zosia. Up close her eyes were dark, black as the night sky with only the faintest suggestion of blue. Her lashes were the same icy silver as her braid. "I'm on my way to visit him."

"What a coincidence," Marynka lied easily. "My *aunt* is sick and we're traveling so we can be with her. My cousin sent a letter begging us to hurry. She's very, very sick."

Janek looked troubled.

"Oh, that's terrible," Zosia said. "But at least your cousin is there to care for your aunt. You see, my uncle is all alone. We have no other family. There's no one but me to care for him."

"Ah, but at least your uncle has *time*. We've been told our aunt doesn't have very long to live. So it's really, really important we get to Warszów first."

Zosia's eyes narrowed.

Marynka's chin came up. She could feel Beata pressing against her side in silent warning, but she'd never been one to pass on a challenge, and something told her that this girl wouldn't go down without a fight—which, of course, made it that much more fun.

The slam of a chest crashing to the floor broke the tension crackling between them as everyone jumped.

Two men carrying luggage over the threshold to load onto a sleigh outside called out apologies. A third man, gray-bearded and barrel-chested, the husband of the woman who ran the inn, joined their circle, slapping a massive hand on Janek's shoulder.

"And where are you girls headed to?" He asked cheerily.

"To Warszów," Marynka and Zosia said immediately. "Janek is—"

"But of course. To find the prince?"

Marynka's eyes widened. Beside her, Beata tensed.

The old man beamed, his gray eyes twinkling. "Funnily enough, that's exactly what the last group of girls had to say. He's very popular, our Józef. He must have amassed at least a hundred brides this season."

"Oh, don't tease," his wife scolded as she stepped into the foyer. She wiped her hands on her apron and smiled at Marynka. "And even if they don't catch the prince's eye, I'm sure there are plenty of nice boys in the city."

Marynka tried not to grimace. Karnawał was a time of costumes and wild parties, a time to fight the gloom of winter with firelight and laughter, but it was also the time of courtship. It was a commonly held belief that there was no better time of the year to search for the other half of your heart. Your soul mate.

It wasn't surprising that there were other girls their age traveling to the capital to find love and a rich husband. Grandmother had said it would help them blend in. Still, that didn't mean she had to *like* pretending she was one of them. Honestly Marynka couldn't understand why girls got so strangely excited over boys that most of the time she couldn't even tell apart.

"Actually, my aunt—"

"My uncle—"

"Janek said—"

Marynka, Zosia, and Beata all started speaking over one another at once. It took several moments for the bewildered couple who owned the inn to make head and tail of the conversation.

"What terrible luck, and at the beginning of the new year too," the old man summed up. "But perhaps, seeing as it's just the three of you and none of you have much luggage, you could all share the sleigh and travel together?"

Marynka and Zosia's heads whipped to stare at him, and the man flinched a little at the speed their heads turned.

Zosia opened her mouth on what was likely another excuse.

"We would, of course, graciously share our sleigh with you," Marynka said.

"You mean *my* sleigh. The one I hired and paid for." Zosia looked ready to start the argument all over again, but then she caught sight of all the other curious faces in the foyer turned in their direction. A flash of uneasiness crossed her sharp features. She seemed to shrink from the attention. "Fine," she muttered, tossing her braid over her shoulder. "We can travel together, since we're going the same way."

"What fun!" Marynka exclaimed, because she couldn't help being antagonistic even in the worst possible moments. "It'll be just like a party with all three of us."

4.

ZOSIA

JANEK'S SLEIGH WAS PAINTED SILVER and lined with fox fur, and it flew fast, dashing through snow-blanketed valleys and slumbering forests, gliding over measureless fields, past black rivers choked thick with ice float. Frost shook free from the trees at their passing, great rolls of steam issued with the snorting of the horses. The harness bells sounded a constant ringing. The gleaming expanse of seemingly endless white made Zosia's eyes ache, made her briefly crave darkness.

Each day they traveled from first light until the winter shadows swallowed the landscape, until the gloom of night caught them in its hold, forcing them to stop and rest in tiny villages at more inns buried knee-deep in snow.

Curled up on the window seat of the room she'd been forced to share, Zosia watched the starry flakes fall to earth. A ribbon of icy shadow twined lovingly around her wrist, forming the briefest bracelet-like coil.

"You don't sleep," a voice accused, slicing like a knife through the quiet.

Zosia didn't jump, but it was close. The ribbon of shadow instantly unraveled, slithering to the floor and dissolving. She tucked her hand beneath her leg. Moonlight filtered through the frosted window.

When she looked over her shoulder, Marynka was standing a little ways behind her smothering a yawn. Her hair was a wild tangle, and there were dark circles beneath her eyes. The heavy sleigh robe they'd dragged inside, a white wolf-skin, was heaped loosely over her shoulders.

"You didn't sleep last night either."

Zosia had tried to, had closed her eyes and hugged the blankets close and chanted the word in her mind as if it were a charm. *Sleep. Sleep. Sleep.* Tossing and turning as quietly as she could to minimize the noise because that was what normal people did, didn't they? They didn't spend the long hours sitting up letting the shadows shape them jewelry.

This was why she hadn't wanted to travel with anyone.

"Neither did you," she pointed out. Beata fell asleep almost as soon as her head hit the pillows, mumbling replies to whatever random thing Marynka was chattering on about, and then she was gone. Dead to the world until dawn. But Marynka...

Restless feet padded across the floorboards and the window seat cushions shifted as she sunk down beside Zosia.

Zosia tensed, watching her with a mix of curiosity and alarm. Not so much because she hated company, but because she wasn't used to it. The witch who had raised her kept her on a tight leash, guarded her more carefully than a precious treasure, always urging her to return home quickly and to talk to no one.

"*The outside world is a dangerous place for a girl like you,*" Black Jaga liked to say. "*You mustn't be seen. Let no one suspect what you are.*"

It would be a great inconvenience, after all, if Zosia were to be caught or destroyed. The witch who ruled the Midnight Forest would be forced to find another girl to serve her.

"Pretend I'm not here," Marynka said, reading the expression on Zosia's face, "and I'll pretend you're not here."

As though that were possible. Marynka changed position and her thigh came to rest against Zosia's. For a breath it was all she could think about. She'd never noticed how starved for contact she was. She almost shifted closer into the touch but caught herself before she could.

Her skin felt hot all over. The air in the room seemed suddenly twice as warm. A phenomenon that happened whenever Marynka got too close. Despite always complaining of the cold, she radiated heat.

"How are you not freezing?" she muttered, wrapping the sleigh robe more closely around her body and tossing back a handful of those wild curls that changed from brown to fiery red depending on the sunlight. Everything about her reminded Zosia of the sun and heat and summer. The sun-bronzed skin, the hint of gold in her hazel eyes, the freckles scattered across the bridge of her nose.

Marynka cocked an eyebrow, catching Zosia staring.

Not that she *was* staring, or anything like that. It was merely second nature for her to pay attention to her surroundings.

Zosia drew her legs up to put space between them. "I don't feel it." There was a fire smoldering in the grate at the far end of the room, and she had winter in her bones. It was as cold here as it was in the mountains, in the starlit depths of the forest where the hour was always midnight.

Marynka leaned forward to huff a breath onto the window glass. She started to draw in the fog with a fingertip, one of her legs jiggling restlessly beneath the sleigh robe. "Why can't you sleep?"

"You first," Zosia said.

"I asked first."

"Is everything a fight with you?"

Marynka grinned, sharp teeth gleaming in the dark. The strangest sense of déjà vu hit Zosia. Why did it feel like she'd seen that grin somewhere before?

Marynka turned back to the picture she was drawing on the glass. A tiny sun. "I don't like the dark," she bit out. "It makes my skin crawl."

Zosia blinked. She felt the shadows throughout the room twitch as though offended. They'd gained a life of their own of late, growing unrulier the more Zosia's magic grew, with every heart she stole and consumed herself instead of bringing back to Black Jaga.

She picked at the hem of her nightdress. "Everyone has something that they're afraid of."

"I'm not *afraid*," Marynka said, indignant. "I just don't like it." She looked at Zosia expectantly, clearly waiting for her to share what was keeping her up, what might frighten her.

"I can't sleep because I'm worried about my sick uncle." In truth, Zosia couldn't remember if she'd ever had an uncle. But it was the safest answer. It wasn't as though she could admit that she *never* slept at night and that sometimes the dark made her skin crawl, too, when she thought too long about what she'd done and started to get paranoid that Black Jaga would appear suddenly from the shadows at her back, come to add Zosia's bones to her collection.

She almost couldn't resist the urge to cast a glance around, to check. It didn't matter how far she traveled from the old wooden house, from the forest; the witch was always there, always present, those bony iron-clawed fingers dug impossibly deep into her thoughts.

She doubted she could get away with this for much longer. The old woman was becoming more and more suspicious. It was exceedingly unlikely that Zosia had been beaten to a heart four times in a row. She could still picture the witch's face, those deep-blue eyes boring into her as though they could see past her too-innocent expression to the defiant thoughts brewing inside her head.

She could still hear the sheer disbelief in that ancient throaty voice. *"My sister's servant got there first? Again?"*

It was useful really, having a convenient scapegoat. If not for Midday and Morning and their rivalry—theirs, and the one between Black, White, and Red Jaga—Zosia's little acts of rebellion would have been discovered long ago.

She took the heart before I could, Grandmother, but I'll try harder next time, I promise!

Zosia wondered suddenly what her fellow servants would think of her actions. Did they, too, dream of escape, of freedom? Had Midday ever looked down at her bloody hands, at a prince's still beating heart and thought to taste? Thought to take that power for herself?

Her eyes flicked back to Marynka, who was looking bored and unimpressed with her answer. She was so entertainingly easy to read.

"You're not worried about your aunt?" If there was a malicious lilt to Zosia's voice, she couldn't help it. Marynka kept mixing up if the woman was her aunt or Beata's before she corrected herself. Zosia was pretty sure the woman did not even exist. "I thought she was practically on her deathbed."

Marynka's eyes narrowed, but she also looked pleased, as if this was some new game, something to distract her from the uneasiness that kept her from sleeping.

"Why are you *really* in such a rush to reach the city?" Zosia said.

That unsettling grin was back on Marynka's face. "I'm going to steal the prince's heart."

Zosia stiffened and then relaxed, amused. It was, after all, in Marynka's case, only a figure of speech. As the owners of the inn where they'd met had pointed out, there were plenty of girls heading to Warszów with the same goal, girls hoping to find love or secure themselves a better future.

And what better time than now to make that happen?

Winter, when the world itself died before emerging again as something new. A time of transformation. The Karnawał season. The period of icy pre-Lenten delights, of masked balls and fetes and parties without end. It was a time when you could be anything you wanted to be. When girls dressed as boys and boys as girls and servants as masters and vice versa. A time when even a peasant girl, even a *monster*, could don a costume and dance with Lechija's most famous prince.

Zosia, too, was going to make herself into something new, something different. She would leave her old self behind like a snake shedding an ill-fitting skin. But she was surprised. She hadn't thought Marynka the type of girl to be looking for a husband. She and Beata seemed very close. Close enough that they seemed to speak their own language of wordless looks and raised eyebrows and incomprehensible in-jokes. Sometimes they even finished each other's sentences.

What was it like to know someone that well? Just the thought made envy curl in Zosia's belly.

She picked at the end of her braid. "You might have competition. You're not the only one looking to meet him."

"Oh? Don't tell me you have your sights set on him too? Aren't you supposed to be doting all over your uncle?"

Zosia allowed herself a small smile, saw it reflected back at her in the frosted window. "I—"

A log on the fire popped, making them both glance toward the grate in surprise. Over on the bed, Beata let out a great honking snore, murmured something in her sleep that sounded like she was scolding someone, probably Marynka, and rolled over.

Marynka and Zosia exchanged glances trying not to laugh.

"Do you see what I have to put up with?" Marynka whispered. "Even if I *could* sleep, there's that."

"It's not the worst I've heard." There'd been a prince whose castle Zosia had snuck into... Not that she could tell Marynka that. She tried to think of something else, something amusing to say. She was surprised by how much she didn't want the conversation to end.

All the village girls she'd risked trying to talk to before had been intimidated by her for reasons she'd never understood. Maybe it was her height, or her stiffness, or her face, which was usually solemn or frowning. People kept their distance, treated her with caution or like a threat, which Zosia couldn't deny that she *was*, but only when she wanted to be.

"Finally." Marynka was looking out the window at the dark

sky beyond, which was not nearly so dark as it had been before. Night's shadows were softening, the black fading, the sky soon to turn blue, even pink and orange, perhaps, as the sun flared to life like a match.

Zosia leaned forward, the tip of her nose just brushing the icy glass. For a second her eyes gleamed bright as a cat's soaking in the light.

Marynka snorted. "You look like a kid who's never seen the sunrise."

Zosia didn't say anything. She would never tire of this sight. Never. The sun-soaked kingdom was another world entirely, one she'd once believed she could only dream of being a part of. If she had her way, she was never going back to the lightless gloom of the forest, where the sun never rose, where the sky never changed.

Had Black Jaga sensed when she left this time just what she was planning? How much did she know?

Still, better to fail and die trying, and Zosia was confident in her abilities. She may not be very good with people, but she had a natural knack for magic, and when she set her mind on something, nothing and nobody had better stand in her way.

She could pull this off. She was getting out. One more heart, Prince Józef's *pure* heart, and she'd gain the magic she needed to finally break free.

No longer would she move through the world as a mere shadow running errands for a witch. No longer would she serve the witch of the Midnight Forest. She wouldn't be someone's pet monster. She would make herself a power to be reckoned with.

She was made for so much more. This heart would change everything.

5.

ZOSIA

MARYNKA STAYED UP WITH HER the next night too. And the night after, and the night after that. It became a kind of contest to see who could go without sleep the longest—Zosia, of course, a fact that seemed to mortally offend Marynka. Zosia had never met anyone who took literally *everything* as a challenge. When Zosia completely by accident hit Marynka in the head with a snowball, it turned into a full-scale war. When they arrived at each inn, they raced to see who could get the better room, tripping and grabbing at each other's clothes like children. Drinking contests lasted until they were both swaying on their feet and Beata started yelling at them for making a scene.

It was the first time Zosia had ever let herself get so carried away. The first time she'd had someone to wait out the long hours with her. It was nice, knowing she wasn't alone, that there was someone beside her in the dark. Almost too soon, Warszów's mighty red gate and mist-shrouded towers were rising before them.

Zosia gaped.

Marynka shoved her fur cap back up her forehead. "We're here, we're here, we're *here*!" she sang, as the sleigh jolted forward, practically vibrating with excitement. Restless strands of red-brown hair were trying desperately to escape her messy braid. The toothy grin she shot Zosia was slightly frightening, but after a week traveling together, Zosia knew that was just the expression Marynka wore when she was excited.

She flung an arm around Zosia's shoulders.

Zosia tensed. She still wasn't used to being touched so casually. It was impossible not to be hyperaware of every brush of contact. The nudges when Marynka wanted attention. The tugs on her arm and braid. She couldn't help keeping a tally of each one. Was this even normal behavior? Was Marynka like this with everyone? Zosia's cheeks grew hot despite the morning's chill. She took a deep breath, drawing the frosty air into her lungs, willing winter to douse the heat of her racing heart.

"Wake up!" Marynka ordered, elbowing a dozing Beata on her other side. "Are you going to dream forever? Oh look, it's snowing again." She reached out a hand to catch the falling flakes. "Why does it always have to snow at the good parts?"

"Why are you always so loud?" Beata smothered a yawn. "For God's sake, it's like this is your first time away from home. How old are you?"

Marynka made a face and leaned away from her, pressing

close to Zosia, sneaking her freezing hands under the sleigh robes and under Zosia's cloak. There were layers of silk and wool between her palms and Zosia's skin, but she may as well have been naked for all the good they did as a shield. The heat of Marynka's fingers seemed to burn right through them. Zosia let out a choked sound. "Marynka!"

"It's cold! Quick, Beata. Come under Zosia's cloak."

Beata looked like she'd prefer to run naked through the snow. Her eyes narrowed on Zosia's flushed face. When she wasn't outright ignoring her, Beata tended to watch Zosia with an intensity that bordered on suspicion. It was like she could tell Zosia was hiding something, as if she knew there was a monster lurking beneath her skin.

"You're cold because you took your gloves off, idiot," she told Marynka.

"I don't like them. They're like prisons for my fingers."

Zosia tried to focus on something else. Anything other than Marynka's hands, and where they were and how they felt. She tried to think about what it would be like to sweep into a city like this one with no plans to steal a prince's heart.

Marynka wouldn't touch you if she knew what you were planning, whispered a voice inside her head. *If she knew all the thoughts running through your mind. Who would want to be near you? Who would want to touch a monster?*

She concentrated hard on the sights before them. Staring as

they swept beneath the great shadow of the city gate, craning her neck as they glided down streets choked thick with snow and ice.

The royal capital was something out of a dream, out of a grandmother's winter fairy tale. Grand and melancholy palaces emerged suddenly from the morning mist, rising from the frozen earth in shades of sherbet and rose and canary blue, trimmed as cakes were with dressings of silver frost. Eaves dripped icicles. Basilica spires glittered coldly and domed synagogues wore little caps of snow. The mist helped soften the city's scars, the gouges and bullet wounds left in stone, testaments to past and more recent conflicts. And there, that must be the famous Golden Castle, rising like a sun above the white-dusted rooftops.

Beata snickered at the look on Zosia's face. She quickly shut her gaping mouth and smoothed her features into their usual solemn mask. But Marynka stared back at her with equal wide-eyed wonder, her hazel eyes turned a dazzling gold in the daylight.

More wondrous than even the buildings were the people. Crowds dressed in finery and rich furs, hunched and huddled against the cold. Fire flashed from the buttons of their silken robes, from the jewels ringing their fingers and studding their feather-tufted fur caps. Zosia's vision swam with all the movement, the shifting colors. She'd never seen so many people crammed into one place. A vast sea of strangers.

The sleigh skidded sideways and the sudden movement had her grasping the edge of the seat. She was so busy trying to take everything in, trying to drink it all in at once, that she missed what Marynka said next. When she glanced sideways, Marynka was already laughing to herself with her head thrown back.

Beata rolled her eyes, pretending not to listen, though Zosia knew she was.

"There's the market!" Marynka cried as the stalls swept into view, strung with glinting ornaments, fantastical masks and cleverly carved wooden clocks, glowing amber rosaries and saintly icons, bolts of gold-threaded cloth, ropes of dried mushrooms, and horse trappings. The air was heady with the scent of mulled wine spiced with cinnamon and cloves. "Quick, tell Janek to stop!"

The sleigh was already slowing. Even the snow, falling in big, lazy flakes from the heavens, seemed to hover in the misty air like moths, iridescent and silver. There was some disturbance up ahead. Movement beyond the shape of the sleighs in front of theirs.

Zosia could hear shouts. Beata muttered something under her breath. Marynka started to untangle herself from the sleigh robes.

"What is it?" Growing unease made the hairs on the back of Zosia's neck rise.

A heartrending shriek pierced her ears. And Zosia shrieked, too, as a monster came swooping out of a narrow side street, lunging at the sleigh on her side, its face a shaggy mass of brown fur and dagger-sharp teeth. Its clawed hands clutched at her arm.

There was a shrill, inhuman whinny from one of the horses. Janek lashed his whip.

The costumed figure shook their shaggy head one final time and danced out of reach. A dozen more monsters were flocking down the street to join it, trying to pull others into their game. They were joined by people dressed as angels and shepherds and snow maidens, each figure seeming to materialize from nothing as if they, like Zosia, could twist themselves out of the wind.

Zosia's heart hurt, it was beating so fast. Marynka and Beata were laughing so hard they were bent nearly in half.

The merrymakers were Karnawał revelers, breathing life into the misty, sleepy city. Like the roving bands of masquerading musicians who made their way from house to house in the villages on the outskirts of the Midnight Forest.

Marynka was wheezing, wiping tears from her eyes. "Your face!"

Heat flamed Zosia's cheeks. "You jumped too. I *felt* you."

Mercifully the sleigh chose that moment to start moving again. Very slowly, though, only crawling along. Even Janek in the driver's seat up front was smiling broadly.

The revelers were still winding in and out of traffic. A woman was plying passersby with mulled wine and salty snacks. A man dressed as a bear pranced through the snow slush on all fours, growling at a group of children clinging to their mothers' skirts. Someone was singing a Karnawał song. The air was full of their merry shouts. Someone else beat a drum.

The colorful retinue accosted another sleigh, and a daring girl in a devil's mask stole the lynx-skin cap from the head of a boy riding in it and skipped away.

Zosia marveled at her nerve. The boy didn't look much older than them, and his shadowy attempt at a mustache was honestly quite sad, but he had to be the blue-blooded son of a magnate family. A member of Lechija's noble caste. He and his friends were peacocks in their fur-lined kontusze of ruby, emerald, and gold, each robe cinched tight by a wide, ornately embroidered waist sash.

The boy leapt from his sleigh to the jeering and cheers of his friends, chasing after his hat. He brushed their sleigh on Beata's side, shoving past a musician and a tall figure wearing a crown.

"The prince!" cried Marynka and Zosia in chorus.

"God's blood," hissed Beata. "You're both *idiots*. That's not Prince Józef. That's Prince *Zapust*. The Karnawał prince? A beggar in a costume. What kind of real prince wears a paper crown?"

Zosia was immediately abashed.

Marynka's cheeks turned an equally bright red, and she grumbled into Zosia's ear. "It's not like I've seen him before to be able to tell." She redoubled her efforts to untangle herself from the sleigh robes. "Come on, let's join them. We're never going to find the real Józef if we just sit here."

She was talking so loudly that a masked reveler overheard and commented, "Not another one! Are there any beautiful girls arriving in Warszów who aren't after our sweet prince?"

His companion, another boy dressed in a matching mask, mock-groaned. "Won't he leave some pretty faces for the rest of us?"

"But if you really have you heart set on him…" The first boy handed Marynka a flyer with a dramatic flourish.

Marynka stared at the paper blankly. Neither she nor Zosia could read. "What does it say?" she demanded of Beata who could.

Beata squinted, lips moving as she deciphered the words. "It's an advertisement." Her tone was dry as she raised an eyebrow at the boys. "For a tailor."

"Only the best tailor in the entire city!" said the second boy. "You see, our great friend the Rusjan ambassador is holding a costume ball. A grand masquerade to help the king forget the troubles of the nation."

"What troubles?" joked his companion, sharply sarcastic. "We have no troubles here. Here, life is perfect." He flung his arms out as if to embrace the world.

"Our prince adores dressing up," the second boy continued. "He's sure to be there."

Zosia looked again at the flyer. So did Marynka. A costume ball that the prince would attend. Catching him alone was always going to be difficult, but at a party it would be much easier, when he was out socializing and could be drawn away into some shadowed corner.

"You may have to fight the other girls for him though."

"I can do that." Marynka grinned like this was exactly what she'd been planning all along.

Zosia had a brief image of her swanning into the ball with a sword, heaving the prince over her shoulder, and carrying him off like a prize. She should probably feel guiltier knowing she was going to *steal* that prize—Zosia often worried that she lacked that thing people called a conscience. She just didn't seem to feel bad or sorry about a lot of things. But at least she knew she was *supposed* to feel guilty; that had to count for something. Probably.

"Good luck to you then," the first boy told Marynka with a wave. He abandoned them to flirt with the occupants of the sleigh behind theirs.

"Hey, don't leave me behind!" cried his companion, bowing to them quickly before running after him. "Take care, beautiful ladies. Don't forget to visit the tailor."

"You can both stop grinning like fools now," Beata told Marynka and Zosia. "Do you think they're going to let just anyone waltz into this ball?"

"It's not like it's the first party we've ever snuck into," said Marynka reasonably.

"Yes, but we weren't in Warszów then," said Beata. "This is the royal capital."

"But it's Karnawał here too," said Zosia meditatively. The time of year when you could become whoever you wanted to be. So long as one wore a mask, even a peasant could dance with a princess, a witch's monstrous servant with a prince. "Everyone disguises themselves so they can have fun regardless of their background. All we need is the right outfit."

Marynka responded instantly. "My costume is going to be so much better than yours."

"Oh, do you think so?" Zosia glanced at the flyer again and then away, tipping her head back. The brilliant bewildering blue of the sky and the glittering sun were so different from the midnight skies and soft moonlight she was used to. "You can let me off at the next corner." She'd find her own way from there. She had the name and address of a woman who owed Black Jaga a favor.

"Say hello to your precious uncle for us," said Marynka.

"Say hello to your poor sick aunt."

Marynka snickered.

Zosia was going to miss this—the banter and their midnight insomnia chats. They'd only known each other a short time, but she was already reluctant to lose this connection. Marynka wasn't bad company, if she was being honest, or maybe it was just that Zosia had been alone for so long that having someone with her, anyone, even someone like Marynka, who Zosia was pretty sure would drive any normal person mad, meant more than it should have.

She hesitated, holding back. They had only traveled together out of necessity and Marynka already *had* Beata. She didn't want to come off as desperate or needy or—

"Maybe we'll see you there," said Marynka easily. "At the ball."

A tightness unraveled inside of Zosia's chest. She smiled. "Maybe."

6.

MARYNKA

"YOU ARE NOT WEARING THAT," said Beata.

"Why not?" Marynka spun and admired herself in the mirror.

"You look ridiculous."

"I look *amazing*. Just like one of the revelers in the marketplace." Marynka laughed in delight. A great furry, hooded black cloak swept the length of her body, falling to her ankles. Beneath it she wore a man's dusky kontusz with a wide, ornate crimson waist sash and crimson boots to the knees, the toes of which were pinched sharp as knifepoints. Her high collar was buttoned with rubies. The cut of the robes made her look incredible and, most importantly, tall. A mask on a stick completed the outfit. A monstrous thing to cover her face. Wicked horns curled back from its temples. Its gaping mouth was full of glittery teeth. She was an elegant version of a turoń. A festive Karnawał devil.

Marynka backed up so she could see the whole getup in the looking glass, nearly tripping backward over an open chest and falling into the pile of previously discarded masks and costumes that they'd spent the last hour giggling over and trying on. They'd taken rooms at the House Under the Moon. The opulent yet gloomy abode of one enterprising and widowed Pani Baranowska who was taking guests for the duration of the Karnawał. Cold crept through the cracks of the creaking baroque town house named for the finely sculpted crescent that graced its lemon-yellow facade. The air was sweet with the musty scent of moth-eaten silk.

Beata buried her face in her hands. "We're trying to blend in. We're here in *disguise*. We're trying to sneak into a costume ball attended by a prince, by the king's nephew. You're not here to make a spectacle of yourself. You can't go as a monster!"

"Pani Baranowska said Prince Józef loves dressing up and seeing everyone's costumes. The more fun they are, the better. You can always change *your* costume if you're jealous, Beatka."

Beata ran on as if she hadn't heard. "You may as well be going as yourself. As Midday."

Marynka cocked her head to the side, seriously considering the idea. "You know, I *could*."

"Don't even think about it. You need to wear something normal. Something pretty. Something to catch a boy's attention. Here, you'd look much better in something like mine."

Marynka cast a disdainful glance at Beata's sad excuse for a costume. She was bedecked from head to toe in white, in a western-style dress embroidered with crystals that dazzled like stars across the bodice and down the length of the flowing skirt. An exquisite wreath of starry flowers, gold straw, and ribbons haloed her fair head. Her face was hidden behind a twinkling gossamer veil.

"If you're going as an angel, I don't see why I can't go as a devil."

"I'm not an angel! I'm a *star maiden.*" Beata held up a glowing paper star on a stick.

Marynka rolled her eyes and turned away, studying her reflection once more, running a finger over her mask's gruesomely sharp teeth.

"You're not taking this seriously." Beata waved her star, stabbing it accusingly at Marynka. "Weren't you the one making a fuss because you couldn't afford to lose this time? You know Midnight's probably been sent after the prince too. Do you want to take his heart before she can? Are you even trying?"

An involuntary shiver that was half dread, half excitement ran through Marynka. "I haven't forgotten." Midnight was never far from her thoughts for long. It was impossible to forget the other servant fully. Marynka couldn't remember the last time something she'd done hadn't revolved in some way around her. She couldn't forget her if she tried.

We haven't had a proper contest in more than two months, Midnight. Isn't that sad?

Marynka tugged the hood of her cloak back, stepping away

from the mirror. "You say that I'm the one obsessed with her, but you're the one who keeps bringing her up."

Beata sputtered indignantly as Marynka started to pace. Even crammed full with richly carved furniture, the room she and Beata were sharing was bigger than the whole of the house in the Midday Forest. The night breeze tapped at the ice-rimed windows, from which, if she drew the thick curtains back, Marynka could see the snowbound Golden Castle where the costume ball would be held and the black ice-choked river that divided Warszów in two. Snow was falling thickly, shining flakes sinking into the depths of the distant water like tiny silver shipwrecks.

"Are you nervous?"

"Of course not," Marynka scoffed. "I live for this."

"You didn't eat anything earlier."

Marynka cast a glance at the heavy tray on the side table. After making the customary protest that she had no food worthy of them in the house, the elderly Pani Baranowska had proceeded to serve them up a full-course meal. Heavy and hearty food to stave off the cold—steaming barszcz and rich bigos stew and kołduny dumplings stuffed with lamb and broth. In the old woman's opinion, they looked like they needed fattening up.

But Marynka had no appetite.

"You've been fidgeting like you do when you're nervous."

"Then stop staring at me."

"I wasn't—" Beata took a breath before she continued. She

removed the wreath crowning her head and the twinkling veil, avoiding Marynka's gaze. "I don't—" she started and stopped.

Her expression was so serious that Marynka raised an eyebrow. "You don't what?"

"I don't like it when you lose," said Beata at last, looking her straight in the eye. "I don't like seeing what she does to you."

She could've been referring to Midnight or Grandmother, but in this case Marynka knew she meant the latter.

Something hot and sticky tried to claw its way up her throat. "Grandmother's only hard on me because she knows I can do better," she said, trying and failing to keep the sharpness out of her voice. "She believes in me. She does. She wouldn't have given me so many chances if she didn't." Deep down, the witch *had* to know she couldn't possibly find a better servant than Marynka. No one was stronger than her save Midnight.

Beata frowned.

"And anyway, you're here. It's you and me together, remember? Morning and Midday against Midnight. You'll wear that boring"—she corrected herself quickly—"*beautiful* costume. And you'll look so stunning that no one in the city will be able to take their eyes off you."

Beata sniffed looked slightly mollified. When Marynka grabbed her hands and turned her like they were dancing a mazurka, her cheeks dimpled with a reluctant smile.

"The prince won't be able to resist you. He'll claim your hand for the first dance and refuse to leave you till the last. He'll lavish you with compliments all night long, and you'll laugh and lean in close to whisper, 'It's a little hard to hear in here isn't it, with all the music?' And then you'll draw him away, out of the ball and into the winter night or into some shadowed nook. He'll fall at your feet bewitched." Marynka suited the action to the word, dropping to her knees dramatically, throwing her arms around Beata's waist. "'Oh, loveliest of maidens, your beauty has enthralled my heart. I love you so that I cannot breathe!'" She grasped Beata's hands and covered them with kisses. "'I beg of you, be mine—'"

Beata turned a delicious red and shoved Marynka violently away.

Marynka fell onto her back on the floor laughing. "And that's the moment when *I* leap from the shadows and rip out his heart!"

"You're ridiculous," Beata said crossly.

"You worry too much." Marynka rolled to stand, picking up the poker from beside the fireplace and stoking the glowing embers. They crackled eagerly at the touch. "I've told you a thousand times before I can beat Midnight. You'll see, I'm going to bring Grandmother Prince Józef's pure heart."

She had to.

She couldn't lose this time.

She would make Red Jaga proud. She wouldn't be an embarrassment. She wouldn't disappoint her again.

This was her final chance.

She had to win at any cost.

The flames flared, dancing in response to the turmoil churning inside Marynka. But she was still cold, even standing directly before the fire. How she hated winter. If she could, she'd have slept until the season turned, buried herself deep in the earth and hibernated until the summer heat returned to wake her.

The wind whispered at the window and ate the sound of Beata stripping off her costume and crawling into bed.

Marynka very carefully removed her own costume, kicking off her red boots and smoothing the furry cloak, setting the monstrous black mask gently on top of the dresser. She wondered idly what kind of costume Zosia would have chosen if she'd still been with them. She half wished the other girl had stayed, if only for the distraction.

She joined Beata in the bed, slipping beneath the blankets and sneaking her frozen fingers down the neck of her friend's nightgown.

Beata shrieked. "Get out! Your hands are like ice!"

"But what if I get sick from the cold, Beata? What if I die?"

"Who cares!" Beata hissed furiously, squirming away. "Mother of God, why can't you be *normal*?"

"Why can't you be *fun*?" Marynka retorted, wrapping her body around Beata's for warmth the way she'd done a hundred times before, but pulling her in a little tighter now than usual. Beata was the one who'd brought up Midnight and ruined her good mood, so she would just have to deal with the consequences.

Her knees tucked into the back of Beata's knees. Her face pressed into the crook of her neck. Morning always smelled so good, sweet as spring, like fresh leaves and branches and new green things.

"Why am I even friends with you?" Beata huffed.

"I ask myself that sometimes," Marynka admitted, snuggling closer, letting the familiar sound of Beata's breathing ease some of the tension knotted through her bones, lull her into something like sleep. Real sleep, of course, would be impossible, what with the shadow of Midnight hanging over them and the pressure of finally proving herself to Grandmother.

She drifted instead, floating in that place between dreams and waking, balancing on the knife's edge of consciousness. Falling, into a shallow but pleasant fantasy, wherein Midnight discovered the prince lying dead with his chest empty while Marynka's triumphant laughter echoed loudly through the halls. Over the years, she'd refined the imagined look of shocked defeat on Midnight's face—the small, stunned O of her mouth, the frustrated fury in those great hollow eyes, the same fury Marynka had felt time after time, defeat after defeat—to a thing of perfection. She pictured the other servant's clawed hands raking the walls in a rage as she cursed the clever and beautiful rival who had outdone her yet again.

Beata rolled over and pressed her lips to Marynka's brow in a fierce kiss. "Marynka?"

"Mmm," came the dreamy reply.

"At the ball tomorrow night? Don't go as a monster."

7.

MARYNKA

MARYNKA WENT TO THE BALL as a monster.

At midnight exactly, the masquerade was opened by Rusja's ambassador and his sour, moon-faced wife. Over three hundred pairs stood in the first mazurka. Polished boots and a glossy floor reflected the fiery glow of chandeliers and candelabras, the blue moonlight washing through the windows. Glass doors, great arching things, lined one side of the ballroom leading onto a terrace, which in turn led down frosted steps into the castle's winter-white garden. The doors were left open, so that every so often the night blew in sparkling flurries of snow. Guests spun by in circles, dancing with a furious energy, sliding, leaping, each couples' feet drumming the floor with such force it was as if they were trying to strike flame with their heels.

Light glittered off the snowflake crown and silver-blue robes worn by a girl dressed as a snow-maiden, off the icy scepter held aloft by a frost demon. A man clinked past in the full armor of one of Lechija's legendary winged cavalry riders, a leopard skin falling from his shoulder and a curved saber hanging from his waist. The city's tailors and hairdressers must have been making a fortune. It was impossible to describe all the costumes, but wings were clearly a popular choice.

Marynka watched it all from behind her black-horned mask, searching for the prince hiding somewhere in the crowd, scowling when Beata refused to dance with her. Which was fine; Marynka didn't need her. Beata would come crawling back soon enough anyway. What other fool would talk and dance with her? It wasn't like she had any other friends.

"I'm going to ask about the prince. I told you not to wear that costume. Stay here and don't do anything reckless." Beata pressed away through the crush of bodies. Marynka watched her stop to flirt with some rich princess, twirling her little sparkling star on its stick. Knowing Beata, she was probably already planning their wedding, dreaming of how they would live together forever in a little house in the woods.

Really, it was quite pathetic.

But she did look beautiful. Undeniably beautiful. And mysterious, with her violet eyes, fat, rosy cheeks, and unknowable smile just visible behind her twinkling gossamer veil. Soft and delicate in a way Marynka knew she could never be even if she tried.

And she had tried.

It wasn't as if she'd never worn a dress. Never combed her hair so it wasn't a wild tangle. Never painted red on her lips.

She had a fleeting pang, thinking she *should* have worn a costume more like Beata's, before she gave herself a shake. No, changing yourself for others was like admitting defeat. Marynka didn't dress to please people. She dressed to startle them, to make them uneasy. She didn't dress so that they would look at her and see something they wanted to touch and taste. She wanted them to look upon her and be afraid. She wanted their knees to tremble when they beheld her. She wanted their voices to crack with visceral fear at her approach.

She wasn't going to make herself into something sweet, mold herself into something more palatable. Something to be gobbled up and swallowed down. She was not a dessert.

Speaking of which…

A servant wheeled past, bearing crystal platters weighed down with sweet things. Karnawał treats designed to suit the season: crusty faworki and almond cookies and cream puffs and glazed pączki piled high into towers. Spicy honey-cake hearts steaming and fresh from the oven. During the Karnawał there were two rules, and the first was to eat as much as you possibly could, to glut yourself on all that was fatty and rich, on all the good things before the strict fasting period.

The second rule was, of course, to dance and drink as much as you ate. So Marynka made a face at Beata—who, glancing back, gave her best impression of never having seen Marynka before. *I've never seen that girl in my life! Who is that mad creature there? Who let that monster in?*—and helped herself to the food.

Not only the sweet, but also the savory, fancy appetizers of smoked sausage and pickled fish and sour radish, washing it all down with shots of vodka glimmering with flakes of burnished gold.

How rich must the people here be, to be drinking actual gold?

Lifting onto the tips of her toes, licking oil from her fingers, Marynka scanned the crowd again. To her left, a boy in peasants' costume was dancing with a firebird. A girl in a half mask wrapped in a glory of golden silk. Brilliant feathers in dazzling shades of scarlet made a crown in her fair hair. Vast wings of living flame flared from her back, shedding sparks as she twirled on small feet. A priest with a big belly started complaining loudly about divine magic being used for unholy purposes.

Marynka snorted. At least Grandmother didn't care what she used her magic for so long as she brought the witch her hearts. That was the biggest difference, that she could see anyway, between divine magic and the kind that she had—the holy kind was supposed to be used primarily for the good of others. It wasn't supposed to be used for petty purposes.

She chewed her lip. What kind of costume would Lechija's prince wear to his death? Was he the peasant dancing with the firebird? The young man there, who'd come as a bear? She even spied someone dressed as a king, which she thought was rather daring considering Lechija's actual king was meant to be here tonight, until she realized the man must *be* the king. The real one.

The man said to have been bewitched by Imperial Rusja's wicked tsarina. Marynka wondered if it was true that he carried a likeness of her in his breast pocket with him always.

As if to prove there was no spell clouding his mind, the king smiled brightly at the beautiful olive-skinned woman at his side. He wore a flimsy half-mask of lace and diamonds, but no proper costume, only a tailcoat and breeches, the foreign fashions he favored.

Most everyone else, if they weren't in full costume, was dressed in traditional Lechijan attire, the sleeves of their robes trailing through the air behind them as they spun across the dance floor. The girls' kontusiki were trimmed with pale fur, the boys' kontusze tied with wide embroidered belts.

Was the prince standing somewhere near his uncle? Was he one of those young men fawning at the king's side? Karnawał was a time when anyone could approach the king, and it was obvious Marynka wasn't the only one to know it. A veritable wall of eager admirers separated them. Young and old all trying to charm their way into his graces, falling over themselves trying to bow low enough.

Marynka grabbed a girl outfitted as an angel roughly by the arm. "Hey, which one is the prince? What'd he come dressed as?"

The girl stared at her, appalled. "How should I know?" She yanked her arm free, rubbed her wrist. "No one does. Prince Józef said his costume was to be a surprise."

What a fool. Marynka scowled, and when another servant swept by, she snatched a goblet of ruby-red wine from his tray. Of course this couldn't be *easy.*

She downed the wine in a single gulp and handed the empty goblet off to some random old man. He tugged his gray mustache in confusion and opened his mouth, but by then Marynka had sidled up to a group of boys and girls who looked to be about her age.

They were gossiping about who was there and who they were there with, and most importantly, about the prince. The way people spoke of him made him sound too perfect to be real. He was a saint, a hero, an ardent champion of freedom. A fierce soldier. A seducer of hearts.

"Did you hear about the time he drove a sleigh naked through the city because he lost a bet?"

"They say he's challenged the ambassador to a duel."

"They say even the Princess Oscik has tried to sneak into his bedroom."

Marynka joined in with the group's hearty laughter, which resulted in several strange looks. A few of the girls exchanged raised eyebrows and snickered in each other's ears. Marynka ignored an uncomfortable prickle of self-consciousness. If they knew who she was, *what* she was, they wouldn't dare laugh at her.

I could reduce you all to ash where you stand. I could burn this castle to the ground.

She took a deep breath and found herself, as she often did

when she was in a bind, imagining what Midnight might do. How would *she* go about this? How would her rival approach her victim? If Midnight were here, would she have already found the prince?

Unless she was already here…

The strangest shiver traveled down Marynka's spine. She was already facing the arching glass doors lining the far side of the hall when the air seemed to change. Candles flared, flickering and guttering as a gasp of icy wind rushed in eager to join the party. Masks and faces took on a newly sinister gleam. Strange shadows jumped up the walls, the dark of night dancing along with the merrymakers.

Marynka turned in a slow circle, pulse thrumming sickly in her veins.

Her eyes caught on a figure standing head and shoulders above most of the crowd, and a sudden hysterical giggle bubbled up her throat, shattering the tension. She made her way over.

"Nice beard."

"Thank you," said Zosia through a mouth full of honey cake, looking down at Marynka from below the shadow of her wide-brimmed hat. She was dressed as a cloud shepherd, as one of the nature spirits that haunted Lechija's mountains. The mercurial creatures carried cold in their rough-hewn sacks and controlled the weather, towing clouds back and forth across the sky by lengths of rope. Zosia was carrying a painted storm cloud on a stick and wore a sheepskin coat and a long, fake silver beard.

She looked ridiculous.

Marynka was unreasonably happy to see her. And she couldn't help but notice that Zosia looked just as happy to see *her*. It wasn't often that people looked pleased to see Marynka—for obvious reasons. Warmth bloomed in the center of her chest. Despite the lingering thought of Midnight, she found herself grinning. "Dressing as a grandfather is *definitely* the best way to catch the prince's eye."

"I thought so," said Zosia oblivious to sarcasm, sounding pleased. "He likes amusing costumes."

"You've seen him?"

"No. Not yet. No one seems to know what he's wearing. Everyone here is looking for him."

"Maybe he's decided to spite them all by not showing up." That would be just her luck. Marynka held out a hand for one of Zosia's honey cakes.

Zosia gave her one and watched, with a fascinated kind of horror as Marynka proceeded to cram the whole thing into her mouth at once. "It's like watching a snake unhinge its jaw in order to swallow prey."

"Shut up." Marynka tried to crush Zosia's foot with her boot.

Zosia dodged, grinning behind her beard. "You look good too."

Marynka stilled, the compliment catching her off-guard. The tips of her ears burned red, and she was glad for the furry hood of her cloak currently covering her head.

"Of course I do," she said, recovering, maneuvering sideways as another person dressed as a devil squeezed past them. The man said something to them both in a language she couldn't understand. She nodded anyway, not wanting to look a fool in front of Zosia.

"You didn't understand a word of that."

"Of course I did."

"What did he say then?"

"He said you have sugar in your beard."

"What?"

"He said"—Marynka stepped closer, standing on tiptoe, raising her mouth to Zosia's ear to be better heard above a sudden swell in the music. Zosia went very still—"that you have crumbs in your beard."

Zosia's hand rose to her face. "I do no—"

Marynka reached out and swiped a dusting of sugar off the corner of Zosia's mouth, licking it slowly off her thumb.

For a heart-stopping moment, Zosia just stared at her wide-eyed. Marynka wondered if she'd crossed a line, wondered if she should have drunk all that gold-laced vodka and then the wine.

Zosia opened her mouth as if to speak, then bit her lip, hesitating. Holding herself back. She did that a lot, Marynka had noticed.

Fortunately, or unfortunately, they were interrupted again. A boy asked if Zosia would give him a dance.

She glanced at Marynka.

"What? Don't look at me, Grandfather." Marynka's voice came out too bright, too loud. She waved them off airily. "Go have fun falling on your face."

Zosia continued to look at her, expression unreadable, but Marynka was already turning her back, chasing off the feeling she should have asked Zosia to dance herself. Her skin felt too tight, too prickly.

God's teeth, this wasn't the time to get a crush. She had important things to do.

The song changed. Shouldering through the perfumed throng, Marynka wondered if Zosia was still dancing.

"Now that," remarked a cheerful voice at her elbow, "is a fantastic costume."

"Isn't it?" Marynka held the horned mask to her face, pivoting and turning to find a young man of bear-like physique—tall and barrel-chested—smiling down at her. Broad shoulders stretched the seams of a kontusz in glorious forest green, the silk fabric embroidered with gold and silver thread to make a pattern like scales. He wore the snout of a dragon as a kind of hat. Its upper jaw and fierce fangs shadowed the upper half of his face.

"Why dress as a star maiden or a firebird when you could come as a devil and look as good as this?" Marynka gestured at herself.

The young man grinned. "You're certainly the best-looking turoń that I've ever seen."

Marynka dipped her head. The compliment didn't mean as much coming from him as it had from Zosia. Compliments always meant more when they were from girls.

"But I thought you looked a little lonely. I feel like more people should be asking *you* to dance."

Marynka waved a dismissive hand. "Alas, no one here has taste."

The young man let out a bark of genuine laughter.

Marynka started to smile, then jumped at the sudden cold touch of snow on her face. She glanced up, thinking she'd imagined it. But snow really was falling, through a great window in the ceiling left open to the night sky. Glittery white flakes drifted down to powder a servant's passing tray of desserts, melted into a woman's raised glass of vodka like sugar.

"Beautiful, isn't it?"

"Mm." How long was he going to keep talking to her? "Why aren't you dancing?"

The young man patted his leg, hand brushing the sheathed saber hanging at his side, a ceremonial blade for formal attire. "Old injury. I'm taking a rest. And"—he looked away, out at the crowd—"I heard someone I used to know was here tonight."

"Someone you want to dance with?"

He laughed again. "Not exactly." He lifted the dragon's snout to wipe away sweat at his temples.

Marynka caught a glimpse of raven-black hair and warm brown eyes, flushed cheeks.

"Please don't tell anyone," he said softly, catching her staring. "I'm really not in a mood to play nice with my uncle and Rusja's ambassador." He nodded his head at the frost demon who had moved to stand beside the king.

Oh.

Oh. Oh, this was *too* good. Oh, this was *perfect.*

Marynka's heart beat faster as they exchanged conspiratorial grins, holding the most delicious of secrets between them.

See? she wanted to shout at Beata. *And you said the prince who loves dressing up for the Karnawał would never approach a girl dressed as a monster.* Prince Józef was clearly a young man of taste.

He tugged at his high collar, pulling it away from his neck. Marynka thought again of his flushed features, and it occurred to her why he might've chosen to stand here to rest, beneath the window in the ceiling open to the night sky, to the cold.

"There's only one trouble with this kind of costume." Her hands prickled with heat, with magic. The air around them shimmered slightly, warming. Still holding her mask in place with one hand, she tugged the shaggy hood of her fur cloak back. Wild red-brown hair spilled over her shoulders. The strands glowed like blood, like fire. "In all these heavy robes, you get so very hot."

The prince patted sweat from his brow again. "I know exactly what you mean."

"I wanted to step outside," said Marynka, looking toward the arching glass doors and the empty snow-dusted terrace lying in shadow beyond. The perfect place for a private rendezvous. "Just to catch my breath and cool down, but my traitorous friends have all deserted me, and I was too nervous to go out into the dark alone."

The prince considered her a moment. His gaze skipped past her, scanning the crowd quickly. Then he smiled and offered her his arm. "Well, we can't have that, can we?"

8.

ZOSIA

ZOSIA HAD FOUND THE PRINCE.

He was standing in the leftmost corner of the ballroom disguised as a priest. Dressed in a midnight-black cassock with a rosary of amber wound round his wrist. He looked like he'd climbed out of the frame of a gilded icon. His features might've belonged to a saint: the lush mouth, the elegantly hooked nose and soulful green eyes, the ridiculously long lashes. He was tall and slender with brown hair that flashed gold in the candle glow, and there was a porcelain-like delicacy to him that made Zosia think if she pushed him over, he might shatter.

He's a handsome boy, our Prince Józef, Zosia had been told, *but he has the saddest eyes.*

Well, this boy had sad eyes and was far and away the handsomest person Zosia had seen here tonight, and if that alone was not enough to convince her, there were the whispers. Snatches of hushed conversation that kept finding their way to her ears as she drifted closer to him:

"Why do you think he came back?"

"I can't believe he dared. He has to be mad to show his face here."

"Do you think he's planning something terrible?"

"Shh! They'll arrest you next, have you marching in chains to coldest Sybera. Look, Rusja's ambassador is coming."

Zosia edged deftly through the crush of bodies. Everything was so loud and bright. A great blur of color, masks, and music. She could barely hear herself think.

A swan maiden's wings tickled her cheek. A boy wearing a bride's flower crown laughed deafeningly in her ear. She maneuvered past a girl dressed in peasants' costume, in a skirt and blouse and apron that honestly looked like something Zosia owned. She couldn't decide if she was more offended or amused.

It was curious, seeing what people chose to be when they were given the choice to be anything. Had they donned their Karnawał masks to transform themselves into who they most wanted to be? Or had they merely *removed* the masks they wore daily, to reveal who or what they had always been?

But it wasn't only the costumes that were distracting. An older man pressed by, blocking her path, hands groping Zosia's waist drunkenly as he pretended to stumble and steady himself. His drooling gaze seemed to stick to her as he moved away, like glue or honey, like saliva, all icky and trailing.

Zosia's skin crawled. A small smile lurked beneath the man's mustache as he joined a middle-aged woman who was clearly his wife. She threw Zosia an acid look as if her husband's behavior was somehow Zosia's fault.

For God's sake. You can have him. The sheepskin coat of her cloud shepherd costume hid the shape of her body. She was wearing a wide-brimmed hat that shadowed her face and a gray grandfather's beard and *still*—

Zosia sucked in a breath.

She hated that dressing like this wasn't enough to keep them from looking at her. She hated how many times she'd been forced to smile sweetly tonight and let men kiss her fingers, let them lead her in a dance, let them interrupt her hunt for the prince and her moment with Marynka. At least she'd managed to ditch the last boy after a single song. Refusing would have attracted too much attention. If you didn't dance, you had to pay a fine in silver to the man dressed as a goat lurking over near the musicians. Karnawał was the time to find the other half of your soul, and the kingdom made a game of punishing those stubborn bachelors and maidens who made no effort to find a partner by the end of the season.

Zosia couldn't afford to cause a scene right now. She was here in disguise, a monster masquerading as a human, pretending to be just another innocent girl come to Warszów eager to snag herself a rich husband.

She had to act normal. Natural. Like everybody else.

She wondered why the prince wasn't dancing, but perhaps he was working up the courage to ask someone. She'd managed to shuffle almost to his side now. She held herself slightly aloof, attaching herself to a group of revelers daring to send flirtatious looks his way, mimicking their posture, the way they held themselves.

Normal. Natural. She could do it. She'd already infiltrated the costume ball with ease as expected.

The prince snatched a glass from a passing servant's snow-dusted tray and gulped down wine like his life depended on it. His gaze kept darting across the ballroom.

Zosia followed his gaze, eyebrows lifting.

It wasn't hard to spot Marynka. While Zosia did everything in her power to blend in, Marynka did everything to stand out. Even if you didn't count the fact that she'd come to the ball dressed as the Karnawał's most famous monster, Marynka stood out like a flame in the dark. A kind of energy radiated off her like heat, a shimmer as bright as the sun.

For a second, Zosia wondered if she'd drunk too much herself. Marynka was laughing and talking with a boy dressed as a dragon.

"Can you believe her?" said Beata, sidling up beside Zosia and looking exasperated.

"I know." Zosia frowned, twirling the wooden storm cloud on the stick she held as a prop. "I would've thought more people would ask her to dance. Don't they like her costume? It's so good."

Beata gave her an appraising look, scanning Zosia from head

to toe. "Never mind," she said, turning and walking away abruptly. "I forgot for a moment that you're also an idiot."

Zosia was about to deny this, but a high-pitched squeal stopped her.

"Kajtek!" A girl dressed as a snow maiden shoved past, followed by an enormous figure in a bear costume. "Oh, it really is you!" The girl latched onto the prince's arm while the bear swept him into a hearty embrace, kissing his cheeks and lips with its snout.

Zosia stilled, losing the grip on the storm cloud's stick in surprise. The prop clattered to the floor.

Kajtek? Kajtek was a sweet way of calling boys named Kajetan, but the prince's name was...

"You're going to make them all very angry," the snow maiden said, adjusting the kokosznik crowning her pale-blond head, "if you keep staring like that at Józef."

Zosia's head whipped back to Marynka. She and the boy were moving; the dragon escorting the black-horned turoń toward the arching glass doors leading out onto the terrace.

Trust Marynka to have stumbled upon the real prince. But this was her chance; now she had an excuse to approach him.

"Wait!" a voice called after her. "Your cloud!" From the corner of her eye, Zosia saw the boy named Kajtek holding the prop she'd dropped. She debated turning back for it, but Marynka and the prince were already slipping out of sight.

She headed after them, navigating past the seats lining the

edge of the room where anxious mothers and the elderly sat watching the dancing, past a girl twirling in the arms of a sweaty magnate and pretending to like it, past two guests newly arrived, shedding their fur-thick winter layers to reveal more glamorous disguises.

A shiver of foreboding ran through Zosia as she noted the way Marynka leaned on the prince's arm and her tipsy steps as she crossed the deserted terrace. Outside, the moon was a scythe in the sky and snow fell in powdery handfuls. There was a wicked chill to the air. Marynka stumbled as she let the prince lead her down the ice-slick steps into the castle's winter-white garden.

What was the fool doing letting him draw her out here all alone?

The prince was supposed to have a pure heart, but Zosia had heard too many stories about boys taking advantage of girls while they were intoxicated.

She followed quickly, silently, unleashing her magic. Night did strange things to a place, to people, splashing shadow over familiar sights and faces, painting the world and its inhabitants as darker versions of themselves.

When Zosia used her powers, something similar happened to her. She knew what she looked like when she became Midnight, knew how her appearance transformed. She'd caught glimpses often enough—in icy pools, in glassy lakes, in the windows and mirrors in her victim's bedrooms, in the terrified eyes of those she visited. The first time she'd been shocked into stillness, mesmerized by her own monstrosity. A strange nausea had risen in her throat, and the prince whose wicked heart she'd come to steal had woken from the trance she'd cast and fled.

He hadn't made it far, of course.

But her mistake had sparked a superstition. The prince had just enough time to warn a cousin, who'd retold the tale to their cousin, who'd told it to a friend and so forth. Households throughout the kingdom nailed mirrors above their beds to ward off nightmare spirits now, in the hope that the monsters would catch their reflection and recoil from it.

Darkness spread from the tips of Zosia's pale fingers, up her hands and wrists and forearms as if shadow was painting her a pair of gloves. It spread like lacework up her neck. The veins at her temples blackened. Her senses sharpened and so did her teeth. Everything looked brighter, crisper. Her fingers tapered to long, lethal black claws. Her eyes were fully dark, two hollows like the empty sockets of a skull.

They passed a row of iced-over hedges, a frozen fountain. The noise of the party faded.

Marynka finally spun to a halt in front of the prince beside a marble sculpture of some old god. The hem of her shaggy black cloak dragged on the ground, picking up a lacework of snow and frost.

Poised in the shadows, Zosia hesitated.

Zosia *never* hesitated. She'd been trained to be decisive, to follow through, and yet here she was letting every what-if play out behind her eyes. Because if Marynka should happen to… If she caught a glimpse of Zosia's true face…

Morbid curiosity gripped her then. How *would* Marynka react to Zosia's monstrous self, to the darkness hidden beneath the innocent exterior? What would she think of Zosia if she revealed the horrifying extent of her powers? Would she recoil and fall into a faint, run screaming for the hills, stand shrieking for help?

The thought alone was enough to chill Zosia to the bone.

You know what happens when someone sees the real you.

Was it worth attacking the prince now, if it meant losing the first friend she'd ever made?

Zosia's heart was pounding.

Of course it was.

She'd known Marynka little more than a week, even if it felt impossibly longer. The pure heart she needed in order to free herself was as good as in her hands. Ready for the taking. Ready for her to reach out and grasp. There was nobody else in the deserted garden. Zosia wasn't about to lose this chance. Not for a girl she barely knew. Not for anyone.

And yet, still she made no move, only watched.

Marynka was laughing at something the prince had said, the words spoken too low for Zosia to catch. She felt a strange unwanted stab of envy as Marynka moved even closer to him, tilting her face up to his, slowly, coquettishly, lowering her black-horned devil's mask.

It took three full breaths for Zosia to understand. Two more, to truly comprehend what she was seeing.

Moonlight illuminated Marynka's face. Her wicked smile. Her hazel eyes. But those familiar features were changing, as Zosia had become Midnight, the girl before her became something else.

Her teeth were too sharp. Her hazel eyes too bright a gold. Night should have snuffed the fire from her hair. But her edges burned. Her wild curls, her skin lit with an unearthly fiery glow. She was Zosia's inverse reflection. A monster with a face that she'd only ever glimpsed from a distance.

This couldn't be real. She was hallucinating, dreaming…

For a moment while Zosia stared, all other thoughts escaped. She lost where she was. She couldn't remember why she'd stepped outside into the cold and what she was meant to be doing there, why the Prince of Lechija stood between them, transfixed, prey frozen before a predator, unable to tear his eyes from Marynka.

But that girl wasn't Marynka, couldn't be Marynka. Marynka was human. She wasn't like Zosia. She wasn't a monster. She wasn't—

A flash and a blade appeared in Marynka's hands, a small scythe, the kind used for cutting grain. She ran the pad of a finger along the curve of the weapon.

Zosia's boots crunched in the snow. Marynka's head jerked up. Golden eyes pinned Zosia.

"Marynka?" Zosia whispered.

9.

ZOSIA

MARYNKA STARED AT ZOSIA.

Zosia stared at Marynka.

Prince Józef of Lechija snapped out of his trance, stared back and forth between them both, and screamed. A high-pitched strangled sound. His hand flew to the jeweled hilt of his saber.

Marynka stood frozen, seemingly unable to tear her eyes away from Zosia. But Zosia was finished hesitating. She darted toward the prince as swift as shadow.

A sudden, violent gust of heat slammed her backward. The heels of her boots drove black lines in the snow, her shoulders hit the snow-covered hedge behind her. She looked up, eyes narrowed.

Marynka met her gaze, eyes glowing molten gold. Her stare felt hot enough to dissolve Zosia's flesh. Her iron teeth were too sharp to make the smile slowly spreading across her face anything but a threat.

Zosia drew a sharp breath. Her own face gave away nothing, but her blood pulsed with a new and strange excitement.

The prince drew his saber with a *snick*. The curved edge caught the moonlight. He went for Marynka, who was closest. His sword slashed down.

Marynka slid her foot backward, twisting out of the way—fast. But not fast enough. The blade scored a vicious line through the fabric of her cloak, across her forearm. Her devil's mask had fallen to the ground. Blood ran down her wrist, dripping with a sizzling hiss from her fingertips to the snow.

Only, like Zosia, she didn't feel pain like a normal person.

Marynka didn't flinch or slow. Instead she immediately swerved and slashed at the prince's chest with her glowing scythe, sending Józef darting back out of reach, cursing. Already her wound was healing. By the time morning came, any sign of it would be gone. The skin smooth, unscarred, flawless once more. The prince's eyes were wide with shock.

Marynka threw her head back and laughed, an all-too-familiar sound.

They came together with a clash. Marynka catching the downstroke of the prince's blade with her scythe, orange sparks flying, the shriek of metal on metal ringing through the winter night.

That, coupled with the prince's earlier scream, warned Zosia that the three of them wouldn't be alone for long.

Their blades slid along each other, singing a lethal duet as they sprang apart and danced in together. The sight was surreal. A monster and a prince going head-to-head in the frozen castle gardens, both dressed in fancy Karnawał costumes. A dragon and a turoń dueling to the death in the falling, whirling snow. Zosia held her breath as they matched each other strike for strike. Unsure who she feared would win. Unsure who she *wanted* to.

The prince whose heart she needed, or Marynka—no *Midday*—because that couldn't truly be Marynka, could it? Marynka—the first friend she'd ever made, the girl with a smile like summer—couldn't be the stubborn, destructive, childish, impulsive, complete *disaster* of a servant who served the witch Red Jaga, who was always getting in Zosia's way.

A fresh whistle of steel brought her back to herself. The sound of a second saber singing out of its sheath followed by frantic crunching footsteps. She dragged her attention away from Marynka.

"Józek!"

Zosia and the prince both whirled at the shout to find Kajetan, the boy in the priest costume she'd first mistaken for the prince, racing through the garden toward them. He was holding the wooden storm cloud Zosia had left behind, or had been, until the moment he drew his weapon.

Kajetan and Józef's eyes met for the briefest instant, but it was shock not relief that lit the prince's face, and the emotion turned quickly to incandescent fury. For a wild second it seemed he might abandon his fight with Marynka and Zosia all together and launch himself instead upon the boy who'd joined them.

Marynka seized on his distraction, catching the prince's saber with her scythe, shoving the blade back, and forcing him off-balance with inhuman strength. Before he could recover, she came at him with her free hand as if intending to rip his pure heart straight from his chest.

Zosia reached for the night, and the night reached for Marynka. Thin, snakelike arms of darkness rose from the shadows to seize her, binding her in their embrace. The prince shot Zosia a look of surprise, but she didn't see what happened next because Kajetan launched himself at her.

He drove her away from the prince, away from Marynka, down a path between the garden's snowbound hedges.

Zosia ducked, sidestepping, his blade slicing within a breath of her neck. The next blow she staved off with her claws, the force reverberating up her wrist.

Vexed, she fell back, ice splintering beneath her boots, irritation surging as she considered her opponent. She was taller by inches, but he was broader through the shoulders and, despite his delicate, saintly appearance, moved with a soldier's sure footing and a dancer's fluid grace.

His expression was fierce. There was no hesitation in his hand. Worse, he didn't care to dodge. He was as reckless as Midday in his attack. *He fights*, thought Zosia suddenly, *like someone hoping to die.*

She could barely move fast enough to avoid the blade slashing at her throat, her face, her chest. She yielded a step, and another, and another. Kajetan swung his sword in an arc that would've carved her open from shoulder to hip if at that moment she hadn't dived behind a sundial.

Breathing hard, Zosia plunged the world into full darkness. A wave of night crashed over them, vanishing the moon and stars from the sky. For a heartbeat, Zosia's body was solid and then it was pure shadow. A second sweep of the blade cut through her harmlessly, as if she were no more than a ghost, while Kajetan spun in a bewildered circle.

She could hear his hoarse breathing as he groped blindly in the all-consuming blackness. The amber beads of his rosary, part of his priest's costume, clicked anxiously. Words of a prayer whispered from his lips, a plea to the saints, to the Holy Mother.

Zosia smiled softly as she gathered herself out of nothingness, re-forming a mere step behind him—dark separating from dark, shadow from shadow, coalescing into the solid shape of a girl with a silver braid and long, ink-black claws held at the ready.

But then, light sparked. Red-gold flames flared to life along the curve of Kajetan's saber, fire searing through the veil of night she'd wrapped around them.

Zosia stood rooted to the ground as he turned to face her.

Divine magic.

The kind wielded by prophets, priests, and saints. She could feel the heat of that holy fire scorch her cheeks. She took a staggered step back. She wasn't a fool. She knew when to pick her battles. She hadn't come to Warszów to risk herself fighting suicidal soldiers wielding blessed blades. And there was the prince—what was happening to him? And Marynka?

Zosia cut her losses, dissolving into swirling shadow before Kajetan's eyes, circling around him once in a whirl of air and darkness, taking one final look at this strange boy before she fled.

Kajetan let out an angry cry and slashed his flaming sword at the empty space where she'd just been.

Let him waste his time slicing his way through the dark. Zosia let the night breeze carry her away with the falling snow. She felt like she was caught in a fever dream; her thoughts were wild, spinning, unfocused. Her mind raced with a thousand questions and one she kept coming back to: That couldn't really have been Marynka back there, could it? She couldn't *really* be Midday?

10.

MARYNKA

MARYNKA'S CRIMSON BOOTS SKIDDED IN the snow. Her back slammed against a brick archway. Air burst from her lungs in a violent gasp as a half circle of royal guards surrounded her.

A rapidly shrinking half circle. Half the men were dressed in uniform and half in colorful costumes and masks. They'd formed a protective wall between Marynka and the prince. A bruise was fading from her cheek and her pulse thundered in her ears. But she was still on her feet. Her gaze jumped from face to face as she counted. "Ooh, five to one."

An angry murmur passed through the guards.

"Try not to sound so excited," snapped the closest man.

Marynka grinned and licked blood off her scythe. Magic rushed hot through her veins and heat filled her bones like sunlight. Where the fingers of her free hand brushed the brick behind her, they left singe marks.

She could take down five men.

They might be dressed as the monsters from their grand-mothers' tales, as talking bears and frost demons, skeletal sorcerers and fire-eyed gods. But she was a *real* monster. She was Midday, loyal servant to Red Jaga. No way was she going to lose. She was—

A blade scraped the wall a hairsbreadth from her neck, splintering her train of thought. She twisted sideways, lashing out with her scythe. A guard cried out and staggered back, bleeding. Before she could strike again, they were all on her at once. Five pairs of hands to her one.

Marynka was slammed against the garden archway, the hand that gripped her scythe pinned. Her skull cracked against the brickwork and red sparks shot across her vision. A fist connected with her ribs. The world slipped out of focus. One of the guards was fumbling with a flask of holy water, and Marynka remembered all of Grandmother's warnings, the reasons why they usually kept to hunting princes in their forests.

Panicked heat rippled off her.

And then light burst forth, sudden and blinding. A brilliant white-gold flare like dawn breaking over the horizon. The scene exploded with it. Blazing sunlight chased back the black of night.

The guards fell back, too, cursing, their hands raised to shield their eyes.

Another hand closed on Marynka's wrist.

She tried to yank free, twisting violently, but the hand only tightened its grip. A familiar voice spoke in her ear. "This way.

Hurry." She was pulled sideways through the archway, tripping over her own feet, past the men and away from the fight.

Shouts soared over the frantic crunching of their boots in the snow, over the sound of their ragged breathing. "There! That way! Don't let them go!" another guard in a lynx-skin cap yelled as they shoved through a hedge. Still that hand dragged her on.

Marynka narrowly avoided stepping on a peacock wandering the frozen grass. She lifted her head, staring at Beata's grim face. "I could've beaten them! I didn't need your help."

"Oh yes, you definitely looked like you were winning back there," Beata said, still dragging her along.

She threaded her fingers tightly through Marynka's. Hand in hand they fled through the falling snow, through the glitter of the winter night, a tattered devil and a star maiden. Through the castle gardens and another brick archway glinting with frost, through a gate and then on, down a narrow side alley, down narrower and narrower streets, through the snow-choked crooks and bends of the royal city.

Beata slipped on a patch of black ice as they took another turn. Marynka caught her by the waist and steadied her, skidding to a halt. Her breath left her lips in smoky plumes. The street was dark save for the silvery gleam of the moon and the constellation of stars glimmering down the length of Beata's white dress.

They were alone. No sound of pursuing footsteps. No angry shouts.

Ears still ringing with the clash of blades, blood singing from the thrill of the fight, Marynka sank to her knees in the snow and laughed and laughed until her stomach hurt.

Oh, this was just too, too perfect.

Finally. Finally, I've met you.

The shadow always looming over had taken shape at last. Midnight was no longer just a phantom presence. She was a person, flesh and blood and real. Marynka knew how her rival moved now, how she walked and how she spoke. She knew her smile and the color of her eyes, knew her figure, so much taller than hers. She knew how Midnight liked to bite the fingertips of her gloves with her sharp teeth to pull them off, revealing long slender fingers and sharp knuckles and the cold blue veins at her wrists that you could see when her sleeves rode up.

Beata was staring at her like she'd lost her mind.

"Zosia." Marynka hiccuped, trying to stop laughing. "Zosia's Midnight."

A beat of silence and then a "*What?*"

Marynka started laughing again.

Beata rubbed her hands up and down her bare arms, shivering. She must've left her cloak behind when she'd rushed to Marynka's aid, as well as the wispy veil that had been part of her costume. "I *knew* there was something off about her. I knew it. Of course the girl you've been flirting with for days is goddamn Midnight."

Midnight.

The name was a song to Marynka's ears. "I wasn't—you were

flirting with that princess! And that was before I knew who Zosia was." She'd never thought of Midnight in that way. Well, admittedly, there'd been that one dream, but who didn't have dreams like that about their nemesis? Even Beata had dreams like that.

"You've always been obsessed with her."

"Because I *despise* her," said Marynka. "Because she's the *enemy*."

They started to walk again, hurrying, back to their rooms at the House Under the Moon. Beata was babbling on, bemoaning their luck, but Marynka barely registered the words. She was barely conscious of the grand palaces passing, of the silvery ring of distant sleigh bells, of the snow catching in her hair, of her own body moving. Her mind was racing.

Those eyes like two pools of shadow. Those wicked teeth and long night-black claws. Midnight speaking with Zosia's voice, wearing her cloud shepherd disguise. That flash of something when she'd glanced up after Marynka had summoned that gust of heat to throw her backward. The focused look she'd given Marynka afterward. So intense it had made her skin prickle.

"You're pale as a ghost," said Beata worriedly. "You're trembling. The guards back there didn't hurt you, did they?"

Thoughts still occupied with Zosia, Marynka failed to answer.

It all made sense now: the way they had been drawn to each other, Zosia's veiled comments about the prince, her not sleeping, the wide-eyed way she watched the sky lighten as if seeing the sun rise for the very first time. The way her eyes seemed to light up like a cat's at night, how she looked at the sights of the city with such hunger—Midnight rarely left her dark forest.

Marynka couldn't believe she hadn't realized. In hindsight it was so, so obvious.

"Marynka. *Marynka.*"

Marynka snapped back to the present. "What?" she bit out, frustrated.

"I *said*," said Beata with the exasperated air of someone repeating their question for the hundredth time, "what are we going to do now?"

Do? Marynka cocked her head to the side in confusion. "What do you mean? She's obviously here for the prince's heart. So are we. I'll have to take it before she can."

And when she did, Grandmother would finally see she was just as good as Midnight. A better servant then her even. A stronger servant. The best.

There was a familiar wary look in Beata's eyes. She was always looking at Marynka like that, like Marynka was about to dive headfirst off a cliff and take Beata with her. She blinked away the snowflakes catching in her eyelashes and asked another question, and again Marynka failed to answer, too busy scheming, lost in thoughts of Zosia again.

Had Zosia known who *she* was? Had she planned this? She wouldn't put it past her. What were the chances they would end up sharing a sleigh? Of course, they were often sent to the same place, sent after the same hearts. Hadn't she often wondered if they'd passed one another in the street, brushed shoulders, not knowing who the other was?

But that they'd ended up traveling to Warszów *together*. Wasn't that too much of a coincidence, too much like fate?

Did it even matter, either way?

"Promise you won't do anything reckless."

Marynka's heel slid a little on the icy path as she caught the tail end of Beata's warning, startled. She'd almost forgotten her friend was there. "What do you mean, 'reckless'? Do you think I can't beat her?"

"I'm saying we can't afford to make a scene. We're here to *very carefully* take the prince's heart so we don't get caught and killed. This isn't like hunting in the forest. Promise you won't chase after her, that you'll focus on the prince. This city isn't some Karnawał arena for you to stage a duel with Midnight."

But that was exactly what this was, Marynka realized, grinning, and she intended to be the victor. How long had she waited for this, the chance to score against the other servant face-to-face, to finally bring her to her knees?

"Stop being such a mother, Beatka. You're not scared of her, are you?"

"Of course not." Beata scowled. "It's just—" She rubbed her arms and blew warmth on her fingers. "You get so worked up when it's her. You're never like this when you have to compete against me."

Marynka shrugged off the long, fleecy black cloak of her costume and, very generously, wrapped it around her friend's shoulders. She couldn't find a nice way to explain that it just wasn't the same. Beating Beata was easy. She didn't count as a proper opponent.

But snatching a heart from Midnight's claws…Midnight, who was so *good* at this, so clever, so powerful.

Nothing compared. Nothing could ever compare.

The rare times Marynka had managed to beat her to the prize, she'd felt invincible. Incandescent. And that was even before Grandmother had showered her with praise.

It probably said something about Marynka, that she didn't find the easy victory appealing, that what she craved most were the encounters that brought her closest to her own destruction.

Beata pulled the cloak closer around her body. "I think—"

"Don't," said Marynka. "You always think too much."

"One of us has to."

"*Relax.*" Marynka rubbed her hands together. "I'm telling you, this is going to be fun." Really, morning could not come fast enough.

11.

ZOSIA

THE NEXT DAY, A STRANGE wind blew through the streets of Warszów. A wind both mischievous and much too warm for winter. It was the kind of wind that *ate* winter, that drove men to madness. In the mountain valley where Zosia had been born, they called it *halny*, and when it blew, the villagers whispered that the devil was about.

Zosia was pretty sure she knew exactly who the devil was in this case, although so far she'd yet to lay eyes on Marynka.

On Midday.

Or Morning. Because Beata had to be the other half of that ridiculous duo. It wasn't that Zosia disliked her rival servants—she never thought about them long enough to hold a grudge. Black Jaga had always kept her far away from them.

"They're nothing to concern yourself with. Midday, especially. She won't last long. The girls my sister picks never do. She always chooses the wrong type. Foolish girls, too reckless and desperate to prove their worth. They burn themselves up trying to please her.

"But you, you are something altogether different, Zosia. A prize. A treasure. They'll never be a match for you. They're weak things. My youngest sister draws her power from the hours between dawn and midday, while my middle sister draws hers from the hours between midday and sundown. They split the day between them. But you and I, we rule the night, from sundown until daybreak."

Zosia frowned, a deep furrow forming between her brows, but no one seemed to notice. The sudden windy weather had failed to put a damper on the festivities. Night had given way to dawn and dawn to day. The city was wide awake, and crowds of people spilled, laughing, into the giant, glittering ice maze the king had commissioned as part of the Karnawał fun.

The snow was lost beneath so many booted feet. The square was usually a market of stalls selling wares, but today a dream-like labyrinth rose from the cobblestones: a curving maze of icy walls and archways, delicate half-moon bridges, and frosted stair-cases spiraling up the sides of towers topped with onion domes. Everything as cold and lucent as crystal. At the entrance, an ice golem waited to greet visitors. People made their way through hand in hand, arm in arm, so as not to lose each other.

Traipsing alone and wide-eyed through the splendor, Zosia might've been forgiven for forgetting why she'd come. She'd never seen anything like it. The ice maze gleamed, catching the rainbowed colors of those passing—the vivid forest greens and peacock blues and fiery reds of robes and sashes, the rich saffron of knee-high boots—and reflected them back, dazzling her so badly that she nearly missed seeing her target.

"Excuse me," she murmured, catching on to an old man's arm for balance, squeezing in beside him. All of Warszów had turned out for the day. Rich and poor, young and old, the cultured inhabitants of the capital and the visitors who'd traveled far and wide for the Karnawał all packing in to witness this latest miracle, at least half of them hoping to catch a glimpse of Lechija's most beloved prince as they explored.

Zosia leaned over the edge of the icy bridge railing. It looked over a kind of courtyard at the heart of the labyrinth. In the center of the space, someone was busy building an unflattering snow sculpture of the tsarina, while to their left a group of grown men and women waged a war of snowballs. It was amazing the way winter made people into gleeful, giggling children again.

Prince Józef was kissing cheeks with another young man. He'd traded last night's dragon costume for a finely embroidered crimson red kontusz. His unruly black hair was hidden beneath a feather-studded fur cap, and in the sunlight Zosia could see his eyes were a warm coffee brown.

She squinted, lifting a hand against the sun, the sleeves of her dusky-blue kontusik billowing in the breeze. Even as the darkness within her hummed—with anticipation, with impatience—her usual caution awoke. *Don't rush into anything*, the echo of Black Jaga's voice warned. Catching the prince alone was going to be even more difficult now, surrounded as he was by overprotective friends and admirers. When she'd tried to get close earlier, a crowd of scary girls had blocked her path.

And then there were the soldiers, wandering the maze in watchful twos and threes. Uniformed royal guards and foreign troops from the Rusjan garrison, the ever-present occupying forces.

The old man leaning over the bridge railing beside Zosia glowered behind his gray mustache and muttered something rude beneath his breath.

Was the prince under heavier guard than usual? If so, Zosia knew exactly who she could thank. At least this would slow Marynka down too. They'd both have to rethink their strategies. Although the prince himself seemed unconcerned.

She was impressed by his nerve. Most people would've locked themselves away after a violent attempt on their lives, but here he was, acting as though nothing had happened.

Perhaps that was the point. Perhaps he didn't want to worry anybody. She'd heard barely any whispers about the attack. Were they trying to hush it up so as not to spark a panic?

There *was* a faint tightness to his smile, even as he flung a word to a friend, shared a joke with another, as he called over his shoulder to a stranger.

Zosia watched Józef turn to greet a pretty girl, doffing his fur cap before him so low its feathers swept the snow. The girl turned bright red and very nearly swooned.

"All he does is flirt," grumbled the old man beside Zosia, mopping sweat from his brow. "And drink and eat and throw parties. Lose money at cards." He made a sound of frustrated disgust. "Tens of thousands of złotys wasted in the first weeks of the Karnawał alone. Why did he bother to come back to Warszów if he wasn't going to be of any help?"

Zosia shot him a half-curious glance.

"Up all night, dancing past dawn," he rambled on. "He stumbled into the cathedral for mass this morning with all his friends still dressed in costume. Priest almost had a fit. Turned purple every time he looked to the pews and saw a dragon saying prayers with a stork and a bear. Oh, you think that's funny, do you? You young people think this is all a game." His voice trailed off, his expression darkening. His arm knocked Zosia's shoulder as he pointed with an unsteady finger. "And there's another one who should have known better than to come back here."

Glancing down at the bustle below, Zosia couldn't make out who he was pointing at, but her gaze caught on the finished snow sculpture of the tsarina. The woman everyone blamed for Lechija's troubles. Even Black Jaga had spoken of her. The tale of her rise to power had sounded like the kind of fairy tale a real grandmother might tell to amuse her grandchild.

"*She was just a simple girl like you once.*"

A simple girl who had been whisked away to Rusja's capital to marry a future tsar. A simple girl who had survived all manner of treacherous court intrigue, who'd had her husband murdered and become the sole ruler of an empire.

A simple girl who, in those first lonely days at court, had fallen in love with a Lechijan boy she had later placed on Lechija's throne. Only to later still, devour his kingdom piece by piece.

Zosia wondered if she would admire the tsarina more if the woman hadn't used the power she'd amassed to invade Zosia's home. She wondered if the tsarina herself had enjoyed turning the tables on all the people who had underestimated her, who had treated her badly. Did she feel it was a victory if in the end she had become exactly like them?

Sometimes Zosia worried that was what *she* was doing. In taking and eating princes' hearts, was she merely making herself into another witch? A witch as terrible as Black Jaga? She wanted to believe she was better than the old woman who'd made her a servant. She hadn't wanted to become a monster. She was only doing what she had to in order to survive.

Suddenly Zosia stiffened, finally recognizing just who the old man had been pointing at, the saintly looking boy she'd fought in the dark of the castle gardens. Kajetan. So he was here too. Hovering a careful distance from the circle of admirers surrounding the prince. He still wore his blessed saber at his hip.

He turned slightly, looking up in her direction, eyes narrowing thoughtfully.

Hastily, Zosia ducked her head, pushing back against a quick, sharp surge of panic. She pasted a vague smile on her face as she pretended only to admire the view, all the while keeping a watch on him from the corner of her eye.

Other people exploring the ice maze were taking note of Kajetan, too, and she realized what she'd mistaken as reverence last night was in truth wariness. Suspicion. Even fury. The crowd watched him as though he were some poisonous animal slithering among them, a serpent about to strike.

The old man muttered and thumped a fist down hard on the railing.

Ice cracked, white lines spreading in quick branch-like veins. Zosia jumped and the old man himself looked startled. He'd gone very red in the face.

He removed his fur cap, pressing a hand to his brow, apologizing. "I'm not feeling myself. It's this sun. This unseasonable wind."

It had picked up again, blowing hot, yanking strands free from Zosia's silvery braid, curling them playfully around her neck. The air shimmered. For a brief moment, she could have sworn there was a girl standing behind the old man, a little farther down the slope of the bridge—red-brown curls, red robes, summer-brown skin, sharp teeth—but then Zosia blinked and the girl disappeared.

Her heart skipped a beat and she squinted, but the sun was shining like a white-hot moon in the heavens, reflecting off all the ice. She could barely see anything through the glare. Her attention darted back to the prince. He was still chatting with his friends.

Zosia's throat ran dry. Was it the sun making her see things? She backed away from the railing and retreated into the shadows of the maze, letting the blessedly cool shade melt some of the heat.

But even here the walls were starting to drip.

They flashed darkly, wetly, as she took a turn that led down to the courtyard where the prince was, some niggling sense prompting her to get closer to Józef just in case. Sweat slid down her spine and between her breasts as she waded through the frustrating swell of people following the same path. Her robes stuck to her skin. Little streams of water trickled here and there, forming pools that soaked the boots of those exploring.

She spied Kajetan first, still standing in the shadow of the icy bridge.

"Are you well?" someone asked as she put a hand to a wall to steady herself, catching her breath as a wave of dizziness made her head spin.

"I'm fine. I—"

It took a moment to realize they hadn't addressed her, a moment to realize she wasn't the only one feeling hot and dizzy and disoriented. But it was only when the searing wind started to whisper in her ears, in the *crowd's* ears, that she really understood.

It started with a snowball hurled at Kajetan's head. He staggered. Someone laughed. Someone shouted in anger. The wind shook with mischief, ripping fur caps from heads. And again, it was that same wind that blew through the valleys back home, through the Midnight Forest, the kind of wind that ate winter and drove men to madness, that leveled entire forests. Violent fights broke out when a wind like this blew. Murders were committed. Men walked into the trees and hung themselves.

Fists flew as a scuffle broke out between a boy who'd rushed to Kajetan's side and the boy who'd thrown the snowball.

Two Rusjan soldiers took issue with the artist who'd crafted the unflattering snow sculpture of their tsarina. Another man insulted another man's mustache, the very gravest of insults.

Zosia stood frozen, slack-jawed, her long braid whipping the air as the world around her descended into chaos. Because Marynka could *not* be attempting to take the prince's heart before all of Warszów, in front of everyone.

That was absurd. That was *ridiculous*.

Oh, what was Zosia thinking? Of course this was exactly the type of wild, reckless plan Midday would come up with—create a commotion with her magic, drive people sick with the heat of the sun, and go after the prince in all the confusion. She had no finesse. No sense of subtlety.

She had always been like that, infuriating and intriguing, mesmerizing and maddening. Her reckless confidence slammed up against Zosia's caution, daring her to unleash this kind of chaos too, to flex her power on a grand scale, to cast off the shackles of her restraint.

The first time Zosia had come up against her face to face,

Midday had taken the form of a fiery whirlwind, blowing in and raising a great column of dust and leaves, lifting the prince Zosia had been painstakingly tracking off his feet and into the air, carrying him off while Zosia stood staring after them open-mouthed.

Across the city, bells started to ring. Twelve strokes to signal the hour. Twelve for midnight and also for midday. The hours of ghosts and devils.

The red sun beat down. Heat baked the air, merciless as any blaze. The walls of the ice maze were melting, slanting sideways under the force of the strengthening wind. Sweat dripped from Zosia's temples. Midday was Marynka's hour, and beneath the fierce sunlight, the dark magic of night receded. Her feeble shadow hid at her feet.

But...

Zosia's mouth curved into an uncharacteristic, almost wild smile. A smile she only ever wore when she went up against her rival.

Midday was powerful, yes. But not as powerful as Zosia. And Zosia had been *growing* her power. She wasn't the same girl she'd been when Midday had first appeared before her. She knew what a heart ripped beating and red from a chest tasted like now, knew the feel of the magic inside her increasing. She could summon the darkness now, even when the shadows were at their shortest. If this was how Marynka wished to play it, then—the veins on the underside of her wrists turned an inky black that coiled up her arms.

Biting the fingertip of a leather glove, Zosia stripped the

fabric from her hands, drawing the nearest shadows to her with the curving of her bare fingers, beckoning them close. They condensed, swirling in her palm to form a dagger, the blade icy and gleaming as black glass.

Zosia scanned the roiling crowd, the circles of shrieking spectators crowding around each fight, the bloodied faces of the soldiers swinging fists, brawling in piles on the ground. Squinting, and searching in vain for the culprit behind the chaos. The air wavered like a mirage. The ominous sounded of ice cracking echoed from every direction. An icy wall slumped and collapsed with a roar, separating the prince from his friends.

Enough of this.

Zosia took a deep breath and snapped her fingers.

Darkness fell like a curtain, like a funeral shroud. For a beat the world was black, cold and still and silent. Everything and everyone wrapped in shadow save a single figure who seemed to burn before Zosia's eyes. Marynka's outline wavered like a flame in a strong wind. Her edges were limned with fiery light. She was looking extremely pleased with herself.

There you are.

The darkness lifted abruptly, before anyone had time to blink or scream or panic.

Zosia knifed her body forward. Her dagger cut through the air with a flash, embedding itself in the white-glazed earth, pinning the billowing hem of Marynka's red skirt to the ground.

She whirled, cursing, her edges solidifying.

"It really is you, isn't it?" Zosia murmured. This was the same girl she'd sat up through the night with, had waited out the dark with. The girl who'd fallen asleep on Zosia's shoulder as the sleigh carried them toward the city. A part of her had hoped she was somehow mistaken. "I thought—" She shook away the thoughts. Priorities. The prince came first. She could have a meltdown over this later.

"You really are Midday, aren't you? Red Jaga's servant. And you've been sent to take the prince's heart just like I have."

Flame bloomed in the cups of Marynka's palms.

Zosia moved closer, holding her gaze. Letting her arms fall to her sides, she pasted her most hurt expression on her face. "It's just I thought we were something like friends."

The wind dropped slightly. Marynka seemed to hesitate, something like uncertainty flashing in those unnaturally golden eyes. She started to move closer too—or tried to—looked down to find her boots held fast to the frozen ground.

The black ice from Zosia's dagger spread like frost from where it pinned Marynka's skirt, over the earth and in thick bands over her boots and up her ankles.

The smile Zosia graced Marynka with was one of pure wickedness. "Oh, Midday, always so careless."

Uncertainty turned to shock, turned to fury.

But it was too late. Before Marynka could retaliate, the ice swept up her shins and thighs and stomach, climbed her chest and arms and up her throat. Her entire body froze solid in less than a heartbeat.

Just like that, the wild wind died down. In the quiet left behind, Zosia heard voices, including the prince's, calling for calm. Her pulsed steadied as she moved to whisper in Marynka's icy ear. "I mean it, you know. I do consider us friends, but this heart's a very important one to me. I can't let anyone else have it. But afterward...afterward, we should enjoy the rest of the Karnawał together. We don't have to lose what we have over this. We could sneak into another costume ball and—" She stepped back at the sound of approaching footsteps and turned to find a young man with a thick black beard and a young woman in green staring past her at Marynka.

"Oh," the young woman said. "Is it—is it broken?"

"I'm never seen an ice golem of that color or design before." The young man frowned and tugged his beard. "I wonder who made it. Why did they want to carve its face like that? It looks so angry."

"It's almost frightening," added the young woman.

"Is it?" Zosia said, giving Marynka's frozen head a pat. She stared at her face, at the lips parted as if to speak, features caught between shock and fury. She stroked her finger down an icy cheek. "I think she's cute. Look at all those vicious teeth."

The young couple gave her a curious look.

Zosia flicked her braid over one shoulder. "Now that it's stopped moving though, it's not very interesting." She stepped around the couple, heading back toward the center of the maze. "By the way, did either of you happen to see which way the prince went?"

12.

MARYNKA

BY THE TIME BEATA HELPED Marynka melt free of her icy black prison, hours had passed. The red sun had sunk into the horizon. The city was lost to darkness. That was the trouble with winter; the days were too short. The hours mere mouthfuls. The darkness too eager to gobble up the world. Midnight held the advantage in the colder months, and she never played to lose.

Marynka tipped her head back to a sea of stars. The air tasted bitterly of moonlight, but she didn't have time to feel humiliated. She couldn't let her mind dwell on yet another failure, on that awful moment when her body had revolted against her, that horrid moment of indecision when Zosia's words had her recalling their journey together, all the times they'd…

Marynka shook herself.

Zosia had taken advantage of that, had *tricked* her.

"Where is she?" Marynka demanded through chattering

teeth as Beata summoned sunlight between her palms, warming Marynka's cheeks and fingers and blue, blue lips.

"You idiot," Beata snapped, ignoring the question. "What if you were really hurt this time? What if I hadn't found you? What if someone had pushed you over and you'd shattered into pieces? Didn't I tell you not to do anything reckless? You couldn't take a moment to call for me?"

Marynka caught Beata's hand, squeezing it in an iron grip. "Where *is* she?" A sudden awful thought occurred. "The prince?"

"Still has his heart," Beata said, slowing the frantic pounding of Marynka's own. "Last I saw him. They blamed the commotion on freak weather and tensions boiling over. He's been surrounded by people all day. I think Zosia didn't want to risk—"

Marynka cut her off with a nod. She didn't need any more of an explanation. If Midnight had actually been as clever as Grandmother thought she was, she would've acted right away, before Marynka had a chance to free herself. But Marynka knew her. She knew so many tiny, insignificant facts about Midnight that probably no one else in the world knew. Midnight was too cautious. She didn't like to risk striking in broad daylight unless she absolutely had to. She preferred to hide herself until her unsuspecting marks fell asleep, to sneak up on her victims in the dark like the creepy ghoul that she was.

And that would be her downfall.

"I know what she'll try next," Marynka said, dragging Beata

after her through the snow. "Hurry up! The prince lives in the Copper Palace, doesn't he? You didn't hear anything about him attending another costume ball?"

"No. But—"

"Then we know exactly where to go."

The small but elegant palace the king had gifted his beloved nephew was named for its glossy copper roof. It was a short walk's distance from the Golden Castle, from the ice maze, and was, of course, watched over by a contingent of the royal guard. Every uniformed figure stood at attention, resplendent in their bright double-breasted jackets and sashes. Each carried a curved saber and wore a glittery mask.

Marynka's eyebrows rose.

"Here." Beata pressed something smooth and icy into her hands.

Marynka turned the half mask between her fingers. It was a delicate, glassy thing that looked to be crafted from crystal. Only its cold told her it was made of ice. Ice, and magic. The moonlight sparkled through it.

"It's another Karnawał game," Beata whispered, the words forming clouds. "They were handing them out while you were frozen, after everything calmed down. Enchanted ice masks. The whole city's wearing them. They're supposed to melt away at midnight, or when you come face-to-face with your soul mate."

Ah, of course, because Karnawał was the time of year to search for the other half of your heart.

"You should have seen how many girls kept trying to approach the prince."

Marynka rolled her eyes, but a fresh disguise wouldn't hurt. There was no string to tie the thing in place, no fastenings, but when she touched the mask to her skin it froze fast, fitting so firmly over her features that she couldn't pull it off.

Beata put on her own and cast a tiny, hopeful, very annoying glance in Marynka's direction. Her shoulders drooped slightly when neither of their masks showed signs of melting. She was quick to recover, though, tossing her golden braids back briskly and adjusting her sapphire-studded fur cap, narrowing her eyes on a pair of guards.

"Go get them, sunshine," Marynka murmured.

This was what Bright Morning was good at—meeting her brought men to misery. Beata didn't even need to transform or use her dainty white claws half the time. Her starry violet eyes bewitched with a glance. The princes she appeared to dug their bloody hearts from their chests themselves and handed them over like gifts. Only this time…

Beata waved a gloved hand back and forth in front of the guards' faces. The men didn't move. Through the slits in their masks, Marynka could see their eyes were closed. They were asleep on their feet.

"God's blood," Beata cursed. Night had come to the Copper Palace and brought sleep with her.

Marynka was already slipping past, rushing through the front doors and out of the cold, boots leaving a trail of mud and snow. She stumbled over a servant lying slumbering on the floor in the magnificent foyer. The man startled awake, so it wasn't as though they couldn't be woken.

Marynka left Beata to deal with him.

Adrenaline fueled her movements. Her blood pulsed with the all-consuming need to win against Midnight. In truth, there was a terrible thrill that came with having the tables turned on you, in realizing you were one lethal step behind, that the victory you'd been so certain of was about to be snatched straight out of your hands.

Marynka both hated and loved this feeling. Beata complained that the witches forced them to play this twisted game, but a tiny part of her relished it. She was convinced a part of Zosia did too.

Keeping her footsteps light, poking her head through every doorway, she made her way through another maze, this time of grand salons and offices and gold-gilded chambers. In every room she peered into, she discovered more servants and guests in glittery masks, slouched in corners, upon staircases, all snoring softly. Even the prince's younger sister lay slumped between a sofa and a great, towering tiled stove, her pretty head resting on a footstool and a fluffy white dog curled up in her arms.

It was only when she reached the prince's apartments on the uppermost level of the palace that Marynka finally made out signs of life. Voices tangled with soft music and the clink of glassware. A tipsy group of young men were sipping from glasses of something steaming poured from a great jeweled samovar.

Quietly, Marynka slipped past the open door, turned a corner, and came face-to-face with a man standing guard outside the prince's sleeping room.

She froze.

The man gave her a knowing smirk. "Come to see if you might be the prince's soul mate?"

Marynka smiled innocently and ducked her head, twisting her fingers together.

The man chuckled and, after giving her a look up and down and dismissing her as just another guest, stepped aside to allow her entrance.

Marynka quickly deduced she wasn't the first girl to have snuck into this room.

Perhaps not even the first girl to do so tonight…

The door clicked closed behind her. The quiet in the prince's sleeping room was thick and heavy. Candles flickered, illuminating shiny ornaments and fine paintings. Vibrant rugs covered the floor, softening her steps. It was almost too dark to make out more than the outlines of a curtained bed and a grand piano. The prince was said to be fond of playing.

A flick of her wrist and Marynka's scythe materialized in her hand. She cast her senses out, a spider in a web, waiting for the threads to tremble.

Where are you, Zosia? Where did you go?

Her ears strained to catch any hint of movement, the sound of breathing.

Nothing.

Nothing but the rapid beating of her own heart, a whisper of wind at the windows.

No shadows moved.

Come out. Come out and—

Abruptly, the double doors at the opposite end of the room flung wide. Marynka instinctively shrank back into a shadowed niche behind the sculpture of a winged rider cast in bronze.

There was a loud crash, followed by a curse, and then an exceedingly drunken prince wearing an elaborate ice mask staggered into the sleeping room, one hand reaching to the furniture for support.

A slender shadow followed after him, stealing through the doors just before they closed.

Marynka was about to call out a greeting, something clever like: *Hello, Midnight, fancy seeing you here* or *We really do have to stop meeting like this.* There was no shortage to the witty and devastating remarks she'd dreamed up over the years, rehearsing for just such a moment as this.

But the prince spoke first. "Who's there?" he called, hand going to the eagle's-head hilt of his saber.

The tall, shadowy figure crept closer. Marynka frowned at the square angle of their jaw, the tousle of brown hair falling over their brow, brushing the edges of an ice mask nearly as elaborate as the prince's.

Who was this fool intruding upon her and Zosia's game?

"*Kajetan?*" The name left the prince's mouth like a curse.

There was a painful pause. The boy in the shadows coughed into his fist and made a vain attempt to muffle his voice. "I think you've mistaken me for—"

"Mother of God, I can tell it's you. Do you think I can't recognize you in that ridiculous mask? Have you lost your mind?" The prince's hand hadn't left the hilt of his sword. "Did you come here to kill me? Your attack at the costume ball failed, so you decided to try again?"

"That wasn't me!" the other boy protested. He crossed the room. "I helped to fend those monsters off. I—" Water dripped onto the rug as his mask began to melt.

So did the prince's.

Marynka didn't think she'd ever seen anyone look as appalled as Józef did in that instant. She recognized the other boy now. He was the one who'd chased after Zosia in the castle gardens. And apparently, the prince's soul mate.

"I came here tonight to *warn* you," Kajetan said now, struggling to regain his composure.

Hidden in the shadows, Marynka's eyes narrowed.

"Warn me?" Józef said.

"It's not safe for you here. You shouldn't have come back. I don't know who those girls were that attacked you. I don't know *what* they were. There was nothing natural about the creature I fought. And that strange wind earlier today... I swear to you, I saw that same monster in the ice maze. A girl with a silver braid. She was watching you. I swear I've seen her here tonight, wearing one of these cursed masks. I don't know who would have let her in."

"I don't know who let *you* in," cut in Józef. "But trust me when I find out—"

"Józek," Kajetan said, clenching his fist, twisting the last syllable of the prince's name into something with a softer ending.

The prince's face was livid.

"If you would just listen. I'm telling you the truth as God is in Heaven. It's too dangerous here. Leave tonight. Leave this instant."

"I'm not going to hide!"

"Return to Ostarr. You need to leave Warszów, get out of Lechija."

"And you need to get the hell out of my room," the prince exploded, fumbling to draw his saber.

"I don't want to fight," said Kajetan urgently. "The vodka's gone to your head. I'm trying to warn you. I'm not your enemy."

"Not my *enemy*?" The glare the prince shot the other boy could have reduced him to ash where he stood. It would have made Red Jaga proud. "You're a traitor to this kingdom. You fought for the tsarina. You rained holy fire on my soldiers. You shot my horse out from under me!"

"How long do you think you'll be angry about that?"

Józef finally managed to free his sword but lost his balance and fell against the piano.

Both Marynka and Kajetan jerked in alarm. At this rate, the fool was going to impale himself on his own damn blade.

"Wait!" Kajetan motioned for peace, hands up.

The prince's sword scraped the wall. "Draw your saber, you coward!"

Kajetan stepped back, and when the prince tripped over himself a second time, he fled the room. "Remember I warned you! Don't let your guard down, and stop drinking so much. Everyone knows you have a weakness for a pretty face!"

The prince started to give chase, and Marynka quickly summoned a gust of wind to stop him from tripping over his feet.

Józef caught himself against a bedpost and cursed, swaying there a moment to collect himself. He let his naked saber fall to the floor and then collapsed onto his back on the bed, an arm thrown over his eyes, chest heaving.

Marynka waited, listening. She wasn't sure what had just happened, but so long as the prince was happy to ignore warnings of danger, of monsters and strange girls, she didn't care. It had nothing to do with her.

A clock chimed somewhere in the room. The prince's breathing slowly steadied. So did Marynka's. Yet still she waited, watching the shadows as if they might come suddenly alive. Had the commotion scared Zosia off? Should *she* seize this chance and act?

Minutes passed in anguished indecision. The candles dimmed, the dark thickening like a fog.

From out of that dark crept Midnight like a wolf, death padding forward on soundless feet. Black Midnight who could enter anywhere, though the doors and windows might be locked and bolted. Midnight who could cast herself into any shape, stretch herself as long and thin as shadow, as flat as paper to slip beneath a door or needle-thin to slither through a keyhole.

Midnight who could cause sleep with a touch, who could trap her victims in nightmares.

Behind the bronze statue, Marynka blinked rapidly to rouse herself. She couldn't put a name to the emotion twisting through her. It wasn't quite envy, nor admiration. But an agonizing mix of the two. Zosia's hair was luminous as moonlight, her robes a spill of lightless black. Her eyes were skull-like hollows. Darkness leaked from her in tendrils. Candles guttered in her wake.

It was a kind of torture, how perfect she looked. Marynka might have loathed the other girl with all her heart, but there was no denying that Midnight was a glorious, glorious monster. And now that she had seen her in both her monstrous and human forms, she could mark the similarities. The hard jaw and sharply pointed chin. The deep-set eyes. Midnight moved with the same grace as Zosia, the same easy poise that came from years of simply being the best.

Marynka's heart stuttered.

Show-off.

Taking care so that her long black claws didn't scrape the mattress, Zosia straddled the prince's legs, settling on his thighs light as a caress. He stirred, eyelids fluttering, caught in that state between dreaming and waking when you weren't sure whether what you were seeing, sensing, feeling was real or simply a product of your imagination.

Marynka had often dreamed of this too—of the heavy weight of another body pressing upon her own, of being held down by hands made of pure darkness, of Midnight with a bored look on her monstrous face as she kept Marynka from rising.

Now, though, Zosia wore a small, self-satisfied smile.

Oh, how Marynka wanted to see her frustrated, furious, desperate, just once. She wanted to see her on her knees. She wanted to ruin Zosia as thoroughly as Zosia did her without even trying.

The candle flames throughout the room jumped, flaring to new life. The monster looming over the prince froze. Its outlines going rigid before they shifted as Midnight quickly reshaped herself.

A second later all that perched on Prince Józef's chest was an innocent black kitten. Its ears twitched. Its tail lashed back and forth.

Again, Marynka was filled with that unwilling admiration, followed by a flash of red-hot jealousy that licked up her bones like kindling. She found it hard enough to transform herself into a dust cloud, to twist herself into a fiery summer wind, but Zosia changed form so effortlessly. Did she really have to be so much better at everything? Why were things so easy for her?

How am I meant to compete with someone like you?

Marynka gritted her teeth and bellowed as loud as she could, "Help! Quick! Oh, quick! A monster is trying to kill the prince!"

A snap of her fingers set the tip of the kitten's tail on fire. A dozen things happened at once: the kitten let out an agonized yowl, there was a terrific crash from outside the room, the prince bolted upright, gasping, the doors swung open so violently they almost wrenched from their hinges, the guard who'd smirked at Marynka burst in, followed by two servants, three boys with their sabers drawn, and the prince's sister's fluffy white dog.

Commotion. Chaos.

The dog let out a joyful bark. The kitten, its tail smoking, streaked off the bed.

Marynka let her eyes fall shut and took a deep, satisfied breath, drawing the sounds of Zosia's audible distress into her lungs. Savoring it.

"Nothing personal," she whispered.

13.

ZOSIA

THERE WAS NO BRUSHING OFF or hushing up the third attempt on the prince's life. Talk spread fast through the city. A thick mist threaded the streets like smoke, and those striding through it wore matching frowns and spoke in low, tense voices. Zosia didn't need to hear what they were muttering to know they weren't chatting about the weather. Fear passed from person to person like a sickness with each new whisper.

A scuffle broke out in front of the Royal Cadet School among foreign soldiers and patriotic students. Sleigh drivers refused to carry passengers down certain avenues. The *Warszów Courier* reported that the princess fainted at a salon party, claiming to have seen a monstrous pair of eyes staring at her through a frosted window. The prince turned down an invitation to another costume ball with the weak excuse that he needed to rest his feet.

"The Rusjans have brought a monster into our city," Zosia heard a young man tell his family as she passed the steps of a snow-capped cathedral. His ruddy face was lit by the glow of a fat beeswax candle. Half the population had crammed into the city's churches in droves this morning to celebrate the midwinter feast day. Everyone eager to have their candles blessed, to take a little holy fire home for protection.

"It escaped the night of the ambassador's ball," the young man continued, gesturing excitedly. "The tsarina's given the ambassador a devil on a leash, and he sets it on those who offend him. Like the prince. He's always hated Józef. He believes he's a bad influence on the king, so now the monster's hunting him."

"Oh, hush," said an older woman, very likely the young man's mother. She had a whole armful of candles pressed to her generous bosom. "All that talk. You're going to blow the candle out."

Zosia glanced down at her own unlit candle, which she was holding simply to blend in. She couldn't risk handling actual holy fire, but for everyone else, it was important to keep one taper burning the whole way home. The eldest in the family would use it to safeguard the house, dripping wax upon the thresholds and burning black crosses into the ceiling beams to scare away misfortune and wicked spirits—and in this case, it was hoped, also the monster haunting the city. The wide, misty avenues and meandering streets were a sea of ghostly, flickering lights. The red-orange flames of hundreds of candles danced like ogniki, like the lost souls of the dead that haunted the Midnight Forest.

Moving on, feeling just the tiniest bit hypocritical, Zosia

glided down a pathway paved with frost, her dark fur-lined cloak whipping at her ankles. Her left ankle twinged with a phantom ache where the princess's fluffy white dog had bitten her as she'd fled the prince's sleeping chamber. It wasn't often that someone managed to turn the tables on her, which made it all the more unbearable when they did.

Things had always come easily to Zosia. It was frustrating, infuriating, when they didn't work from the beginning. This was the one area where she had no patience. She wasn't like Midday— always rising from the ashes of defeat. Midday, who knew what it was like to have to work hard at something.

She should've known Marynka wouldn't go down so easily. Where other people, where any normal person, would've given up, Marynka charged on regardless, stubborn and determined. There was a fire in Midday that never failed to make Zosia's heart race. The idea of giving up would never even cross her mind.

Marynka was likely oozing with satisfaction right now, but not for a second was Zosia going to let her come out of this victorious.

A lesser person might have focused on revenge, and she had cast a quick look—all right, maybe several quick looks—about for the other girl, but she was above that. She had self-control. The main thing was to concentrate on the goal. If she *did* happen to run into Marynka, she was definitely going to murder her with her bare hands but for now…

The prince came first.

The best kind of revenge, after all, was success.

Figures flashed ahead, blurs of darkness among the mist. Ice splintered beneath Zosia's boots as she crossed the street, keeping a careful distance, eyes on one figure in particular. The prince was dressed casually, in clothes that would blend easily into a crowd, but even if she hadn't been watching since he left the Copper Palace, she would've known him from his broad shoulders and solid build. After holing up indoors for three whole days, Zosia supposed he'd grown bored or tired of hiding. Or maybe he'd just wanted to join in with the feast-day festivities like everyone else. Whatever his motives, they didn't matter.

She slowed when he slowed, quickened her pace when he did. Paused when he paused—to stop and crouch down to relight a crying child's candle with the flame from his own. Zosia sneered a little. But the sight gave her an idea.

The group of young men accompanying Józef kept their hands close to the hilts of their sabers. One, with tawny skin and a scar crossing his temple, was dressed in the uniform of the king's elite guard. He was also clearly a friend and kept teasing the prince, trying to make him confess the name of whoever had made his enchanted ice mask melt the other night.

Zosia was grateful for their loud voices and laughter. It made it easier not to lose them. The mist held on to the city with dissolving hands, but it was annoyingly stubborn. Growing thin and insubstantial one moment, only to unexpectedly thicken and steal the prince from view the next. That and the constant flickering of the candles played tricks on her eyes. Figures and frost-laced buildings faded in and out of sight. Grand old palaces were suddenly there, then not there, like ghosts.

Her skin prickled, but she couldn't tell if it was because of all the divine magic or something else. The prince and his friends turned a corner. Picturing the map of the city in her head, Zosia hurried down a different side alley, intending to loop back and come out ahead of them. They were heading away from the Copper Palace and the Golden Castle and the Ice Maze, moving in the direction of the abutting Christian, Jewish, and Muslim cemeteries.

She would orchestrate a crash meeting—pretend to clumsily bump into the prince, pretend the blessed flame of her candle had died. It was a tactic she'd used before to get close to a target.

Zosia was panting as she stepped to the mouth of the alley. The mist was thick as soup here, and she ran blindly into a shorter body. She dropped her candle. "Why are you *here*?" she ground out, exasperated.

"Why are *you*?" Marynka shot back. "Find your own misty avenue to ambush the prince. Aren't you too cautious to be stalking him in broad daylight?"

"And you? You wouldn't be about to launch another ridiculous attack in front of half of Warszów?"

Black ice snaked over the ground, sweeping over Marynka's boots and up to encase her body, but Marynka knew better this time. Heat shimmered around her like a shield. Where the cold darkness touched her boots, it melted.

Her lip curled as if she were amused. "You'll have to do better than that." She fixed her sun-gold gaze on Zosia. A glowing scythe materialized in her hands. Her teeth were gleaming points. "I'm not falling for that trick again."

Zosia ripped a glove off, calling to the shadows. An icy ink-black dagger formed in her palm an instant before Marynka's scythe came singing down. Zosia's blade shattered on impact, and she hissed as slivers of ice cut into her fingers.

Shadows swirled across her skin, coiling up her wrists like smoke. Her wounds healed in seconds. Her fingers tapered to long, lethal claws. "You really do not want to go toe-to-toe with me."

"Don't I?" Marynka bared her teeth in challenge, and Zosia couldn't help it; she grinned back. For a moment their faces were a mirror image of each other's.

What even *was* this? Zosia fought to wipe the grin from her face. How could she even feel like this, so excited, whilst at the same time feeling so incredibly irritated? It shouldn't make her heart beat faster that Marynka could stand her ground before her, that she wasn't afraid, that she didn't flinch from Zosia's monstrousness, that she smiled at it, so clearly pleased with even the worst parts of Zosia that Zosia could barely stand it.

That she could even *catch* Zosia's arm as she lashed out—

A foot hooked Zosia's ankle, and she stumbled backward as

Marynka threw her weight forward, pressing Zosia back against the unforgiving brick of the alley wall, gripping her wrist so hard it almost hurt.

Zosia winced as the hardness of the wall met her shoulders, driving the air from her lungs. The burning edge of Marynka's scythe scraped against her throat. A slip of her hand… It would be nothing for Midday to end her.

Just as it would be nothing for Zosia to tear Marynka open from stomach to hip. Her free hand pressed between their bodies, long, ink-dark claws digging into the other girl's navel. "Don't hold back on my behalf."

The air sparked. "I am going to cook you inside your own skin."

"Try it," Zosia said, throat straining away as the glowing edge of the scythe pressed a red line into her skin. "I'll tear you in two."

They were at a stalemate.

Marynka's fur cap had fallen back. Her hair was on fire in a spill of pale sun filtering through the mist, a stray curl skewed across her forehead. She leveled Zosia with a look that might have been intimidating if she hadn't had to tilt her head back and look up to lock eyes.

They were standing chest to chest, breath fogging the air between them. Both daring each other to make the first move, to be the first to retreat.

This close, Zosia could count the freckles dusted like kisses across Marynka's nose, could feel her breath, see the way her lips were chapped with cold. Those lips were dangerously close, and for a heartrending moment, Zosia seriously considered what would happen if she leaned forward, leaned down, and pressed their mouths together.

Would Marynka freeze?

Would she scream?

Would she *bite*?

A hundred inappropriate thoughts Zosia had buried during their journey together came surging back. The unfairness of it all stuck in her throat and she gritted her teeth, sucking in a breath through her nose as she fought desperately to ignore the heat pooling in the pit of her stomach. Marynka was Midday. Her opposite. Her rival. Her... Was there even a word for a rival who you also wanted to kiss? Whatever she was, Marynka was the very last person she should be having those sorts of thoughts about.

"I wish," she said bitterly, "that I'd never met you."

"Oh?" snarled Marynka. "I'm so glad the feeling is mutual."

"When are you going to give up? How many years have we been competing for hearts? Remind me again, how many times have you lost now?"

"Who knows," Marynka said. "A few times. Not a lot."

"You've lost twenty-four times."

"Twenty-*three* times!"

"So you *have* been keeping count—"

The crunch of approaching footsteps had them both tensing.

"Step back," Zosia hissed.

"Or what? You'll slice me open in front of half of Warszów? In front of whoever walks around that corner?"

"You'd love that, wouldn't you? They'll *see* us. They'll know us for what we are. You're going to get us caught."

"Then we'd better enjoy this while we still can," Marynka said, not moving an inch.

"Only *you* would find this fun."

"Oh, don't try to pretend like you don't."

The footsteps drew closer. Zosia could make out voices. Muffled laughter. Any second now, whoever it was would pass by the mouth of the alley and find two monsters at each other's throats.

Zosia's heart stuttered in her chest. The scythe bit into her skin, tilting her chin slightly up. There was a reckless gleam in Marynka's eyes that said: *If I'm going down, I'm taking you with me.*

How was this fool even still alive?

A hot trickle of scarlet ran down Zosia's neck and into her fur collar. The cut healed instantly but the blood remained. It was far from the first time the two of them had caused a scene, but this felt different, more dangerous. It was the first time there had been so much at stake.

Sweat beaded at Marynka's temples.

Zosia let out a breath.

At the very last moment they drew apart. Zosia's claws vanished. Marynka hid her glowing scythe behind her back. Her eyes faded from incandescent gold to a human shade of hazel. The prince passed by right in front of them.

He didn't even glance their way, but one of the boys he was walking with did. He looked a little startled to find two girls in red and black cloaks staring silently at him from the misty entrance of the alleyway.

Zosia shrank from the attention but Marynka loved it and waved.

The boy raised an amused eyebrow. The prince and his company moved from view. A beat passed. Another. If they'd raced to follow immediately, they would have missed the final boy stalking his fellows' steps, trailing a careful and deliberate distance behind as Zosia had.

His fur cap was plumed with costly peacock feathers, studded with a giant ruby, and drawn low over his brows to shadow his saintly features. The thick collar of his coat ate up his slender neck.

Still, Zosia recognized him. Kajetan. "Why is he always—"

"Him again," Marynka said, peering round the side of the building, elbowing Zosia out of the way.

Zosia elbowed her back, both of them spilling into the main street. "Do you think he's also after the prince? Why else would he—"

"No, the other night he tried to warn Józef against us. He's the prince's soul mate."

Up ahead, the prince and his friends had paused. Kajetan paused too. Zosia dragged Marynka to a halt before they ran straight into his back.

A sleigh dashed by on their right, speeding down the center of the street, through the snow. The bells on the horses' harnesses ringing sweetly.

The bright flame of the blessed candle Kajetan carried stuttered in its wake, wobbling until he curled his fingers around the glow. Then it blazed with unnatural steadiness. It hurt Zosia's eyes to look at it directly. Her skin itched. Kajetan's lips moved as if in prayer. The mist curled around him like a pet.

"I thought it was you playing tricks with the mist," she murmured, "trying to make it hard to follow Józef."

"I thought it was *you*," Marynka said. "I even got separated from Beata in it."

They were both silent for a breath.

Zosia cast a glance sideways. Marynka's single raised brow said it all: *Shall I kill him, or do you want to?*

A dozen paces or so ahead, Kajetan started walking, only to find himself suddenly dazzled by a blinding burst of sunlight burning through the mist. He threw a hand up to shade his eyes, and a searing gust of wind ripped his fur cap from his head.

He leapt after it, cursing, skidding, and slipping gracelessly on the glossy footpath as ice melted beneath his boots and shadow snatched at his ankles. Arms pinwheeling madly, he went tripping headfirst into the middle of the road, into the path of an oncoming sleigh.

A panicked shout went up from the driver. He stood, yanking hard on the reins. There was a terrible cry as the horses spooked and reared.

Zosia didn't stay to observe the results. She and Marynka were already weaving through the bustle of the other walkers wearing expressions of carefully crafted innocence. It surprised Zosia how well they worked together when they weren't actively trying to sabotage each other. She might even have shared a pleased smile with Marynka, if at that moment the ice beneath *her* boots hadn't gone slick, melting.

She slipped. Staggered. Flailed. Regained her balance and tore after Marynka who'd dashed around the corner ahead in the direction the prince had vanished. Caught a fistful of her red cloak and yanked.

When the brief shove-fight and subsequent squabble ended in another stalemate, Marynka puffed out, "Wait...*wait*." She stopped trying to set fire to Zosia's hair. "Can you see him?"

Zosia released a fistful of Marynka's collar. Her gaze swept up and down the avenue. The mist had thinned as they'd fought. The skeletal outlines of poplar trees lined the edges of the road. A sleigh was pulling to a halt outside a dilapidated palace. A group of girls were busy trying to blow out each other's blessed candles.

But there was no sign of the prince.

Had he and his friends disappeared inside one of the buildings?

A door flung open, spilling out music and warmth. Maybe even now he was watching them with his coffee-brown eyes, looking out from behind a frosted window with a mouthful of mulled wine made all the more delicious for the knowledge of the cold outside.

"Wonderful," Marynka said, righting her clothes and fur cap. "We've lost him. And now he'll go hide in his palace again with all his guards." She crossed her arms, her gaze raking over Zosia. For a moment she sounded almost pleased. "I guess that makes this round a tie."

Frustration flared in Zosia's chest. This wasn't like their usual clashes. This wasn't a competition. There was so much more at stake. If she didn't take this heart and Black Jaga realized what she'd been doing, she'd never have her freedom.

She whirled on Marynka. "This isn't a game."

"It's always a game."

"Well, *I* want to stop playing."

"So give up and go home, then." Marynka flapped a hand at Zosia as if she was shooing away an insect. "I'll take his pure heart back to Grandmother. I'm sure Black Jaga will forgive you returning empty-handed for once."

Zosia couldn't have said what pulled the confession from her throat. Afterward, she didn't know what possessed her. Exasperation. Fury. A sudden mad desire to be understood. Because if anyone could understand, it should be Marynka. She might be the only person in this world who could.

The words spilled out, defiant: "I'm not taking his heart for Black Jaga, you absolute fool; I'm taking it for *myself*."

14.

MARYNKA

MARYNKA'S FACE WAS BLANK WITH shock.

"What?" she croaked out, with a fear in her voice that hadn't been there even when Zosia's claws were pressed to her stomach. Terrified that the wind, the witches might somehow be listening. "Don't *say* things like that." She stared at Zosia, aghast.

Zosia stared back.

Marynka's gaze roamed the other girl's face, wary, trying to determine if Zosia was leading her into some trap. A terrible, almost hysterical laugh bubbled up her throat. "You're serious."

"You've never thought of taking a heart for yourself?" Zosia said, her voice nearing its usual calm, though the light in her eyes was still defiant. "You've never stopped and thought, 'Why am I risking my life, spending my efforts feeding the witches more power when I could take it for myself?'"

"Oh yes," Marynka said, deeply sarcastic. "I think about stealing from Grandmother *all* the time, but, oh, then I remember the witch will *eat me* and decorate her house with my bones if she finds out." She glanced over her shoulder, then back at Zosia. Why was she telling her this? Had she lost her mind? A bitter breeze blew down the street, and she pulled Zosia into the closed-in gloom of another narrow alley between the buildings, barely wide enough for two people to walk side by side. The temperature felt strangely warm out of the violence of the wind.

For a moment Zosia didn't speak, and when she did, Marynka could barely hear her over the pounding of her heart. "That won't happen," she said dismissively.

"No," Marynka said. "It really would."

"I've done it. Taken hearts for myself and gotten away with it."

Marynka was speechless. "How?"

Zosia tucked a stray strand of silvery hair behind her ear. "I told Black Jaga you did it."

"You—you *what*?"

"I told her that you had taken the heart she sent me after. It's not as though you don't beat me to the prize sometimes. Occasionally. Very, very rarely. Our little rivalry has been very useful to me. She doesn't talk often with her sisters, so she didn't realize I was lying. I did it before that too. Four times. And now I'm going to take the Józef's pure heart for myself." The way she was looking at Marynka, those midnight-blue eyes so piercing, made it less a confession and almost a challenge.

There wasn't a flicker of guilt on that face. She didn't even have the *decency* to look ashamed.

"She's going to find out," Marynka said. "She's going to *kill* you."

I am going to kill you.

"She can try," Zosia said. "But by then it will be too late. It's true what they say—a witch is as strong as the number of hearts she's devoured. And it's true for us too. Every heart I've eaten has grown my magic, made me more powerful."

Marynka flinched like she'd been slapped. Was this why Zosia was so much better than her at everything, because the whole time she'd been *cheating*?

"If I take Józef's heart, I'll gain enough power to face even Black Jaga. I'll be strong enough that I can escape this life, strong enough to take my freedom. Look at us," Zosia said fiercely. "Look at what we can *do*. And we just obey the witches without question? We could be so much more. We could *have* so much more. They need us more than we need them. They can't even touch someone blessed with a pure heart like Józef. They need us to do it for them. Imagine being free. We wouldn't need to be monsters. You would never have to go back to the Midday Forest."

But what if I want to go back?

The Midday Forest was home. Marynka *liked* the old wooden house at its heart with its strange carvings and pale, unsettling decorations of bone. The skull lanterns. The lingering scent of drying red poppies. The locked chests full of treasures dead princes had left behind. The strange carvings that crested the front door, the monsters cut into the dark wood that bared their teeth at wayward visitors. Zosia made it sound like wanting to return there was a bad thing, when Marynka had worked so hard to prove she was worthy of staying.

"You've never thought of running away?" said Zosia.

"Running away from what?" Marynka snapped, raising her chin in unconscious defiance. "There's nothing to run away from." Her heart was racing again. Her skin felt too tight. The burning desire she'd felt when they'd fought, the violent urge to tear out Zosia's throat with her teeth returned with a vengeance. "Grandmother *saved* me. She gave me a second chance. A new life. Magic."

Wasn't it the same for Zosia? Weren't they all, Midday, Morning, and Midnight, three tragic girls who had been saved and taken in by the witches, three girls who had escaped the funeral shroud, three dark miracles? Or was Zosia something wholly different?

"I know they saved us," said Zosia. "But do you really want to waste this new life of yours slaving away as a servant? Aren't you tired of scrubbing the blood from their floors and fetching their firewood? Do you really want to spend eternity groveling and bringing them offerings, being punished horribly when you fail to complete a task? Don't you want more? I do. I was made for more than this. I can't accept this is going to be my life forever. I won't go back to that forest with its never-changing sky. I won't stand in the shadows with my head bowed and my hands laced behind my back, waiting for instructions. I am tired of always living in the dark. I am tired of being someone's pet monster. I am tired of all *this*."

She gestured between them and sucked in a breath. Let it out. Her gaze swept Marynka from head to toe. "You should come with me. You deserve more than this too."

Marynka choked on a laugh. "Are you asking me to run away with you?" Didn't she realize who they were? Didn't she care about all the times they'd fought? "You do realize that we are *enemies*."

"I've never thought of you as my enemy, Marynka. You've been my rival, my competition. But we're not enemies."

Marynka couldn't make her throat work. All the breath had left her lungs.

"You could help me take Józef's heart. We could do it easily. So easily. You and I, we'd be unstoppable."

The way she said it, just like that, like it really *would* be that easy.

"With my new powers, I could help you too. We can help each other. Come with me and—"

"And what?" Marynka said, her voice harsh. "Be your servant? Cook and clean for you as I do for Grandmother? Eating hearts and taking servants. Is that your goal? You want to become a witch instead of a monster?"

"No!" Zosia protested so vehemently that Marynka was

ALICIA JASINSKA

startled back into silence. "I'd never make someone a servant. I'm not going to become like them. I don't want to be *anything* like Black Jaga. So, so after this, I'll stop taking hearts. I'm going to stop acting like a monster. I'm going to be something different."

"Different," Marynka repeated. "Did you hit your head in the chase the other night?"

"No."

"Are you sure?"

"I didn't… Why are you being like this? Why do you hate the thought of us working together so much?" Zosia sounded confused now, defensive, like she couldn't understand Marynka's reaction. "What would be so wrong with being with me? We got along well enough when you didn't know who I was."

"Exactly!" Marynka said. "Because I didn't know who you were! I didn't know you were Midnight."

The rival servant who had driven her to despair for years since they were children. The enemy she'd sworn to beat. Just hearing her name had been enough to make her feel sick. And now Zosia wanted to work together? Working together meant defeat. Working together meant giving up on ever hearing Grandmother tell her she was the better servant.

Marynka's fingers clenched into fists. She'd had to work for this. While Zosia had been glorying in her wins, she'd been fighting to survive, groveling for approval, trying desperately not to disappoint Grandmother, always fearing she'd be replaced.

You have no idea what it's been like for me.

You have no idea.

"You…" Marynka said, taking a step closer. Zosia held her ground, looking down her nose at Marynka from an insurmountable height. The tumult of feelings inside Marynka swirled into an incandescent fury. She put as much venom into the words as she could. "Are the *last* person in the world I would ever team up with."

Zosia's eyes widened slightly. Her jaw clenched tight with hurt.

A delicious shiver of satisfaction ran through Marynka.

"This can't be all you want."

"Don't tell me what I want. I know what I want." *I want you in shreds. I want you ruined. I want you to feel every bit as helpless and defeated as I have.*

Heat rippled off Marynka. The morning sun glowed white behind the haze of mist. The air sparked and shimmered, and the icicles hanging from the eaves of the buildings in the alley began to melt.

To drip.

Darkness leaked from Zosia in tendrils, swirling around her like a wind. Shadows jumped up the walls. "You won't win."

"Do you know what your weakness is? It's your overconfidence." A scythe appeared in Marynka's hand. Her eyes had a dangerously golden sheen.

Before either of them could strike, the mist grew hands that caught them up and sent them spinning, staggering backward, forcing them apart.

"Are you both entirely brainless?" A furious Beata stood at the head of the alley, hard color in her round, rosy cheeks. "Oh yes, did you forget that I'm here too?" She stalked forward, glowing with a murderous aura. Her face was so suffused with light that the shadows didn't dare touch her. She gestured at the thawing buildings. "You do realize the whole city is watching for even a hint of dark magic? Are you trying to get yourselves caught?"

Marynka and Zosia stared at her in stunned silence. Their eyes met for the briefest second, and Marynka had a sudden wild urge to laugh.

She could've sworn Zosia's lips twitched too. But then she turned on her heel, turned away, and the warmth that had risen between them turned to ice. The air lightened; Zosia seeming to suck the darkness back into herself. She stalked past Beata, not bothering to spare her a glance, as if Marynka's friend was beneath her notice.

Marynka bristled.

"Think about it." Zosia's voice was cool and her words were for Marynka alone. "I've gone too far to stop now. I'm going to take the prince's heart and accomplish what I set out to do. So you can join me." She looked back and their eyes locked. "Or you can get out of my way, because if you try to stop me, Marynka, I will remind you exactly which of us is the stronger servant."

15.

MARYNKA

"SHE'S MAD," BEATA SAID WHEN they were alone and back in their room at the House Under the Moon, after Marynka had told her everything. "Utterly mad. We should send word to Red Jaga. No, *Black* Jaga. Traveling on a good strong wind, she could be here in less than a day. She could be here tomorrow, sooner even, and while she's dealing with Zosia, we can take the prince's heart. This will all be over. We win."

"No," Marynka said immediately.

Beata narrowed her eyes. "It's the perfect solution. You're the one who said you can't afford to lose this time."

"I don't want to beat her like that. I'm not so weak that I need help. I want to win with my own power. And—" Marynka gnawed on a nail.

And if they told Black Jaga what Zosia was planning, then Zosia…

Marynka shuddered to think what Grandmother would do

if she suddenly discovered Marynka had been stealing hearts from her, if she learned Marynka had lied to her face and was planning to run away. She'd strip her of her magic. She'd snap each one of her thieving fingers and rip out her iron teeth. Leave her defanged and defenseless, lying in the dirt where she'd found her—and that was only if she didn't eat her.

Zosia really *was* mad.

Mad and reckless and fearless.

All the things Marynka was supposed to be. The thought made her even angrier. Midnight was meant to be the cautious one, the careful one. So why was it Zosia daring to do this? Why was it she, Marynka, who was trembling at the thought of betraying Grandmother? When had they switched places?

Marynka stared at the scrollwork on the ceiling.

Why is it when I'm with you I always feel like I'm losing? Why are you always one step ahead, always so far beyond my reach?

"I would've thought you'd leap at the chance to get her in trouble," said Beata watching Marynka closely, combing her twin braids out with her fingers. Her hair was so long now that it dragged on the floor when she sat at the dressing table.

Marynka wanted to tangle her hands in the strands, let the familiar sensation soothe her. She just needed this all to stop for a moment, for a heartbeat, just so she could catch her breath, steady herself long enough to make sense of everything. Sometimes she had trouble making sense of her own feelings. They were all so overwhelming.

"You're not worried about her, are you? I thought you hated her. I'd think you would *want* her to run away."

"Of course I hate her!" Marynka snapped, flushing. The sheer violent intensity of this feeling—it had to be hate, didn't it?

Beata reached for a hairbrush.

Marynka kicked the post of the great hulking bed in the center of the room and paced up and down the carpet. She kept hearing Zosia's voice in her head, the same words over and over again.

"Our little rivalry has been very useful to me."

Useful! Marynka retrieved the advertising flyer they'd been given when they first arrived in the city from beneath an armchair and crumpled it in her fist.

"With my new powers, I could help you too. We can help each other."

Smoke rose between her knuckles, drifting up. When she uncurled her fingers, nothing remained of the flyer save powdery ash.

"This can't be all you want."

As if Marynka didn't know what she wanted, as if what she wanted was something bad. And yet…

"You should come with me. You deserve more than this too."

It was the first time anyone had ever said she deserved more.

"Don't you want more?"

She only vaguely registered Beata babbling on.

"Can't afford to attract more attention. Honestly, the whole city could be on fire, and you'd still be trying to fight her."

Marynka stopped pretending to listen. The fire in the hearth was almost dead, the last embers flickering a desperate red. She found a poker and stabbed at them moodily.

What had possessed Zosia? What was she even thinking?

"You've never thought of running away?"

Of course, when things had gotten particularly awful, when Grandmother had punished her, Marynka had occasionally fantasized about fleeing. She'd dreamed up elaborate escape plans, imagined feeding the witch to her own oven. But she'd stayed because running away had felt too much like giving up, like admitting defeat, like admitting Midnight *was* better than her, and Marynka never backed down from a challenge.

She'd stayed *because* of Zosia, and now *Zosia* wanted to run away?

She couldn't give this up. She wasn't allowed to stop playing their game. The end of this was supposed to be Marynka's moment of triumph. It wasn't meant to be Zosia abandoning the fight.

How dare Zosia try to cheat her of her victory?

She *needed* her there. It went beyond desire, beyond ambition. Aiming to outdo Midnight gave Marynka a goal, a purpose, something to strive for, something to look forward to. It kept her mind off everything else, everything she didn't want to think about. When she couldn't lash out at Grandmother, when anger and self-loathing ate her up, Midnight had been her outlet, her target, her someone to fight. She hadn't realized how much she'd come to rely on her presence. When had Midnight become so integral to her life, when had their constant clashes stopped feeling like an intrusion, a threat, and started to feel vital?

And if Zosia could walk away, just like that, as if *she* didn't care…

The fire flared, leaping in the grate. Marynka gritted her teeth, swallowing down the sting, the bitter realization that she was not to Zosia what Zosia was to her. That had always been the question lurking in the back of her mind, hadn't it? Did Midnight care as much about their rivalry as she did; did she care so much it hurt?

Now she had her answer. Midnight didn't. Because she could walk away from this as though none of it even mattered.

"Marynka? *Marynka.*"

Marynka jumped at the sound of Beata's voice, spinning away from the fireplace, dropping the poker. Shocked to find her friend standing so close. She'd sunk so deeply into her own thoughts that she hadn't heard her approach.

Beata's violet eyes were wide with worry. "Are you okay?"

"Yes."

"Are you lying?"

Yes. "No."

She was just on edge. The unexpected thought of Zosia leaving, of her vanishing for good on the next wind, had knocked her off-balance. It felt like she'd have to climb out of her own skin to shed all she was feeling.

Beata reached out and tucked an errant curl behind Marynka's ear. It took all Marynka's self-control to keep from slapping her friend's hand away.

"You'd never leave White Jaga, would you?"

"Of course not. Do you think she'd let me?" Beata's tone was scornful. "Besides, she gave me a home. A second chance at life."

Marynka nodded, slightly reassured. It was a little different, of course, with her and Grandmother. But she understood. She wouldn't run away either. As the witch was so fond of pointing out: *Who raised you? Who puts food on your plate? Who pulled you from the brink of death and gave you power, gave you magic?*

There was a part of her that couldn't not love the old witch for that. She'd made her into Midday, into somebody powerful and new.

And the most awful thing about Grandmother was not that she could be cruel, but that she could also be kind. Was kind. She had fed Marynka and clothed her, taught her how to find the best mushrooms and how to groom a horse, had nursed her when she was sick. She'd stroked her hair and praised her when she triumphed. And those moments, those rare, fought-for moments, caught like thorns in Marynka's skin. She couldn't forget those memories, couldn't stop remembering.

She picked the candle Beata had brought back from the church off the dressing table, playing with the pale-blue ribbons tied around its width. A livid red flame jumped to life in her palm, and she lit the wick, holding her breath a moment, half expecting the blessed taper not to accept her fire.

Smoke curled black toward the ceiling.

Marynka inhaled the heady scent of beeswax. For a heartbeat, she was back in White Jaga's house in the forest where it was always morning, warming jars of dark-gold honey between her palms and complaining loudly about how annoying Midnight was while Beata stirred a pot of duck's blood soup and baked fat braids of bread in the pale dawn light.

She hadn't realized how much she actually enjoyed complaining about Midnight until the thought of no longer having reason to…

Marynka shook herself. She needed to stop thinking about Zosia. Climbing on top of the bed so that she could reach, rocking the entire frame with her weight, she used the candle to burn a smoldering cross into the wooden ceiling beam.

Beata snorted. "You know people do that to keep monsters like us out."

"I know, but I've always wanted to try it."

It wasn't as if she had anything against divine magic. She might even have practiced it had things turned out differently. Since becoming Midday, she'd mostly forgotten her old life, but she sometimes wondered who she would have been if Red Jaga hadn't burned away her past, her history. If her parents had lived, would her mother have taught her how to speak to the moon and stars, how to carve amulets with the names of angels? Would her father have helped her gather herbs to be blessed in church? Would he have lit candles like this one?

"Why would Zosia even want to—" she started.

"Maybe she's grown a conscience," Beata said, peering at her reflection in the dresser mirror, taking out a file to sharpen needle-sharp teeth. "Maybe Zosia doesn't want to be a monster anymore. Maybe she feels guilty and she's decided what we do is wrong."

"Wrong?"

"Don't you think there's something wrong with us?" Beata's eyes found Marynka's in the mirror. She'd asked this question before, once, when they were younger, after they'd walked away with a heart together.

"Do you think there's something unnatural about us? Do you think when they made us into monsters something got left behind?"

"What?" Marynka had laughed. *"Like our souls?"*

She gave the same answer now as she'd given then. "There's nothing wrong with us." She liked being a monster, even if Zosia had suddenly decided she didn't. This was a gift. A blessing.

And she wouldn't give it up for anything. For anyone.

She had earned this power. She wasn't about to let it go, to return to being an ordinary girl. A weak thing of flesh and blood and nothing more.

"You don't feel guilty?" Beata said. "Ever?"

"Not a bit."

"I forget you don't feel shame like a normal person."

Marynka grinned weakly.

"I still think we should tell—"

Marynka didn't let her finish. "And I said *no*." The candle flame surged, and wax coursed down the sides of the burning taper, scalding her fingers. Marynka didn't mind the heat, but she hissed in surprise anyway and dropped the candle. "The witches don't need to know about this." It felt cheap to stab Zosia in the back like that, running and telling tales like children. She deserved better from them both. "It's between us servants."

Beata shot her a look she couldn't read, and came and picked the candle up, taking it away from Marynka before she could burn the whole room down.

"Promise me," said Marynka.

"Fine," Beata bit out. "But only if you stop trying to do everything yourself. Otherwise I *will* call Black Jaga here."

Marynka was struck momentarily speechless by the ultimatum. She'd known Beata long enough to know when she was deathly serious. This threat was one she would go through with without hesitation.

"We follow my lead this time," Beata said. "I'll deal with Zosia, and you—"

"No," Marynka said again, worried now.

"Why?"

"Because…because…" *Because I don't want you to*, she thought but didn't say aloud. "That's not a good idea."

"I have beaten both of you to a heart before."

Marynka blinked, remembering, but honestly that time didn't count. Beata had cheated. The one time she had turned the tables on them, it was because Marynka and Zosia had been too busy sabotaging each other's efforts. Beata had sauntered past and snatched the prince's heart for herself—a dagger to Marynka's pride when she'd least expected it.

She knew it was a weakness. Her tendency to fixate, to hyper-focus on Midnight, made her relentless, but it also left her wide open.

"It's you and me together, remember?" Beata moved closer. Her voice was firm. Fierce. Marynka spared a half smile at her friend's protectiveness. "Morning and Midday against Midnight. So, let's use that. You're not the only one who was given this task. Think about what will happen to us if we return home empty-handed."

A shiver ran down Marynka's spine.

"Don't let her get to you. Midnight's always won. I thought you wanted to even the score. You're not going to roll over and give her this victory too, are you?"

"Of course not," Marynka said, wavering. Maybe that's all this was, another ruse of Zosia's meant to rattle her.

And if Zosia didn't succeed in taking the prince's heart, then she'd *have* to stay, wouldn't she? She wouldn't have the magic to stand up to Black Jaga. Even if she hated Marynka for it, at least she'd still be here.

"I know how we can approach the prince," Beata said.

"How?"

Beata smiled with all her teeth. "Do you remember the girl I talked to at the costume ball that first night?"

"The princess you were drooling all over?"

Beata turned pink. "I wasn't drooling. You know I... You know there's only one person I like."

Marynka cut her eyes away, shifting uncomfortably. Did she really have to bring that up right now?

"We were discussing horses," Beata finished after an awkward pause. "And she told me something interesting. It'll be the perfect opportunity to get the prince away from everybody."

16.

ZOSIA

ANOTHER MIDNIGHT, ANOTHER BALL, ANOTHER
bright day of revelry to follow. There was no end to the parties
during the Karnawał.

The prince and his friends danced past dawn, retreated to nap,
awoke at noon for late breakfasts that slid into dinners of steaming
bigos and roasted deer, wild duck and fish in colorful sauces. Sweet
and meat pierogi and poppy seed puddings vanished from the
table in seconds. And then everything began again. The musicians
tuned their instruments, feet stamped the floor, fresh costumes were
paraded. Endless days of celebration just like at a wedding.

Three nights slipped by with a blink.

Three sleepless nights and Marynka still hadn't given Zosia
an answer to her offer to team up. It gave her too much time to
think. Every spare second, she kept coming back to their conversation, and every time, her uncertainty intensified. Should she have
trusted Marynka with her secret, with what she was planning?

For that matter, why was Marynka so adamant that what she was planning was bad? Why did *she* not want to run away? Was Zosia the strange one? If Marynka couldn't see a problem with how they were treated, did that mean Zosia was overreacting?

To distract herself from the thoughts, Zosia kept busy. The prince was still on his guard, always surrounded by friends and admirers, soldiers and protections.

So she switched tactics. Instead of waiting for a chance to ambush him in the street or trying to approach him directly, she got close to one of his friends, to Esterka, the beautiful daughter of two Jewish merchants. Esterka's father supplied the army, her mother lunched with the king. Her grandfather was the famous Maggid of Koźniewo, whose blessings, advice, and healing remedies were sought by men of all faiths.

She was also the current subject of the prince's affections. "*He even visited the orchard on St. Katarzyna's Day,*" a girl told Zosia, "*and cut a branch from a cherry tree and placed it in his room in a jug of water. All because he heard that if the branch bloomed before Christmas, it would be a sign his love was accepted.*"

For her part, Esterka seemed only vaguely amused by the prince's antics. She took an immediate liking to Zosia, though, pronouncing her wide-eyed appreciation of the city charming, and swept her under her wing as if she were a cousin or younger sister.

Which should have pleased Zosia because it was what she'd been aiming for, someone to vouch for her presence, but it also made her feel strangely embarrassed, as well as a little defensive. She wasn't a *child* and she could look after herself. She wasn't some clueless peasant girl about to have her heart broken by some rich magnate. If anybody was going to lose their heart here, it was the prince. Literally.

Esterka tucked an errant strand of wood-brown hair behind her ear and handed Zosia a glass of mulled wine. "It'll help with the hangover."

Zosia shot her a disbelieving look.

"Did the stars teach you that trick?" another girl asked, crunching toward them through the snow and referring to Esterka's magical talent to speak with the heavenly bodies.

Esterka smiled, the curve of her mouth mischievous and her brown eyes sparkling. "No. This." She winked at Zosia, raising her own glass in a toast. "I simply learned from experience."

Zosia tried to mimic her smile. She wasn't used to so much drinking. So much talking. So much noise. Her head was spinning tipsily, and she worried that when the prince next approached Esterka and she finally managed to get him alone, she'd trip over her own feet and start giggling helplessly before she could get her claws out. For once, she found herself thinking longingly of the Midnight Forest. Of the dark, starlit sky and the cold quiet.

She clasped her hands around the glass Esterka had handed her. What she wouldn't have given instead for something more homey—soup, sour żurek with sausage and root vegetables and hard-boiled eggs mixed in with the broth. Oat cakes, melting with soft goat's cheese.

Today the prince's entourage had taken a break from dancing to gather on the edge of a frozen lake on the wooded outskirts of the city with skates and sleds. Smiling figures spun over the ice in their finest clothing. In the very center of the lake, on a tiny island, stood another of the king's residences, the Silver Palace, glittering like a jewel set into the winter landscape.

"He's watching you again," said the girl who'd joined Zosia and Esterka. She was fat and rosy-cheeked with a braid as blond as Beata's. Zosia couldn't remember her name. It was probably Ola or Kasia or something. "Why does Kajetan dislike you so much, Zosia? Did you refuse to dance with him?"

Zosia shifted, spying a familiar lithe figure from the corner of her eye. Kajetan Pilawski, who must have the devil's own luck, had by some miracle managed to survive her and Marynka's attempt on his life. The near-death experience hadn't dulled his efforts to keep an eye on the prince; if anything, it seemed only to have made him more determined.

"Why does the prince dislike *him* so much?" Zosia said, changing the subject. "Why does everyone?"

Lurking a small distance away, Kajetan was pretending to watch a sled dump its shrieking occupants into a snowbank. He wore the grimly mulish expression of someone who knew exactly how unwelcome they were, but was going to crash the party anyway.

"You mean you don't know?" said Ola or Kasia, wide-eyed.

"Zosia's from the country," Esterka said. "She's not up on all the gossip." She leaned closer, dropping her voice to a whisper. "He and Józef used to be close friends."

"*Very* close friends, some people said," Ola or Kasia added, giggling.

Esterka cut her a look.

Ola or Kasia sobered.

Esterka continued. "They both attended the Royal Cadet School here in the capital. The school the king started. You would never see one without the other. They were inseparable. But, well, you know what happened during the war."

Zosia nodded slowly, fitting the pieces together in her head.

She didn't know the details, but it was common enough knowledge, even among the villagers in the mountains, that a group of Lechija's richest magnate families, families who held more power than the king, who shod their horses' with golden shoes and owned palaces far greater than the royal residences, together with several high-ranking members of the church, had supported the Rusjan invasion in the hopes of protecting their own wealth and privileges.

"Kajetan sided with his family when his father decided to ally with the tsarina," Esterka said. "He fought against our army. Józef was devastated."

"And furious," put in Ola or Kasia.

"But I think even then he understood." Esterka sipped from her glass. "He loves his family too, of course. When the king surrendered, all the generals wanted Józef to move against him. They wanted him to seize control and lead the army, to keep fighting, but he couldn't bring himself to betray his uncle like that. He refused."

Zosia's eyebrows rose. Was this why so many people put their trust in the prince, because he wasn't seeking to lead, to grab power for himself? Was that what it meant to be blessed with a pure heart?

Did that make her his wicked opposite then, as she was seeking power *only* for herself?

"I know he wrote to Kajetan," Esterka said. "Many times, but—"

"Ah, ah, ah!" A boy with black hair and an infectious grin popped up beside them. He brought a reproachful finger to his lips. "Darling," he scolded Esterka. "You know we never speak that name. Have you forgotten that Kajetan's evil and we hate him?"

He waved away the glass Ola or Kasia offered him. Selim was Muslim and didn't drink alcohol. He was another close friend of Józef's, the soldier with the scar Zosia had seen walking with the prince the other day. One of the king's elite uhlan guards.

She'd have to find a way to deal with him before she attempted anything.

"Kajetan's *your* cousin," Esterka said.

"Distant cousin! Very distant. My grandmother's sister converted and married into his family," Selim explained to Zosia quickly. "It's not like I actually *talk* to him. And if he tries to approach Józef again, I'm going to shoot him."

"He is so very beautiful though," commented Ola or Kasia. "It's such a shame. He looks like an avenging angel or a saint. And he rides so well, like someone born to the saddle."

"Obviously," Selim said. "He gets that from our side of the family."

"And his clothes are always so fine and terribly expensive. Have you seen the kontusz sash he's wearing today? He's like a silk-clad present you just can't wait to unwrap." Ola or Kasia let out a dreamy sigh.

Esterka smothered a laugh behind her hand at the scandalized look on Selim's face. Zosia looked between them both, unsure how she was supposed to react.

"Who looks like a gift you'd like to unwrap, Oleńka?" called a deep voice.

The darkness in Zosia's blood stirred. The prince looked resplendent in emerald green as he joined them by the lake's edge. "Are you talking about me again?"

"You'd like that, wouldn't you?" Esterka said.

Józef slotted in beside Selim. Heart skittering, Zosia met his gaze for the first time since the night of the costume ball. She'd been a monster then so he shouldn't recognize her. Still she wasn't sure what to expect, but the prince's expression was friendly. He raised one eyebrow slightly.

"Panna Zofia Zborowska," Esterka said, introducing Zosia by the name she'd given her earlier. The Zborowskis were a noble family with so many offshoots that the addition of an extra fake cousin shouldn't be questioned. "She's staying in Warszów for the Karnawał."

Seizing her skirts with her fingers, Zosia curtsied.

Józef made a soldierly bow, smiling at her with unsettling warmth. His brown eyes lingered for a second on the long silver braid trailing over her shoulder.

A flash of red at the corner of her eye made Zosia tense, but it was only Kajetan in his crimson kontusz and ruby-studded fur cap skulking off to the side, staring at the prince intently.

The prince spied him too. A spark seemed to pass between the two boys as they watched each other. Zosia couldn't place the expression on Józef's face, but Kajetan wore a look of such longing that Zosia actually shivered.

"We're honored to have you join us," Józef said, seizing her hand and using it to draw her closer. He made a show of it, taking a deliberate, almost malicious pleasure in kissing her fingers as though they were holy relics. His gaze flicked back to Kajetan.

It turned out that, despite his pure heart, Lechija's prince had a petty streak.

"And now I beg you'll excuse me." Józef's grin widened as he let go of Zosia's hand. "For I fear the snow is melting."

"Melting?" Esterka asked.

The prince pulled his other hand from behind his back, revealing a snowball that he proceeded to shove down Selim's collar.

Selim yelped. "That"—he bent, scooping up a fistful of white powder—"was a mistake! You're going to regret that!"

The prince was laughing and backing away. "Is that a threat?"

"No. Just a promise."

Józef ducked behind a nearby tree as a clod of white exploded against the bark.

"Honestly," Esterka muttered as snow hurled through the air. She tugged Zosia and Ola out of the line of fire, but her eyes were gleaming, and when Selim took another hit to the shoulder, icy diamond stars catching on the rich amethyst of his robes, she shrieked: "Don't let him win, Selim!"

"Esterka!" cried the prince, feigning hurt. "You break my heart."

Ignoring him, Esterka handed their empty glasses off to a servant from the Silver Palace who offered them a tray of Karnawał roses in return. The crisp golden pastries were shaped like the flowers, dusted with white sugar and filled with wild-rose jam.

The first bite melted in Zosia's mouth. The whole scene felt surreal. Like a dream. The sweet treats and the gracious servants, the frozen lake and the grand palace rising from its icy center. The prince and his friends rolling in the snow. The richly dressed, sophisticated, older company.

Standing among them all, amid the chatter and the laughter, she could almost trick herself into believing that she was someone else, someone who belonged here.

But you don't, do you? the shadows whispered. *You're just a monster, playing at being normal.*

Because at the same time she'd never felt so acutely just how different she was, how different a life she'd led. There was an unsurpassable gap between these young men and women and herself.

But that was the reason she was running away, wasn't it? So she could live a different life. One where she wouldn't be confined to the dark. A life where she could be a part of things.

Was that even possible though, for someone like her? Could she ever truly change herself?

Zosia cast an uneasy glance at the sky. The hour was far from late, barely past four o'clock, but already the sun was beginning to sink, painting the kingdom deceptively warm shades of pink and orange and red. Another day gone.

And still no sign of Marynka.

A mischievous breeze blew sharp off the lake, catching up the lightly falling snow and making it dance, keeping the cold flakes from touching the ground.

Where are you?

The prince was here. Mere steps away. Close enough so that if Zosia really wanted to, if she let her magic loose, if she revealed her claws, she could rip his heart straight from his chest.

A call to the shadows, a flick of her wrist, was all it would take to plunge the scene into darkness.

So why don't you? whispered the voice in her head, sounding too much like Marynka now.

Because it isn't safe, she would've answered. *Because I'm not a reckless fool like somebody.*

Because a witch had kneaded caution into Zosia's flesh. If she struck now, everyone here would know what she was. Selim and Józef still wore their sabers. There was Kajetan to think of, lurking somewhere in the background, and Esterka had her own divine magic.

The world was watching. She might not move fast enough. They would kill her before she could flee and...

You're waiting for her.

Waiting for Marynka to make her next move. She'd grown too used to it, having Marynka—Midday—always compete with her. There had been a strange kind of comfort in knowing the other girl was there, that she existed, another monster bound to the same fate as Zosia, a servant like her. There had been a thrill in the knowledge that Midday would likely be tracking her steps, going after the same hearts.

Wasn't Marynka going to come after her now? Wasn't she going to challenge her for the prince's pure heart? What was she doing? Four whole days. Marynka wasn't known for her patience.

It made Zosia uneasy. It felt far too much like she was being ignored.

Where are you? Come after me.

She tried to focus on the people around her. Józef and Selim had called a temporary truce. A couple more boys crowded round. There was talk of going hunting. Zosia perked up. The forest was her natural hunting ground. Then more gossip about people she didn't know, mixed with jokes and references she didn't understand. She shifted her weight from foot to foot restlessly.

Thankfully the tide of conversation turned next to talk of dangerous things, of uprisings and revolution. Zosia was fascinated despite herself. Beyond the gloom of the forest so much was happening, had happened. The world was so *big*. There was so much the witch had kept from her.

Rumors were swirling about another graduate from the Royal Cadet School who was gathering allies and support in other kingdoms. There was news of riots, of the Lechijan army being forcefully disbanded and its soldiers conscripted into the tsarina's forces. More gossip, from neighboring Prusja this time, where the king spent his days seducing handsome men and joking of consuming Lechija mouthful by mouthful.

Zosia watched the figures around her bristle with indignation.

This at least was the kind of talk she could relate to. This made her think there was a chance she could fit into the world outside the Midnight Forest. If this was how ordinary boys and girls spent their days: drinking and dancing and dressing up, but also dreaming of better worlds and plotting the downfall of empires. Longing for the freedom to decide their own futures.

Maybe she was not so very different from them after all.

A faint furrow formed between Zosia's brows as she struggled to keep track of all the facts. Everyone was talking over each other and switching languages with ease. Her struggle must've been obvious because Esterka asked softly, "We're not making you nervous, are we?"

Zosia hesitated, uncertain how to respond. The prince was watching her closely without seeming to. Selim, too, and a few others. She wasn't sure if it was a trick question. A test. To see where her loyalties lay. People had been snatched away in the night for speaking such things, threatened with beatings and arrests and exile. Maybe they thought she might report them to the tsarist authorities. Maybe they thought she was a traitor like Kajetan.

"It's okay if you are," Selim said gently. "I'm nervous too. I'm afraid what it will cost us to stand against them. My uncle was arrested. I don't want to lose anyone else. But I'm even more afraid of a world under the tsarina's rule."

"Come," said the prince, clapping a hand on Selim's shoulder. "Dear hearts, enough talk. Before the light goes, I want to skate once more around the palace."

Coming from Józef, it was as much an invitation as it was a command. There was a flurry of movement. Selim excused himself and left them. Zosia glanced at the lake's frozen surface with trepidation. Still, here at last was a moment she could take advantage of.

She copied the others as they strapped metal blades to their boots. Esterka stepped daintily down onto the ice, gliding away, and then another boy, and finally the prince.

Gingerly, Zosia stepped onto the lake, letting out a shrill gasp and flapping her arms exaggeratedly as her feet slipped and slid every which way.

Józef looked over his shoulder in concern. He started to skate back. Zosia fell, reaching for him. He went to catch her, but a different pair of arms intercepted them, wrapping around Zosia's waist from behind and yanking her upright, pulling her flush against another body.

17.

MARYNKA

"DON'T WORRY, I'VE GOT HER," Marynka reassured the prince. The smile she gave him might've been called charming if it hadn't been full of so many teeth.

"Go away," Zosia hissed under her breath.

Marynka's smile didn't falter. "You look strangely unhappy to see me, Zosia. Didn't you miss me?" She tightened her grip on Zosia's waist before adding in a louder voice, addressing Józef. "I'm Zosia's friend. Well, aren't you going to introduce me?"

Zosia looked like she was going to kill Marynka in broad daylight, which was likely going to put a damper on the Karnawał festivities.

Józef's curious gaze darted between them. His eyes lingered on Marynka, though that could just have been because she was dressed in boys' clothing in a coral-orange kontusz over a gold zupan and loose trousers tucked into her favorite red leather boots. Her long hair was hidden beneath a fur cap decorated with a peacock feather. She liked to think that she could pass for a hetman's nephew.

Józef's lips parted. Before he could speak, a figure came speeding to a stop beside him with a spray of ice. Cackling, a boy dressed in vibrant purple thrust a snowball down the prince's collar and took off.

The prince gave chase, leaving a startled Marynka and Zosia blinking in his wake.

"I wasn't about to take his heart right here in front of everyone," Zosia said after a pause. "You didn't need to literally throw yourself at me."

"What do you mean?" Marynka let go of Zosia's waist. "Who threw themselves at you? I was merely joining in the festivities and happened to see you tripping like a fool all over the ice. Shouldn't you say thank you?" She pushed her fur cap back so it was no longer falling down her forehead.

Zosia watched her, gaze sharp and measuring. "What are you thinking after what I told you?"

Marynka gave a deliberately careless shrug. "There's not much to think, is there?" She swiveled on the spot, starting to skate backward, arms behind her back. "I already told you that you're the last person I would—"

Zosia's hands whipped out, seizing the front of Marynka's robes.

Marynka flailed for balance. "What are you—let go!"

Zosia clung on, her legs as unsteady beneath her as a baby deer's. "Pull me to the lake's edge."

"You can't be serious!" Marynka's entire body flushed with heat as Zosia's hands climbed her chest to settle on her shoulders. "I thought you were pretending so the prince would hold your hand. You can *freeze* shadow into daggers. How can you not know how to ice skate?"

"It's not like I didn't want to learn. It always looked fun, but Black Jaga doesn't let me out to play—" Zosia blanched.

A flock of skaters rushed by either side of them, colorful robes and trailing sleeves and braids of hair whipping the air behind them. Zosia recoiled, trying to twist out of the way. Marynka grabbed her around the waist again, but it didn't help. Zosia lost her balance and they went down with matching expressions of horror on their faces, Zosia dragging Marynka on top of her as her back hit the ice with a solid *thwump*.

For a moment they just lay there, staring blankly at each other, stunned. Marynka could taste coppery blood where she'd bitten her lip.

Then Zosia moved, fingers releasing their death grip on Marynka's shoulders, reaching to either side of her body to push herself up. Marynka reacted purely out of instinct, catching Zosia's wrists and pinning her arms above her head.

Zosia's eyes grew wide as saucers. Her pupils were so dilated that her eyes were almost black.

And haven't you always wanted her beneath you like this? whispered the loudest of the voices currently vying for attention inside Marynka's head. The second voice, which sounded awfully like Beata's, was shouting that this was *not* a part of the plan.

It occurred to Marynka, as she watched a single snowflake catch like glitter on the bow of Zosia's lips, that Zosia could probably have broken out of her hold by now. If she'd wanted Marynka off, there would've been bruises up and down her body.

A shiver that had nothing to do with the cold raced down her spine. Her heart skipped a beat. Another. She didn't know if it was just their position or her usual reaction, the way her pulse always raced when Midnight was close. The red in Zosia's cheeks felt contagious. She could feel the press of her body even through all their layers of clothing.

"Do you need help?" someone asked, skating up to them.

Prickles of heat danced over Marynka's skin and she blinked, realizing to her horror that she'd been staring. "No!" she snapped, coming to her senses, hyper-aware of how high her voice came out. She let go of Zosia's wrists and jerked back, trying to make withdrawing her hands look like a natural course of action rather than a scrambled retreat.

They fell another three times attempting to stand. Marynka was pretty sure everyone was watching and laughing at them. They looked utterly ridiculous with Zosia being so much taller yet clinging to Marynka for dear life.

"God's blood!" she bit out. "Don't overthink it. Lean your weight *forward*."

Zosia did so, face flushed, mouth a grim line, holding tight to Marynka's forearms. Marynka gripped Zosia's forearms in turn because it wasn't as if she was going to hold Zosia's *hands*.

Her own hands, in their fur-lined gloves, felt much too warm and much too sweaty. She skated slowly backward once more, towing Zosia as they were swept into the current of skaters drawing circles across the frosted surface of the lake.

"I never expected *you* to be so bad at something."

Zosia frowned, clearly disturbed to discover there was something she didn't excel at. "Like I said, it's not as though I was let out to play. Was it different for you? Did Red Jaga teach you to skate?"

Marynka almost laughed. Grandmother would never... She couldn't remember who had taught her. It was something she'd learned long ago before she'd met the witch, before she'd come to live in the Midday Forest. "No. I can't remember now who taught me. But Beata and I would try spins on the pond near White Jaga's house."

"You make it look so easy. And that," Zosia added as the falling snow melted before it could touch Marynka. "Conjuring heat. You don't even have to think about it."

Marynka raised an eyebrow. "It's just practice. I could melt a hole in the ice beneath your feet, send you plunging into the depths of the lake."

Zosia's grip on her arms tightened.

"Grandmother's…strict. She wants me to be the strongest, to be able to beat you. She wouldn't even let me go after a prince until I could travel on the wind all by myself. Was your training any different?"

Zosia looked surprised. "You could already travel on the wind when she first sent you out? How old were you?"

"Twelve. Why, couldn't you? How old were you when you could?"

"Fourteen," Zosia admitted reluctantly, scowling.

Marynka blinked, and then a great blinding grin spread across her face. "Oh?"

Zosia's scowl was even more pronounced.

They'd almost reached the far edge of the lake now, where Marynka had planned to strand her rival. Instead she skated on, pulling Zosia into another loop across the ice, not quite knowing why and knowing that she shouldn't. If Zosia thought anything of it, she didn't comment or try to stop her.

"When were you first able to control the shadows?" Marynka demanded. "Were you ever sent after anyone who wasn't a prince?"

Pale flakes fell like a veil around them, separating them from the other skaters. There was only the two of them in a whirl of white, anchored tightly to each other.

"Did you have to deal with all the princesses and peasant girls coming to beg the witches for help?"

"No one ever made it that far through the dark," Zosia said. "Black Jaga hates visitors. She'd send me out to attack anyone who dared disturb her. I was thirteen when I learned to control the shadows. Do you ever imagine what life would be like if we hadn't been taken in by them?"

"Sometimes. Are there other creatures living in your forest? I'm friends with our rusałki. Grandmother used to make them chase me. She says I learn faster under pressure."

"She sounds exactly like her sister. Black Jaga thought it was hilarious when a dragon returning to its cave up in the peaks tried to eat me."

The words poured out between them, an exchange of strange and traumatic childhood tales. Stories Marynka had never thought to share with anyone, save Beata, because they wouldn't have understood. She ignored the niggling thought that she was giving too much away, eroding the boundaries between them.

"I think the worst was when she'd make you polish the skulls of the other servants, because you knew she was only making you do it as reminder that you could end up just like them." Zosia's strides were steadier now. She spoke overly casually and in the past tense, as if she were already trying to distance herself from all of this. "I was always glad when she sent me out to find a prince."

"You'll miss it," Marynka said. "That thrill. The danger." The mad race to get to the target before your opponent. The challenge. The possibility of failure. That rush that was like nothing else. "Do you really intend to run away? Do you really want to give up being Midnight? After everything? Don't you enjoy it at least a little bit?"

Zosia was supposed to feel the same way she did.

"Don't you *like* knowing you have the strength to twist a man's head from his neck, to break every bone in his body? Don't you like being able to walk the shadows knowing you're the monster and not the victim?"

"I don't like people recoiling from the sight of me like I'm something terrible."

"That's the best part though! When they cower and tremble. Look, I'll—I'll keep your secret." *Out of rivalry respect*, Marynka told herself. "You don't have to tell Black Jaga you took the other hearts; just pretend like it never happened. Don't do anything reckless."

Zosia didn't need to respond with words because her look said it all: *I cannot believe you are saying that.*

"Shut up," Marynka snapped, heat rushing up her neck into her cheeks. "Just *think* about it."

Think about what you're giving up, what you're leaving behind.

"You're not like them." She jerked her chin at the other skaters. "No matter how much you like to pretend. No matter how you disguise yourself, you'll never *be* one of them. There's too much darkness in you. You can't escape that. You don't have a place here. You don't belong here."

Zosia belonged with her, and Beata, and—

175

"They're not so different from us," Zosia said. "And I don't belong in the forest anymore either. I've tasted freedom. I've tasted hearts and it's *changed* me. I couldn't cram myself back into my old self now if I tried. I don't hate being Midnight."

A wash of relief rushed through Marynka.

"Not always. But I don't want to be someone's pet monster. I want to decide my own fate. I meant what I said before. You should come with me. Don't make the wrong choice here."

"You know you saying that just makes me *want* to refuse you."

"Then why come speak with me at all?"

"Maybe I'm just here to distract you."

Zosia smiled faintly. "You know I thought you'd be glad to be rid of me. You're making it sound like you don't want me to leave. Are you worried you'll miss me?"

Marynka gritted her teeth. "What I'm *saying* is that you can't run away because I still need to show everyone that I'm better than you."

"And how is that going?"

"I think I'm making progress."

"You haven't won yet."

"Always so overconfident." Marynka tightened her grip on Zosia's forearms and then she spun them in a wild circle.

Zosia hissed through her teeth. "*Marynka.*"

Marynka threw her head back and laughed.

"You'll miss the darkness. I've seen the way you always squint in the sun. You'll miss the quiet and hunting princes. You'll never get to ride Black Jaga's special horses again."

"How did you know about the horses?"

"I—" Marynka slowed out of the spin. It was one of the precious facts she'd obsessively unearthed whilst trying to learn more about Midnight, her weaknesses, her habits, what she was like. But she'd rather die than admit that aloud. "You told me. On the journey here, that your grandmother keeps horses."

"I never told you that."

"Well, it's not like it's a secret," Marynka said, flustered. "We have been stuck with each other since we were twelve." They'd been each other's competition, each other's rival for six whole years. The only other people she'd known for that long were Grandmother and Beata. "No one knows you like I do."

Zosia's eyes widened slightly.

"I'm sure you've picked up things about me too."

"Like your overdramatic tendency to burst onto the scene as a whirlwind and your penchant for driving people mad?"

Marynka's mouth curved into an involuntary grin. "See? You know me too."

Zosia shot her a look she couldn't quite decipher. "Then why not keep sticking together?"

"Because…" Marynka had to work hard to keep her temper, to keep everything she was feeling from spilling out.

Because, because, because.

Because she couldn't just shrug off all the resentment that had built and built within her.

Because she couldn't give up on taking Prince Józef's heart. She couldn't disappoint Grandmother again.

And because…because she wasn't ready for this game of theirs to end.

"It's not that simple."

"You make it difficult."

"That's part of my charm." Marynka could read Zosia's face and knew she was trying her patience. She'd seen the same expression worn by Grandmother and Beata when she'd done something stupid or childish or reckless and it had been up to them to clean up the mess.

"Why do you even want me to come with you?" she burst out. It wasn't what she'd meant to say. She'd meant to cut back with an insult. The words to turn Zosia down balanced on her tongue, but instead different words kept spilling out, and she heard herself repeating all the things Grandmother had said to her. "I'm impulsive. Careless. Stupid. I don't think. You don't really want to team up with me. You're just saying that because you're worried we'll attract attention if we keep fighting. What happens if we do run away and I do something you don't like? What happens when I try something reckless? What will you do when I lose my temper or get distracted or lash out and try to hurt you—"

There was a single long blast from a trumpet. A sound so shockingly loud it shivered the air.

Zosia's head whipped toward the noise. Marynka had never been so thankful for an interruption. She skidded to a halt at the snow-crusted edge of the lake. The sun had disappeared into the horizon. Dusk brushed the blue of evening over the snow, sky, and surrounding forest.

Figures shouldered past, everyone scrambling off the ice, choking on their fur collars as they bent to unstrap their skates. Fiery torchlight bobbed here and there through shadows. Only the two of them stood motionless.

"I'd yell at you," Zosia said, still gripping Marynka's forearms, pulling her attention back. "If that happened, if you did something I didn't like or tried something reckless, *when* you try something reckless, because I already know you will. I know we'll fight. I *like* fighting with you. You never back down from a challenge. You never give in. You're incredibly strong and unbelievably stubborn, and you adapt so fast. Why wouldn't I want someone like that with me? I meant it when I said together we'd be unstoppable. And if you think you can actually hurt me…" She paused, chin lifting defiantly. "You can't. You won't. Nothing you throw at me will break me. Believe me."

Marynka swallowed around the sudden tightness in her throat. She'd always believed Midnight thought of her as someone weak and unworthy, someone beneath her notice. But now she was looking at Marynka like she truly meant what she was saying, like she really did want her to come with her. Like *Marynka* was a prize, as rare and unobtainable as a prince's pure heart.

It wasn't fair.

It wasn't fair that it had to be Zosia. Why couldn't it have been someone else? Of all the people in the world. No one had ever looked at her like that. Not Grandmother. Not even Beata. She wanted Zosia to keep looking at her like that forever. All those hours, all those years, obsessing over Midnight and thinking she was someone unattainable, someone beyond reach. For the first time since all this started, Marynka felt like she finally had the upper hand.

"But what if," she whispered, "I don't want to believe you?"

18.

ZOSIA

"MARYNKA—" ZOSIA STARTED.

"MARYNKA—" Zosia started.

Marynka stepped off the ice. Zosia stumbled after her, legs failing to adjust back to solid land. She didn't know what to make of the emotions playing across Marynka's face. She reached out a hand. Marynka moved to take it.

An explosion ripped through the heavens.

Zosia's head snapped up. There was a second explosion. A third. A fourth. Flowers of fire unfolded in violent bloom, in fantastic shades of violet, gold, and vibrant red.

Fireworks.

Some sparkled. Some crackled. Bright color fractured, scattering in every direction. Falling, only to explode again. Cries of delight and the clapping of hands met the sight, followed by loud cheers as arrow after arrow of light squealed and shot toward the deepening blue of the evening sky.

The bank of the lake was black with shadows, writhing with

people. A stream of emerald stars burst from another flare, coloring the snow, illuminating a sea of eager, upturned faces.

Zosia looked to Marynka in wonder, but she had vanished. The space she'd so recently occupied was taken up by a boy Zosia didn't recognize. A prickle of unease raised the hairs at the nape of her neck. Quickly, she knelt to unknot the straps tying the metal skates to her boots.

Her shoulder was jostled by someone shoving past. The air was full of chatter and the prince's hearty laughter. "Now we'll have some fun," he said, appearing at her side, making her jump.

Józef was looking very pleased with himself. He offered his hand to help her stand, inclining his head. Zosia followed his gaze. Further up the slope, from the edge of the snow-powdered pine trees appeared first one sleigh and then another, and another, gliding gently toward them.

Zosia's lips parted in a small O.

She'd seen kuligi before, those torchlit sleigh parties of the nobility that raced through the black of night, over the snow like ships on the cresting waves of a river as they swept through the ice-glazed valleys and soaring highland passes, past the edge of the Midnight Forest every winter. The icy chiming of the bells, the ruddy blaze of the fiery torches, the drifting shouts of laughter had always drawn her to watch from the shadow of the trees. She'd snuck among the valley's peasants, among the gaping villagers who'd felt the mountains shiver when a sleigh came asunder, and run to help drag it from a snowdrift. It was an old Karnawał tradition to travel this way from estate to estate, to arrive without warning and eat your neighbors out of house and home. And then, once you'd feasted and drunk and warmed yourself, to kidnap your host and their family and take them with you as you set off to the next estate and so on. The sleigh party growing like an avalanche, like a stone collecting snow as it rolled down a slope.

But she'd never seen anything quite so bewitching as this. The torches in each sleigh formed halos of gold. The flames flickered like prayer candles, spreading light across the white-glazed earth. At the head of the cavalcade rode a dozen of the king's uhlan guardsmen, resplendent in their bright double-breasted uniform jackets and sashes. Behind followed ten four-horse sleighs crammed with musicians: violinists mixing sweet melodies with the sleigh bells' silvery ringing, pipers and flutists with their instruments held ready, percussionists waving jingling tambourines. At the rear of party were another ten—no, twenty; no, thirty; no, more; Zosia gave up and stopped counting—whimsical Karnawał sleighs. Each was drawn by six snow-white horses, each gloriously decorated. They were carved in the shape of swans with long, slender necks, in the shape of snarling wolves and griffins and eagles.

Half the sleighs were full. The other half were empty. And beside those sleighs rode even more splendidly dressed figures on horseback, their mounts donned in glittery harnesses, in the finest of festival trimmings, their breath pluming before their noses like dragon's smoke.

A light snow was falling over everything, delicate flakes glinting in the glow of the fireworks, falling in gentle pirouettes, dusting Zosia's cheeks and shoulders and catching in the prince's eyelashes.

Józef rubbed his hands together. "Ah, how I've missed this! There's truly no place like home. No place like Lechija. From here we'll go first to the Sapphire Palace, then to the princess, my royal cousin, then to the Wojewoda of Połock. He's a sour old thing, but he keeps the finest cellars and pantry in all the city."

"You arranged all of this?" Zosia said, astonished.

The prince was amused. "Did you think somebody else did?"

"No I thought..." Her voice trailed off. *You thought what? That Marynka had managed to magically conjure up a royal sleigh party? As what, some kind of diversion?*

"And for the last, we'll invade my uncle's castle."

Zosia only caught the tail end of what the prince was saying. She cut him a sharp glance, wondering just how much of the flirtatious party boy was an act. A ruse to fool the tsarist authorities and anyone else who might be watching. A kulig was often arranged with ulterior motives. Organizers would deliberately plan the sleigh route so feuding neighbors would be forced to visit one another's homes and have to make amends with those they'd quarreled with. What ulterior motive might a rebellious prince have? What a convenient excuse a sleigh party was to visit with and unite all the most powerful families in Warszów.

"Józek!" called a girl in green velvet. "Come ride in my sleigh!"

"No mine!" called another.

"Mine!" shouted a third.

The prince was laughing. Inspiration seized Zosia too. "Your Highness," she said quickly. "Why don't you and I ride together?" She could use her shadows to drive the horses faster, have them pull ahead, away, into a dark grove in the forest somewhere, and once they were alone...

She cast another look about for Marynka, biting her lip. This was the perfect chance for them to act.

Before Józef could reply, the crush of bodies at the lake's edge surged forward, running to join the torchlit procession. A girl elbowed in front of Zosia, a boy blocked her path, and she lost sight of the prince completely.

A sleigh swept by, its runners almost cutting over her feet. The air hummed with the sound of drunken singing. She could hear the Arlekin, the jester-like individual who would ride ahead to warn people of the kulig's coming, scolding a man dressed in foreign clothing. "No tailcoats! It's forbidden to join the party in foreign costume!"

"Zosia!" Esterka waved as she climbed into a sleigh carved in the shape of a silver bear. "Over here! There's room in this one!"

Zosia smiled at her briefly. A group of children ran out from nowhere, towing a sled, shrieking with excitement, almost falling beneath a bay horse's hooves. The stallion reared and its rider called out a flurry of good-humored curses. And then finally, finally, Zosia spotted the prince again.

There, stroking the nose of another horse. A midnight-black mare in a shiny halter. Frost iced its whiskers and a white star blazed in the very center of its forehead. It looked like one of the horses belonging to Black Jaga. A beautiful animal.

He put a hand to the pommel of the saddle. Selim jostled his shoulder, shoving him playfully out of the way.

The prince backed up. Someone else caught his elbow, tugging him toward a sleigh shaped liked a wolf.

Zosia started after them.

A hand caught her wrist. "If you want to ride in a sleigh, you can ride with me."

"No, thank you," Zosia said coldly, whirling to face Kajetan. His handsome face was grim. She tried to yank her arm free. "I'm not interested. I'm riding with the—"

Kajetan's grip tightened. "It wasn't a request."

Zosia gritted her teeth. "If you don't let go, I'll scream."

"Scream, then," Kajetan said. "Do you think I can't recognize you, monster? You might have fooled everyone else, but I know what you are. I know why you're here."

"I don't know what you're talking about." Zosia took a step back.

Kajetan stepped forward, following her. His free hand was on the hilt of his saber. "I am not going to let you harm Józef."

It took everything in Zosia not to let her veins darken and her fingers taper to claws. The only thing keeping her from committing violence was the fact that they were surrounded by so many witnesses. She tried again to jerk her arm free, glancing back over her shoulder toward the line of sleighs, toward the prince.

Her eyes widened as they landed on another familiar face.

Beata was dressed in boys' clothing like Marynka. Zosia had forgotten all about Morning again. It was always like that; when Marynka was in front of her, she couldn't see anyone else.

Beata gave them a wicked grin, then raised her hands above her head and called, "Have you heard it said, Zosia? Morning banishes Midnight. She opens the gates of heaven so the red sun may rise."

Kajetan frowned, twisting toward her voice.

Zosia grasped for the night's dark, for the shadows, but she wasn't fast enough.

Blinding light erupted from Beata's palms and the sky, the scene exploded with white fire. Zosia and the sleigh party were reduced to silhouettes.

She threw a hand up, shrinking from the brightness. Far brighter a light than that of the fireworks. Bright enough to illuminate even the darkest of nights. Bright as the morning sun so that for a breath, dusk became dawn. Even with her eyes shut, Zosia could still see it.

Kajetan's grip on her wrist loosened and Zosia stumbled free.

The light burned where it touched her. Tears dripped down her cheeks. Dark shapes, bodies, writhed at the corners of her vision.

She heard the prince shout.

The rest of the kulig mistook the cry for joy or merely saw his sleigh setting off and took it all as the signal for the party to start. The shout went up from a hundred throats: "Hey! Kulig! Kulig! Kulig!" Trumpets blared. The pounding of hooves and the playing of wild music drowned out Józef's distress and the truth of what was happening.

How could they not realize what was happening?

For a horrified second, Zosia stood frozen. Then the sound of Kajetan's voice knocked the ice from her bones and she was moving again.

"Mother of God," he murmured, rubbing his eyes as she rushed past, running after the sleighs, running for the nearest horse.

Why had she ever thought they could be friends, that they could work together?

Furious with herself, with Marynka, Zosia caught the closest rider's boot and ripped him from the saddle with monstrous strength, vaulting into his place on the horse's back.

Kajetan was a step behind her.

Zosia shouted down at him, kicking the horse into a gallop, pointing after the procession of sleighs. "You're worried for your prince? Then don't let them get away!"

19.

MARYNKA

"FASTER!" BEATA URGED THE SLEIGH driver.

Marynka didn't see the bewitched young man whip the horses into a frenzy, but she felt the sleigh jerk forward. The dark trees lining the road through the snowbound forest flashed by like phantoms.

"You were supposed to melt the ice and drown her in the lake," Beata snapped. "You were supposed to distract her while I went after the prince. What happened?"

"I don't know."

"What do you *mean* you don't know?"

"I just don't know!" Marynka might've said more to defend herself if, at that moment, Prince Józef hadn't knocked her sideways, fighting to free himself.

The two of them fell against Beata, against the hard seat, grappling wildly as the horses gained speed, carrying them away from the frozen lake and the Silver Palace, rushing the prince away like a whirlwind.

Sparks filled Marynka's vision as his fist struck her chin, snapping her head back. The anger in her blood turned to fire. Her palms glowed the red of molten metal, and Józef cried out in agony as her touch burned through his sleeve, through fur lining and silk and tender skin.

"You," he gasped out, wrenching his arm free and clutching it to his chest, cringing away from the lethal heat rippling off her body. It shimmered the air and melted the snow swirling around them. Flames licked up Marynka's arms as she shed her human appearance. Her eyes were living embers and her teeth glinted like daggers.

"Me."

A biting wind, like a cold breath, nipped the nape of her neck, tearing the fur cap from her head.

Marynka twisted, looking back, hair streaming in the air. The rest of the sleigh party was dashing after them, and at the head of the cavalcade, gaining fast, were two riders galloping like demons.

A girl and a boy by their clothing. Great sprays of snow and mud flew up from their horses' hooves. Torchlight traced the path of the girl's long silver braid.

Beata let out a hiss.

Marynka felt a jolt of something close to guilt. She shoved the feeling—and the prince—down, climbing and kneeling atop the seat, gripping the back of it, facing the riders pursuing them. This was how it was supposed to be, this desperate struggle between them. This was all she needed. This was what she'd wanted. The two of them unhinged and breathless and wreaking havoc. No room for confusing feelings, no thoughts, just adrenaline and the thrill of Zosia chasing after her.

This is all you need.

"Lose them!" Beata shouted to the sleigh driver.

They drew ahead, veering from the main road with a spray of frozen earth, flying into the trees to a clamor of sleigh bells and the eerie, joyful music of the kulig, following what was likely only a hunting trail.

The forest swallowed them up.

Their pursuers didn't slow.

They came, driving their horses on, riding knee to knee. Galloping across the treacherous ground at breakneck speed, black branches and needles of ice lashing at their faces like moths drawn to a flame. Night descended; the dusky blue of the sky deepened to black. Shadows bled over the landscape, oozing up from the ground, reaching to embrace them.

Oh, Midnight, is this all you've got? If you're going to hold back here, you're going to lose.

The cold hit Marynka's teeth as she barred them in a grin. The prince shielded his eyes as Beata lit up like a living sun. Light seared the air with its incandescence. The night flinched back, the white radiance emanating from Beata devouring the shadows.

But still they lingered, a pack of writhing, monstrous black shapes, snapping at the sleigh's runners like wolves chasing down prey. The night had claws, and it was fast and hungry. The darkness leapt.

Marynka shrieked as a talon of shadow caught at her robes, trying to drag her from the seat. She jerked back, fabric tearing, but Beata reacted faster, shoving her sideways out of the way. "Get down!"

A second talon curled around Beata's torso. Her violet eyes widened. She let out a choked sound, and then she was gone. Ripped from the sleigh with a rush of air, her cry echoing in Marynka's ears, drowned out by the thunderous drumming of hoofbeats.

"Beatka!" Marynka screamed, hanging over the back of the seat. "Beatka!"

And still the riders were coming on, Zosia and Kajetan, leaning forward so their faces pressed almost to their horses' manes, the beasts foaming with sweat. And beyond them, the rest of the sleigh party.

A blistering, soul-deep fury filled Marynka. In that moment she hated Zosia as she'd never hated anyone in her entire life. Paint bubbled where her hands gripped the seat, peeling away to reveal the charred wooden bones of sleigh.

Józef was shouting at the driver. But the man stared blankly ahead, still under Beata's spell. Marynka stopped thinking of the prince and his heart; there was only the furious pounding of her blood, the heat at her fingertips, only Zosia. Everything else fell away.

Sparks skittered off her skin. Heat scorched and steamed the winter air.

Another talon of shadow lashed out.

Magic shuddered through Marynka's bones and down her arms. She threw her hands out and fire exploded before her. A whirlwind of flame howled through the air, searing the shadows, burning the darkness to tatters.

Terror seized the horses. The sleigh swerved wildly, bowling and jolting down a slope. The breeze rose to a shriek, carrying sparks, great clusters of them like fiery birds.

Stray branches caught aflame. The forest glowed a hellish red. The scent of charred pine filled Marynka's nose. A scorching wind lifted her hair.

The forest groaned. Trunks swayed. Great roots pulled out of the frozen soil as if the ancient trees were fleeing. The wind screamed like a thing alive. A kind of horrified wonder seized Marynka, awe at the clash of their magic as it bent and broke the forest. The sound of it was terrible, ruthless: the dry crash of splintering wood, the howls of terror from those in the sleigh party.

You and I, we'd be unstoppable.

Her eyes locked with Zosia's, and Marynka thought vaguely that if she died in the midst of this fight, she wouldn't care. She wouldn't mind if they went down together here. Suspended between the cold dark of night and the furious heat of day. She half hoped Zosia *would* end her now, so she would be caught in this moment always.

She recoiled as a branch caught her across the cheek. Blood spat hot down her collar.

The sleigh flew out of the trees, listing sickeningly around a bend, saplings snapping beneath the runners. The sky opened up, bright stars flashed overhead.

There was a cry of alarm from the prince. The slope of a hill rose on their left; to the right, the ground was rapidly giving way to a deep ravine. The path was narrowing.

A flutter of panic filled Marynka's chest. A tiny voice was screaming at the back of her head that they needed to slow down, to stop.

But Marynka had never been good at stopping.

Night reached for her with another claw and Marynka spun, throwing both hands out, pushing back with everything she had. Fire streaked the wind. She looked to Zosia and saw her eyes widen, felt a fleeting flash of triumph.

But Zosia wasn't looking at her. She was looking up the steep slant of the hill to their left.

There was a great rushing roar like that of a river. The trees bowed as an avalanche of snow came crashing down the slope. Impossibly fast. Impossible to avoid. Marynka had one last fleeting glimpse of red light glinting off the belled harnesses of the horses, off the distant sleighs of the kulig still following. She saw Zosia's lips move, her mouth forming a single word before the wave of snow washed over them and she was dragged under by a cold, white sea.

"Marynka!"

20.

MARYNKA

ZOSIA. ZOSIA.

Marynka's eyes shot open. There was ice in her mouth, in her ears. Snow, wet and heavy, clung to her clothes and skin and hair. The deep blue-black of the sky stretched overhead, spinning and dipping in and out of focus. The snowslide, the force of it, slamming into the sleigh had thrown her from the seat like a rag doll. There was a stabbing pain in her side. A gash on her forehead that wasn't healing was weeping hot blood into her eye. If she'd been fully human, she wouldn't have been moving.

The other members of the sleigh party were not so lucky. Terrible groans floated through the dark. Someone nearby was whimpering softly. An awful gut-wrenching sound.

"Zosia!" Marynka wheezed, sucking in an agonized breath to shout.

No answer. Only silence where her rival's voice should have

been. Even the wild wind had died down, gone silent to listen. Not even the slightest breath stirred the branches of the trees.

"*Zosia!*" There was a taste like ash in her mouth. The heat of her fury had cooled, and without it, all Marynka had left was the awful fear pounding through her. She dragged herself up onto her hands and knees. Her fingers brushed something soft.

She recoiled. Frost crusted the skin of the too-still form sprawled in the snow beside her.

Her heart banged hard against her ribs. Dread clawing up her throat, Marynka forced herself to look. But it wasn't Zosia. Or the prince. It was the young man who had driven the sleigh. If not for the unnatural bend of his neck, he seemed only to sleep quietly.

Shameful relief burned through Marynka even as a voice in her head whispered: *But isn't this what you wanted, what you were aiming for? To beat Zosia. To break her.*

To win.

Marynka pushed quickly to her feet and gasped. It felt as though someone had driven a hot knife up through the sole of her foot. She stumbled over the dead sleigh driver, reeling as the world spun, passing more crushed and broken bodies—limbs snapped to reveal the white of bone, skulls caved in, blood black against the snow. Past splintered branches, uprooted trees, crashed sleighs, and wounded figures lying half-buried, quivering, kicking, clawing. She ignored somebody's cry for help. That wasn't who she wanted. She didn't care about *them.*

"Zosia!" With every breath and step her body protested, pain shooting through her ankle each time her foot hit the ground. The snow was deep here and she sank with every step. But the thought of the other servant lying somewhere like the driver…

You're not allowed to leave me.

In all the years they'd competed against each other, in spite of everything, she had never once truly wished Midnight dead. What was the point in winning if your opponent wasn't there to see you do it? What was the point of it all if Zosia wasn't there to admit Marynka had bested her?

Ice that had slipped past her collar and turned to meltwater trickled down her spine. The cold was so sharp it cut her skin.

There was nothing fun in the thought of succeeding if there was no Zosia to look down on, no Beata to share her triumph—*Beata*. Marynka's heart lurched. The memory of those great claws of shadow closing around her friend replayed in her mind. But Beata was strong. Zosia was strong. Her shadows would surely have shielded her.

Marynka staggered past an overturned sleigh carved in the shape of a wolf. Then stopped, swaying, cold horror spearing through her when she spied the horse.

The midnight-black horse Zosia had been riding. The horse with the white star in the very center of its forehead. Lying broken and half-buried now, unmoving, flung down like a discarded toy.

Marynka moved like a sleepwalker, like someone trapped in

a nightmare, a passenger in her own body, feet drawn forward, compelled by an outside will.

You've killed her. You've—

She fell to her knees beside the animal and dug feverishly, desperately, through the snow until her fingers were stinging and burning and bleeding. Her nails, such fragile human fingernails, cracked and broke. Fresh snow started to fall from the sky. But she kept going, kept digging.

Don't die. You're not allowed to die.

If you die, I'll—

If you die, I'll be so bored.

There was a sound like a clap of thunder. A sharp and earsplitting crack.

Marynka jerked sideways, a white-hot blast of pain searing through her left side. She cried out, clasping a hand to her shoulder, blood soaking through her glove in an instant.

She looked around wildly, searching for who had—

Standing on a crest of snow, silhouetted by the rising moon was a boy in a fur cap tufted with feathers, holding a trembling, gleaming silver pistol. His voice shook with fury. "What in God's name *are* you?"

Marynka knew that voice. It belonged to the boy from the prince's bedroom, the boy who'd trailed Józef through the streets to protect him. Kajetan.

He dropped the pistol and drew the curved saber at his hip.

Marynka reached for her magic, but it was like grasping at air. There was nothing there. She'd burned herself out, given all she had to turn the wind and darkness back against Midnight. The heat that sang through her blood had turned to ice, leaving her brittle, aching, and powerless, feeling like winter inside and out.

It was an awful reminder that she wasn't invincible or as powerful as she liked to think.

Her ears caught the whispered words of a prayer to the Holy Mother. Kajetan's saber burst into flames, great swirls of heavenly fire racing crimson red along the steel blade, setting the whirling snowflakes alight, illuminating his face. He looked like an avenging angel. A saint facing down a devil.

Desperate, Marynka called again to her magic, but there wasn't so much as a spark. No heat burned the air. She still hurt, was still bleeding like a weak, normal person. She'd lost her grip on her only weapon and now stood facing her foe with empty hands.

Kajetan shouted to someone over his shoulder. More voices echoed a reply. There was the sound of many feet.

Marynka turned on her heel and ran. Tripping frantically over the snow, stumbling, staggering. Falling, face-first into a ditch of endless white. She forced herself up as angry shouts and crunching steps pursued her, gaining on her as she fled into the forest.

21.

ZOSIA

ZOSIA CAME BACK TO HERSELF slowly, a steady throbbing at the back of her skull pulling her into the present. Dazed, she cracked open an eye and tried to make sense of her surroundings.

Black. Everything was black. It was as if she'd been tossed back into the Midnight Forest, back into those woods where the sun never rose, into that inescapable darkness. She cracked her eyes open a fraction further, and bright spots, stars, blossomed across her vision. Everything *hurt*.

Where was she? She remembered—sparks. Fire. Marynka's face. Her features lit with fury. Her eyes burning gold as day. It all came back to her in pieces. Marynka. Beata. The kulig. The furious chase through the trees. The horse she'd stolen galloping faster and faster and faster, the raging wind, the clash of fire and shadow. The towering wall of snow crashing down…

Panic seared through Zosia like lightning. She tried to sit up and quickly discovered that she couldn't.

She was lying on her stomach. One arm pinned beneath her chest and the other trapped beneath a solid weight of ice. The cold pressed down on her body like a boot heel grinding an insect into dust. She tried to turn her head, but it was like a hand gripped the back of her skull and was holding her in place. She'd been buried. Snatched from the saddle and dragged under by the full force of winter herself.

Breathe.

She had to remember to breathe.

Think.

Zosia's breath rasped out in ragged puffs, spit icing on her lips.

You're going to get out of this—and then you're going to murder *Marynka.*

She tried to shift her legs, but a searing pain tore through her calf.

Move.

She would die down here if she couldn't dig her way out. That was the danger of snowslides. Only those pulled quickly from the slush survived. The corpses of those who didn't reappeared each spring when their white shrouds melted away like rain-soaked cobwebs.

Move.

But the snow, the ice, weighing on her was as stubborn and unforgiving as stone. It refused to shift, and the throbbing in her head sharpened painfully with each failed movement.

Zosia reached desperately for her magic, for the darkness that bled through her veins, that slept deep within her bones. And found…

Nothing.

She was all hollowed out. Empty. Completely drained of power. She couldn't summon her monstrous strength or call on the shadows to free her. She'd given everything she had fighting Marynka. She had not a drop of magic left.

Horror clawed at her insides. She squeezed her eyes shut and tried again, reaching deep, deep, deeper inside of herself. Denial warred with outrage, with fear. Impossible that she'd spent all her magic and still been overpowered. Impossible.

You're going to die down here, whispered the voice in her head. *Alone. In the cold, in the dark.*

Like you were supposed to all those years ago.

When one winter's night, Zosia's mother, not much more than a girl herself, had abandoned her by the side of an ice-rimed road for the wolves or the mountain spirits to find. For a witch to find.

"Be a good girl and wait for me, Zosiu. I'll be back soon."

Only her mother hadn't come back. Zosia couldn't even remember what the woman had looked like, who her father had been, whether or not she'd had other family. She could only recall pieces of things: the phantom touch of someone's hand stroking her hair, the snatch of a hummed lullaby. She'd sometimes dreamed of trying to find her mother. "*Look,*" she'd tell her. "*Look, I'm alive. I came back.*" Only the faceless woman always recoiled from her as if she were some bloodsucking upior crawled out of the grave.

"*That's not my daughter. That's a monster.*"

The tiniest whimper escaped Zosia's throat. It was getting harder and harder to breathe. Pain throbbed through her with every jagged hammer of her heart. She was so spent of magic that she didn't even have the power to heal herself. Had she really defied Black Jaga, stolen all those hearts, become a monster just to die down here in the dark?

No. No, she refused to let it end like this. She would not die quietly here in the cold. She would *not* be buried here. She wasn't going out like this—whimpering over her wounds. She wasn't finished yet.

She was *Midnight.* The strongest and most terrifying of the servants who served the three witches of Lechija. The most powerful. She couldn't be beaten. Midnight didn't lose.

She ignored the pain that lit up every nerve as she pushed herself to *move.*

And that was when she heard it, the faintest sound filtering through her despair. A shout, muffled and distant.

Zosia stilled. There was only silence now. Had she imagined it? She screamed as loudly as she could, until her throat was raw, the effort making her head spin violently. Her pulse thundered in her ears. But if she could let them know she was down here. If someone…

No one had ever answered her prayers. But just this once, just this *once*.

Please. She prayed for help, for a miracle. *Please, I'm begging you. Someone. Anyone.*

Time passed in small eternities. Zosia fought to keep conscious, to keep from slipping into that beckoning dark, her tired mind sinking toward sleep, until, through a fog of haziness and pain, she felt something shift.

The weight on her back lessened, eased slightly. There was a sound of frantic scrabbling. Someone seized her arm.

Zosia sucked in air through her teeth, filling her starving lungs as the darkness gave abruptly to shards of moonlight. A pale face swam into view above hers, and a pair of worried, coffee-brown eyes.

For a moment she could only stare, unable to comprehend why Prince Józef of all people would try to save someone like her.

With the help of two more boys, he freed her from her icy prison, from the snow's hold, shouting as he did so. "Good, good. Here! Quickly, she's frozen through."

Zosia surfaced into a scene of chaos and devastation. Debris surrounded them. Shattered trees and giant branches lay half-buried beside overturned Karnawał sleighs and...bodies. Some moaning. Some still. Beyond the prince, a foam-streaked horse was rearing, hooves clawing the air, whinnying in high-pitched distress as a woman leapt for the reins. Voices called to each other through the dusk in low, urgent tones. One repeating the same name over and over. Another praying. Flaming torches carried light through the dark. More blurry figures huddled together in shock.

"Where?" Zosia croaked out. Where was Marynka? If the prince was here—

"Shh," Józef hushed her. "Don't try to speak. Selim, quickly, over here!"

A new pair of hands swaddled Zosia in thick sleigh robes.

"We're going to get you someplace warm," Józef said, his breath escaping in ghostly plumes. "It's all going to be okay."

Zosia stared at him, thoughts spinning wildly. He pressed a leather-gloved hand to her cheek as a comfort, and then he was moving on, calling firm, concise orders, searching the snow for the injured, for more survivors. "Staszek, bring the lanterns this way. Watch for the edge of the ravine."

She grabbed after him weakly. "Wait, don't—" Her fingers brushed his trailing sleeve, and the last of her strength deserted her. Her arm flopped loosely to her side. Her vision slid in and out of focus. *Don't go. Marynka. Where is Marynka?*

Oblivious to her silent protests, a massive pair of arms swept her up, cradling her as if she were something fragile made of glass. Zosia's head lolled against the broad wall of the man's chest as he staggered through the snow, murmuring soothing words as he carried her away from the carnage.

22.

ZOSIA

THEY HURRIED ZOSIA TO THE closest shelter, to a monastery built hundreds of years ago atop a hill rising out of the
forest where the sleigh party had come to ruin. Those still in
one piece, mostly those who had been riding at the rear of the
kulig, did their best to carry their injured friends. The monastery's monks rushed among them like ghosts in their pale habits
and hoods, lining the wounded up in neat rows along the floor
on rough pallets, treating patients grimly, chanting spell-prayers
of healing.

Zosia wasn't used to enduring physical pain, wasn't used to
feeling bruised and battered. She was used to being impossibly
strong. Her body had been shaped into a weapon that carried her
through deadly missions and desperate fights. But now, with one
split-second clash, it had been rendered useless. She could barely
stand or sit up without her head spinning. Her body was so weak
it felt like it belonged to somebody else, to a stranger. She couldn't

stifle a cry as calloused hands attempted to rub warmth into her limbs. She wanted to bite the monk who was trying to force her to drink some kind of broth. She did not want to be touched.

Never in her life had she felt so horribly vulnerable. So exposed and powerless. The closest she'd come to feeling this way was when she'd awakened for the first time in the old wooden house in the dark depths of the Midnight Forest. She'd tried to run away then, too, tried to stab Black Jaga with a small knife she'd stolen when her back was turned. The old witch had caught her hand before the blow landed and snapped the bones in Zosia's wrist like they were kindling. "What a stubborn creature you are," she'd laughed. "What a little monster. But if you wish to hurt me, child, you'll have to grow much stronger than that."

So Zosia had. She hadn't had a choice. Powered by spite and the dream of one day making the old woman eat her words, she'd taken it as a challenge. She'd clenched her teeth as the witch poured magic into her, as eager fingers of shadow pried between her teeth, forced her mouth open, and reached down her throat into her core, into her heart, filling her veins with darkness.

She'd learned to use that darkness, learned how to fold herself into shadow until she was a slither of the night itself, learned how to grow claws and steal prince's hearts. She'd learned to bide her time and wait for the best moment to strike.

Really, Black Jaga could hardly claim to be shocked by Zosia's actions. She was the one who had shaped Zosia into what she was, the one who had raised her. Wasn't she the monster the old witch had wished for? The monster she'd crafted in her own image.

You made me, Grandmother. Am I not everything you wanted me to be?

The witch had only herself to blame.

Zosia bit her cheek against the pain and forced herself up onto her elbows. The hall was a blur of haunted faces and flickering candlelight. Voices rose and fell, urgent echoing shouts and the singsong words of prayers. Everyone speaking over one another until it all mixed into meaningless sound. The dry bones of deceased monks decorated the walls, the skulls of the faithful dead watched her silently from either side of the room.

Nausea rushed Zosia and she gagged. She had to give it to Marynka. She'd never been in a fight before that had exhausted her to the extent that she had nothing left. Black Jaga had warned her it could happen if she pushed past the limits of her magic. A grim kind of admiration undercut her shock. That Marynka had managed to push her this far...

She had to applaud her. Marynka had actually managed to best her this time. She wondered if this was how *she'd* felt all the times Zosia had beaten her. Frustrated. Furious. And yet strangely exhilarated. Every nerve in her body ached to hunt the other servant down and wrap her fingers around her neck.

So *this* was Marynka's answer to her offer to work together. She should've known better than to think that they could ever—

"How are you feeling?"

Zosia blinked, lost for a heartbeat in the haze of her own thoughts. A skeletal figure loomed over her.

"You're at the monastery. We're trying to get a little warmth back into you."

Zosia nodded, squinting, gaze sliding past the monk, an elderly man with summer-blue eyes and wild, overgrown white brows. On the opposite side of the hall, another equally elderly monk was treating the prince, who, to Zosia's unending relief, had been bundled into the monastery's guest house soon after her. The monks had exclaimed over Józef's frostbitten hands in horror, over his blistered face, his bruises, and the raw red skin at his wrist. The imprint of what must be Marynka's fingers burned into his flesh.

They were attempting now to dress the wounds, bathing them with holy water, smearing his injuries with a salve mixed from church-blessed herbs. Only Józef kept pushing to his feet to comfort and reassure people. His words put heart into everybody, but Zosia could see he was exhausted. There was a haunted look in his eye and a helpless fury in the clench of his stubbled jaw. She wondered if he blamed himself. He had arranged the sleigh party and Marynka had come after him.

She watched him lay a soothing hand on an agitated figure's shoulder. "You're hurt, Staszek. Rest, get warm. Let Brother Aleksander look at your arm. We'll keep searching for them, I promise. Why don't you sit down here?"

The young man followed the directions wordlessly. Since coming to Warszów, Zosia had seen girls and boys flush red when Józef so much as smiled in their direction. She'd seen them practically melt if he deigned to speak to them. She'd thought it was just his royal title and his good looks, but she was starting to think it might be something more.

The old monk bent over her again, blocking her view. "Don't push yourself. You're as bad as he is."

Zosia squirmed, trying to see past him. Her attention flicked over the other rough pallets, to the door. A tired Selim, ever close to the prince, caught sight of her and frowned, a question in his eyes.

A shiver of unease ran through her. How much had he seen? How much of what had happened did he understand?

How much did he suspect?

For now, at least, she didn't think anyone knew what she was. She doubted she'd be lying here being cared for otherwise. And she couldn't see her momentary ally, see Kajetan, anywhere. Perhaps it was a blessing in disguise that she didn't have the magic to mend herself just now. If her cuts and bruises had healed instantly, there would definitely have been questions.

Zosia feigned exhaustion, slumping back against the pillow, playing innocent, speaking softly so only the old monk could hear her. "I wanted to see if the others were all right, Father. Have they brought anyone else in? A girl with curly red-brown hair, with freckles across her nose? She's small and talks loudly. Have you seen her?"

The monk's brow furrowed and he shook his head sorrowfully. "There won't be anyone else brought in now. Not with the snow coming down heavy and the wind picking up. I'd be surprised if this storm settles before morning."

In the pause that followed his words, Zosia heard the wind outside, whimpering like a forgotten child. She and Marynka had stirred it into a frenzy it wouldn't easily calm from.

"They'll have to call the search off."

"But the prince—" Zosia said.

"Wants to carry on into the night," finished the monk with a heavy sigh. "I know. He's not thinking clearly. He's more seriously injured than he looks. It's all a great tragedy." The old man bowed his head and crossed himself, and then he did the worst possible thing. Tearing a passage from a prayer book, he set the crackly paper aflame and blew the ashy smoke onto Zosia's injuries and into her face.

It happened so fast Zosia couldn't stop herself from inhaling.

His magic hit her, filling her lungs, sudden and bright, lighting her up from the inside. Heat lanced through her body and to anyone else it might've been healing, but because she wasn't fully human, because she was a monster, the heat became a fire that scorched through her veins, setting every inch of her ablaze.

For a breath Zosia thought her entire body would crumble to ash.

She gasped and grasped the monk's wrinkled hand with a strength that made him wince.

He misread the action, took the pain on her face for a spasm of grief, because he said, "I am sorry for the loss of your friend."

"She's not dead." The words rushed out of Zosia, an instinctive denial. Her grip tightened on his fingers as a strange swell of protectiveness surged through her. Marynka was alive, of that she was certain. She had to be because Zosia was going to kill her herself.

She held the thought in her mind like a talisman. Of course Marynka was still alive and out there somewhere, waiting and plotting her next move. She would appear any minute now, loud and reckless and infuriating as always. It didn't matter if it was storming fiercely, the wind howling an unholy lament, the snow coming down thick and fast. It didn't matter that Marynka was weak against the winter cold, against the darkness, that she might be injured like Zosia was now.

Nightmarish scenarios paraded through her mind: Marynka buried beneath the snow, wounded, dead, gone. What if the blizzard was too much for her in her weakened condition?

Zosia crushed the niggling thoughts. Marynka wasn't a friend to worry over. She had made it painfully clear that she was nothing but an enemy.

Her gaze darted toward the door.

Footsteps scuffed against the stone floor. A second figure peered over the monk's shoulder, drawn by the sound of Zosia's agonized gasp. "Is she well?" The prince knelt beside her pallet. "How are you feeling?"

Zosia glanced up at him, startled.

"Come," the monk said, looking worried, trying to free his fingers from the death grip she still had on his hand, trying to reassure her. "You should rest. I know you wish your friend alive—"

"I do *not* wish her alive," said Zosia vehemently. "I don't care what happens to her." Anger trembled through her, mostly anger at herself for letting her guard down, for letting her focus drift, for imagining for even a second that she and Marynka could be allies. There was too much antagonistic history between them both for it ever to have worked. When Marynka had appeared before her all those years ago, when she'd swept in as a literal whirlwind, Zosia had thought she might not be alone in the world, had thought there might be someone who was the same as her, another like her.

But she'd been wrong. They were too different. The servants of night and day, claimed by opposing factions, set against each other from the start.

She should have known that trying to reach out to someone like Marynka was only asking to get burned.

The old monk tutted. "She's worried about another of the girls," he explained to Józef. "Her friend. A girl with red hair."

"She's not my friend," said Zosia. "I never liked her anyway." She knew she sounded childish, petulant, but pain was a constant throb in her bones, and it made her irritable and want to lash out.

Curiosity crept into the prince's gaze, and he looked at her with more attention, giving Zosia the kind of look she could *feel*— as though he could see right through her, pick the thoughts straight out of her head.

A lock of unruly black hair fell across his forehead and into his brown eyes. Something in his expression softened. "It's strange, isn't it?" he said. "You would think it should be impossible to feel two such contradicting emotions about a person at once. To hate someone so much you wish them dead, while at the same time the thought of them being hurt is unbearable. You can't stop yourself from worrying even when you know you shouldn't, can't stop yourself from looking at the door in case they might still walk through it."

Zosia's breath stuttered in her throat.

Józef gave her tired smile. "You should get some rest." He nodded at the monk. "God guard you both. Please keep a close watch over her for me, Father."

Zosia let out a breath as he moved away. He was right. She did need to rest, needed to give her body a chance to recover its strength so she could take his heart and put an end to all this.

Murmuring softly, the monk smoothed her blankets. Zosia wanted to turn her back on him, but then she'd be lying on her sore ribs, so instead she shut her eyes, ignoring his presence. It didn't matter what he said. Marynka was alive. If Midday were so easily killed, so easily beaten, Zosia's life would have been so much simpler.

23.

MARYNKA

MARYNKA WAS SO COLD SHE couldn't even feel it anymore. Only stubbornness and a fierce effort kept her on her feet, kept her limping forward. She'd lost Kajetan and the rest of her pursuers among the trees. She could only hope they'd given up or fallen into a ditch or the snow had swallowed them. It was falling freely now, coming down thick, as if it wished to bury her sins beneath a sea of pristine white.

It was already burying her tracks. Her faint footprints and the red bread-crumb trail of blood trickling hotly down her wrist, dripping from her fingers. The bullet had gone straight through her shoulder. It was a miracle she'd made it this far, a miracle she was standing. Still, she struggled on, forcing one numb foot in front of the other. Soldiering on through the dark of the winter night with nothing but the moon to guide her, staggering over hidden roots and rocks, all alone now save for her treacherous thoughts.

You won. You beat her. You won like you always said you could, just like you've always wanted.

Marynka followed a narrow band of moonlight falling through the black pines. The air glimmered with floating flakes of snow.

You won and that's all that matters.

You did what you were supposed to do.

"I win," she whispered into the wind. "I beat you."

So why, then, did she feel so defeated? *She* was the one left standing, so why did she feel empty? Why, when she'd finally won, did she feel like she was still losing?

Marynka choked back a sob.

It wasn't her fault. It was Zosia's. If she hadn't chased after the sleigh, if she hadn't attacked Beata, if Beata hadn't tried to help.

The guilt churning in Marynka's stomach twisted into a more comforting, blazing anger. Her hands balled into fists. Why hadn't Beata been quick enough to dodge? Why had she come up with that ridiculous plan in the first place? Why had she insisted on pushing herself into their fight?

You know why.

Because Beata worried about her even though she didn't deserve it. Beata cared about her. Beata *loved* her. Marynka had always known how Morning felt about her. She just pretended not to, as if by ignoring her friend's feelings, they would magically disappear. She'd known. She hadn't wanted…

Life had taught Marynka that love was something you had to

earn. Only through blood and sweat and tears and endless effort could you prove yourself worthy of it. Beata's love made her uneasy. It felt like she was trying to play a trick on her. She couldn't trust a love so easily and freely given. She didn't know what to *do* with that kind of love.

Out of the corner of her eye, Marynka caught movement—the shadow of something large skittering away. There was a crack—a sound like a twig snapping. By the time she spun around, whatever it was had already gone, vanished in the darkness.

She waited, straining her ears. But there was no sound save for her ragged breathing and the rapid *thump-thump-thump* of her racing heart. The sleeping trees bent close as if they too were listening. The wind picked up, carrying through the branches to whisper of cunning things, of monsters and men crouched in wait.

Had she imagined it? Was she seeing ghosts in the snow? Had it been a wolf? Something worse? Another of the fearsome and wicked creatures that made their home in Lechija's forests? Marynka was only one of such creatures, although she didn't feel particularly wicked or fearsome right now. Not without her magic.

Help me, she might've begged the trees. Only this wasn't the forest where the hour was always midday and the sun was always shining. The forest was a different place at night.

A surge of deep primal fear shot through her body. Panicking, Marynka started to run, shoving snow-choked branches aside, letting out a cry as she lost her footing on a hidden root and slipped.

She rolled once, twice, three times, tumbling down a sharp incline and landing hard at the bottom, smashing her injured shoulder against a rock. Searing heat burst down her arm. Lightning fractured behind her eyelids.

She couldn't muster the strength to rise.

Lying facedown in the snow, chest heaving and body on fire with pain, it all caught up with her. Everything. Zosia's eyes as that wall of white came crashing down, her lips forming the shape of Marynka's name. Beata's features bright with shock. The way she'd started to reach for Marynka before she was snatched away by the night.

Marynka breathed into the snow and screamed.

And kept screaming, pressing her face harder and harder into the snow, wanting the cold to freeze away everything she was feeling, gulping in lungfuls of frigid air between each sob.

She could feel the blood slowly freezing in her veins, feel the snow starting to pile heavy on her back, her shoulders, her head. The sky weeping icy tears to match those frozen to her cheeks.

There was a distant part of her that knew she had to get up. Get up and keep moving, or she would freeze to death here.

But in that moment, all she could do was lie in the snow and sink into the cold. It felt like she'd spent her whole life coaxing her exhausted mind and body just that little bit further. One more step. One more try. Because this time things would be different. This time she would triumph. This time she'd make Grandmother proud.

It felt heavenly to lie here flat and still, to let herself rest, to not force herself to keep going. Sleep beckoned to her, tempting her with wicked dreams of warmth, with seductive visions of the Midday Forest in the middle of summer, of a wooden house belonging to a witch all decorated with bone wreaths, nestled in a field of blood-red poppies. She'd lost the prince in the avalanche. What would Grandmother say when she learned the pure heart she'd wanted was buried beneath a mountain of snow?

This time it was not Marynka's imagination. The cry of a night owl broke the cathedral-like quiet. And then—there. A definitive crack of branches. A crunching as heavy boots broke the snow crust.

Marynka struggled to her hands and knees as the shadow moved out of the trees.

Kajetan. His robes rigid with cold. His saber unsheathed and glinting in the moonlight. His brown hair a cascade of frost.

He'd caught up to her, tracked her despite her disappearing trail. Marynka wanted to laugh, but didn't have the energy. The snow was falling so fast the air was white and the world was spinning, exhaustion dragging her toward the darkness eating at the edges of her vision.

She surrendered to it, slumping back on her heels as he came forward. Kajetan's lips moved, but she couldn't make out the words. He raised his saber, and fire licked once more along the curve of the blade.

Marynka let her eyes flutter shut, and the scene wisped away like a candle flame blown out, everything going dark.

24.

MARYNKA

MUCH OF WHAT HAPPENED NEXT was lost in a fog of semiconsciousness. Marynka vaguely recalled being dragged, carried, the sound of a deep voice cursing, boots stomping on ice, the shadowy shape of a woodcutter's hut materializing between snowbound trees and the creak of a door opening, but the memories had all the haziness of a bad dream. They were grayed and blurry at the edges.

She *did* remember being unceremoniously dumped onto a supremely hard floor. The shock jarred her wounded shoulder. The ache of it had faded to a dull throb. When she finally opened her eyes, she could make out the red gleam of firelight playing over the sagging beams of a wooden ceiling. The frigid air was thick with dust.

Footsteps and a sneeze told her she wasn't alone. Rolling onto her side, Marynka found Kajetan staring down at her. He'd started a fire with the dry logs stacked beside the hut's crumbling stove and bound her wrists in front of her, and her ankles, with bloody strips torn from the hem of his żupan.

Lying on the hard floor Marynka shivered violently.

Such bonds would not normally have held her, but Kajetan had soaked the cloth with holy water from a flask he carried. It scalded her skin, and without her magic, she couldn't summon the strength to rip the fabric apart.

Outside, the wind had turned vicious. The roof gave an ominous creak. Shuddered, but held. The wooden walls groaned so loudly it seemed as though the whole hut would collapse. Wild gusts of air scuttled down the chimney, whirling sparks into their faces that threatened to set the place ablaze.

But at least then they wouldn't be cold. Even Marynka's fiery red-brown hair was frozen into stiff, icy curls.

She watched Kajetan beat the ice from his robes, remove his sodden, snow-crusted fur cap and sweep a hand through his hair. With a grimace, he picked up the blanket moldering on an old cot in the corner and glanced at Marynka. His handsome face pinched with indecision.

"Ooh, are we going to cuddle together for warmth?" Marynka's teeth started to chatter. She bit the words out around the clacking. "How romantic. I bet you're wishing it was the prince here and not—"

Kajetan dragged her across the dusty, leaf-strewn floor toward the stove by her collar.

Marynka cursed at him, kicking and spitting, only her heart

wasn't in it. She was so tired still, and it was warmer lying closer to the stove anyway, with those glorious flames throwing a red glow over everything. She wanted to stretch her hands to the fire, let the heat wash over her thick and slow, crawl in among the embers and let herself burn.

Kajetan shook off one boot and then the other, dusted the snow from both, and set them by the fire to dry. His brown hair was touched with gold in the flickering light. It made Marynka think he'd been as blond as Beata as a child.

He sat down cross-legged in front of her, back to the glowing warmth, sweeping the blanket around his shoulders like a cloak, blocking most of the heat. He gripped his saber in one white-knuckled hand. "What in God's name *are* you?"

It was the same question he'd asked after he'd shot her. Marynka smiled, but did not answer.

"A witch? A devil?"

"A monster," Marynka said. "Midday. The Red Rider. Faithful servant to Red Jaga who rules the hours between noon and night-fall." She preened as best as she could with her hands and ankles bound. "You've probably heard of me."

"I haven't," said Kajetan, which made Marynka scowl. "Wait—Mid*night*? You saying you're the midnight demon?"

"Mid*day*." Marynka glowered.

"Then no," Kajetan said. "I've not heard of you. Did the tsarina send you after Józef? Are you some manner of dark creature that she summoned?" He paused, gaze flicking past her to the shadows of the hut before returning. "Did my father send you after him? Szczęsny Pilawski?"

"And if he did?" Marynka asked. "Perhaps you should free me just in case."

Kajetan scoffed. "I'm not freeing you. I'm taking you back to Warszów. So Józef can see for himself that I was right to warn him. So that you can answer for your crimes."

"He's probably dead," said Marynka. "The prince. Buried beneath the snowslide. Rather than chase after me, you should have stayed and searched for him."

Kajetan's expression didn't change. "Józek's too stubborn to die from such a small thing as that."

"Well, you would know," Marynka said, rolling onto her back, fitting the pieces together in her head—Kajetan's questions and the accusations she'd heard the prince hurl at him back at the Copper Palace. "Seeing as you tried to kill him before I did."

The words struck a nerve. Kajetan's green eyes flashed. "Who is the other girl?" he demanded.

"Other girl?" Marynka stared at the ceiling, listening to the wind screech. She wondered vaguely if this was what it was like for Zosia living in Black Jaga's house in the Midnight Forest, surrounded by darkness and the cold pressing in through the cracks. "I don't know any other girl."

"The one with silver braid. She tried to stop you."

"Did she? She didn't succeed." Marynka turned her head toward him, started to sit up, voice going sharp. "Why, did you see her?"

"Not since we were caught up in the avalanche." Kajetan was watching her closely. "Afraid she'll come after you again?"

Marynka slumped back to the floor. "No."

I'm afraid that she won't.

She started to laugh. Loud and unsteady and sharp.

Kajetan stared. "What is wrong with you?"

Marynka huffed out a breath that was almost a sob. "I wish I knew."

"Why did she try to save Józef?"

"She's not your ally, if that's what you think. She only tried to stop me because she wants to take his life herself."

"You said you serve Red Jaga? Who is she?"

"A witch."

"Where can she be found?"

"Beyond the mountains, beyond the forest."

Kajetan's eyes narrowed. He continued to ask questions, demand answers: *Is she working with the tsarina or the King of Prusja? Where in Lechija is the Midday Forest? Why does the witch wish to hurt Józef?*

Marynka lost interest. She was beyond caring by now and so tired of it all. Even the snap and crackle of the flames nibbling on the wood in the stove had become a distant thing. Her body ached. All her senses were numb with cold. She just wanted to stop thinking. About Grandmother. About the prince. About Zosia. She would kill this fool in the morning when she'd recovered her strength and magic, when she was warmer. No matter how dark the night, a new day always dawned. The sun never, ever failed to rise.

Or so she told herself.

She shut her eyes, ignoring her captor, and slept. For an hour. Maybe longer. Waking with a racing heart, choking on memories. Waking to complain that Kajetan was making too much noise heaping more wood on the fire.

He muttered something unkind and lay down across from her, his back to the stove, beneath his blanket, saber still in hand.

In retaliation, Marynka waited until his eyes fluttered shut and then rolled closer, wriggling to join him under the blanket, pressing her freezing fingers to his neck.

Kajetan's body went rigid. The sound he made was completely worth it.

"Don't worry, Kajtuś," Marynka reassured him, using an overly affectionate form of his name, pressing her body closer, anything to feel warm. "And don't flatter yourself. I'm just tired of being cold. I don't like boys."

"And I don't like monsters," he snarled back. "So keep your cursed hands to yourself. Do you have any shame?"

"Not really. Oh! Don't tell me this is your first time? You've never slept with a girl before?"

Kajetan's face was as brilliant red as the coals he'd just stoked. "I am going to murder you."

"No, you won't. You would've already if you were, and you don't want me to freeze to death before you can drag me before the prince, do you?" Marynka pulled the itchy wool blanket over her head and gave an exaggerated shiver, and then a contented sigh. Finally, finally she was starting to get a little warm. The feeling was creeping back into her numb fingers and toes, making them tingle with a pleasant kind of pain. "I'm like your penance. You betrayed your prince, fought for the enemy, and now you're trying desperately to redeem yourself. You think by protecting Józef you'll earn his forgiveness. Am I wrong?"

For a long moment, she thought he would not answer. Then he said, voice barely audible, "If I could choose a single moment, if I could go back." Kajetan swallowed audibly. "I prayed to the saints he'd kill me on that battlefield. I already know I can never make amends for the things I've done. I don't deserve his forgiveness. I don't expect it. I wouldn't ask it of him."

His words were punctuated by the pop and spark of a burning log in the fire.

Marynka was quiet.

They both slept this time, surrendering to exhaustion. All night the winter storm raged on and morning broke without a sun. Marynka had hoped to sense the world warming beyond the wooden walls of the hut, but those hopes were dashed. There was no venturing outside in such a blizzard. The brutal wind and heavy snowfall were unrelenting. They were lucky for the wood stacked inside the hut so they could keep feeding the fire. Less lucky to have no food with them, but Kajetan woke Marynka when he melted a little snow for them to drink.

She was awake again now, listening, watching the steady rise and fall of Kajetan's chest. There wasn't much to do save wait and rest. He murmured something in his sleep, a word she didn't catch. Little more than an exhale, but she read the shape of the prince's name on his lips. There was a deep furrow between his brows as he clutched his saber to his breast. His clenched fingers had locked around the jeweled hilt as if he didn't dare venture into his dreams without it, as if he intended to take the weapon with him to fight the horrors in his mind.

Marynka had felt him jerk out of more than one nightmare.

She hadn't tried to comfort him with empty reassurances, hadn't tried to weasel into his good graces—it wasn't her style— hadn't whispered in his ear that it was all just a bad dream the way Beata did for her. That was a lie anyway. The thoughts and fears that kept Marynka up at night were all too real, and she had the feeling it was the same for Kajetan.

Ever so carefully now, so as not to wake him, she raised her bound wrists to her mouth. Reaching, in vain, for her magic. Her teeth still wouldn't turn to iron, nor lengthen to vicious points. Red welts from the holy water Kajetan had soaked the cloth with marred her skinny wrists.

Still, it wasn't anything she couldn't bear or couldn't work with. Sucking in a deep breath, Marynka pulled and *pulled* against the bindings until they bit into her skin, gnawing at the cloth at the same time and—

Kajetan shifted, blinked, groaned, and dragged a hand down his face at the sight of her, which was honestly kind of rude. "How many times are you going to try that?" His voice was gravelly with exasperation.

"As many times as it takes."

He raised his eyes to heaven.

Marynka's stomach grumbled loudly. She thought longingly of kaszka with molten butter and brown sugar and cinnamon. "Are you sure there's no food?"

"If there was I wouldn't waste it on you." Kajetan staggered upright. His clothes were rumpled and his movements stiff, a gift from sleeping on the cold, unforgiving floor. He shivered as he retied the wide, ornately embroidered sash wound several times around his slim waist.

Marynka hadn't paid much attention before, but really his clothes were very fine. His fur-lined kontusz was a rich red heavily embellished with patterns of silver thread, and the contrasting żupan he wore beneath it was a brilliant silken gold. Pearl buttons drew a glittery line up his torso to his chin. It was a pity he was so much taller than her. She could've taken the outfit from him when she finally freed herself.

Kajetan bent to the stove, stirring the sullen embers back to life, frowning grimly at their dwindling pile of wood.

"How much longer, do you think, until the wind dies down?" said Marynka. "Until it stops snowing?"

How long do you think we'll be trapped in here?

Kajetan settled another log into the embers. "For our sake, you should pray that it's soon."

25.

ZOSIA

ANOTHER NIGHT PASSED WITH THE snow falling fast and thick and heavy. The howling wind piled white domes atop the monastery's rooftops until only the spindly black spire of the church speared through. It wasn't until the dawn of the following day that the winter storm finally broke and quiet fell, and then only for a moment, for that was when the monastery's bells began to peal.

The sharp sound shattered the icy morning. It was a call to prayer and also to action. Fat in their fur-lined robes, faces shadowed by stubble and feather-tufted caps, figures rushed to shovel paths through the solid whiteness holding everyone captive. The whole kingdom seemed to have become a single white field, and the recovered members of the sleigh party looked to the blue sky with unconcealed eagerness. It wasn't just the cold and gloomy halls of the guesthouse they wished to escape. Shock and grief had shifted into a deeper dread. Rumors hinted that the old monastery, with its walls of stacked bones and skull-lined archways, was, in fact, haunted by a demon.

We're trapped in here with a devil for all that this is a holy place.

Trapped inside with some dark spirit, some creature from nightmare and legend. A night nymph or a blood-sucking strzyga, with hair like starlight and long claws of dark shadow. Two girls had glimpsed the monster slipping into a prayer room and fled from it screaming. Even now people were conjuring circles of light with blessed candles to guard themselves.

Annoyance stirred inside Zosia's chest. Was she really that terrifying? She'd only transformed briefly as a test. She was feeling much better, more herself. Her strength and magic were returning, and her wounds had healed, although she was careful to conceal the fact. The prince had taken to checking on her frequently while she pretended to recover. She'd heard more than one voice whisper that she was fast becoming his new favorite.

The thought sent a thrill to the darkness inside of her. Everything was finally coming together. All that was left now was to put an end to the game. Marynka had delayed her, but she no longer stood in the way.

"How are you feeling, Zosieńka?" Józef asked now, coming to stand by her side, adding an extra syllable to her name, making it a term of endearment.

"I've felt better."

"Don't push yourself."

"I could say the same for you, Your Highness. Aren't you supposed to be resting?" Yesterday, Selim had threatened to sit on Józef if he didn't take a moment to rest.

The prince's smile was full of mischief. "I can't help it. I can't bear not doing something." He leaned in close to whisper. "Please don't tell Selim."

Zosia could feel envious eyes watching them. With first light had come not only the steady chiming of the morning bells, but a procession of fretful guardians, parents, siblings, aunties and uncles. All anxious to discover what had become of the ill-fated kulig they'd expected to arrive at their palaces. It was almost impossible to move through the guesthouse hall without tripping over someone.

"Please don't tell Selim what?" A hand brushed Zosia's arm, lightly, as if afraid of startling her. Zosia still stiffened at the touch, but it was only Esterka. Pearl drops shining at her earlobes, a hint of apology in her dark eyes.

"You're looking much better." Esterka's voice softened. "Is there no one in your family coming to collect you?"

Zosia shook her head. "I don't have family in Warszów."

Esterka's brow furrowed and Józef's lips parted on a question, but a voice called to him then and the prince made his excuses, moving away. Selim appeared before Zosia could even think to follow, insisting on showing her and Esterka the holy amulet that had saved his life in the snowslide.

"And now it's protecting me from the monastery's ghoul!" he declared, drawing it from beneath his robes. A leather pouch hung from a string around his neck, and within it was a tiny scroll inscribed with verses from the Quran written in saffron ink.

Looking at it, Zosia couldn't help but shiver. She could feel the hum of divine magic in her teeth. Selim dangled the amulet nearer and it took all her control not to flinch. Was it paranoia or was Selim watching her closely? But then he started talking again as if nothing were out of the ordinary.

"If you visit my village," he told Esterka. "I can ask our healer to make one for you. She's so powerful she can control and summon dżinn. I'm going to ask her to make one for Józef."

Esterka was fascinated and immediately started comparing the magical formula on the scroll to several Jewish ones she knew.

Zosia took advantage of their distraction to slip away, winding through all the embracing families, edging away from these reunions she had no place in. This was the moment, she knew, where she was supposed to feel guilty, where she *should* have felt guilty for plotting to take their friend, their prince from them.

But there was only that familiar hollow emptiness where the feeling should have been and a thrill-like anticipation of the task to come.

She had to remind herself that she didn't actually enjoy this. She couldn't, because that would make her more like Black Jaga than she wanted to be. She was just doing what she had to in order to survive.

Leaving the hall, she turned down a dark corridor and shifted into the form of a cat, black paws padding over cold stone, silent as the wraith everyone was whispering about. Her nose was full of the scent of incense, dust, and candle smoke. The black-socketed skulls of grinning saints followed her progress, observing silently as she listened at each door, moving on when she didn't find what she was searching for. The mummified monks, devotees long dead, stood vigil in carved niches along the walls, still dressed in their habits. Each held a flickering candle cradled in their hands, and wax dripped, filling their cupped palms, spilling through their fleshless fingers onto the floor.

Really, this place reminded her far too much of home. If Zosia ignored the crosses and the biblical verses inked upon the yellowed skulls, the distant drone of voices mingled in pious prayer, she could almost imagine herself being back in Black Jaga's house in the starlit forest. Surrounded by the bones of previous Midnights and the other unfortunate souls the old woman had eaten. Who knew witches and monks had so similar a taste when it came to decorating?

She heard Józef before she saw him. His voice was raised. A closed door stood between them, but it wasn't enough to deter her. There was nowhere that night could not enter.

Zosia let her body dissolve into shadow. She curled like smoke beneath the crack at the foot of the door, sweeping across the floor to join with other less sentient shadows lurking in the corner of a small, private chapel where she formed herself into a cat once more. Her little triangular ears pricked.

The prince and his uncle, the king, were in the midst of a heated argument.

"… asking that you help me keep this peace. We need to tread carefully. You must be sure of who you're throwing blame at. The girl came after you."

"Yes, the girl, that monster came after me, and we both know who would have sent such a creature."

"Rusja's ambassador swears the tsarina wasn't involved. She knows how much I care for you. She has her own troubles to focus on at home. It's more likely it was the revolutionaries wanting to kidnap and take you hostage so they could convince me to join their cause."

Uncle and nephew stood stiffly in the center of the otherwise empty room. The king brushed a black curl from his forehead, and Zosia could count the lines of worry there.

But it was the look on the Józef's face that stopped her cold. She had never seen him look so weary, so young and lost. The illusion of the lighthearted prince had crumbled, and she saw for the first time the boy beneath the mask. Not a carefree flirt, but a prince burdened beyond his years. A prince torn between his duty to his family and his duty to his kingdom.

"I would have stayed away if you hadn't called for me," he said. "Why did you summon me back to Lechija if it wasn't to change things?"

"For my safety," said the king, desperation bleeding into his tone. "Because I need someone by my side who I can trust. You have a way with people. The soldiers respect you. On one side I have the magnates and the bishops and the tsarina's cursed ambassador breathing down my neck, asking if I have any control over my own country. On the other I have the King of Prusja eyeing more land."

"And who will you bow to this time?" The weary look in the prince's eyes hardened into anger. "You were supposed to stop it. You should have raised the whole country, should have led the army yourself. If you had only fought then, I wouldn't need to now. You have made the world like this. How could you surrender? How could you give in when so many of us were still fighting?"

The king was turning a small object over and over in his hands. "You're still so young. You couldn't understand—"

"Then make me," said Józef, stamping a childish foot. "Explain it to me, please, Uncle, because I do not wish to fight with you. Do you think I wouldn't rather spend my days arranging costume balls and parties, that I wouldn't prefer to waste my nights drinking and dancing? I want to cry and mourn and not have to think always of who is watching and listening and who it is safe to speak with. I want to feel something other than despair. I want to arrange a kulig for the fun of it and not because I need an excuse to visit certain people. I want to scream that I too cannot see a way out of this for Lechija. I do not want to have to fight to save this kingdom."

He dragged a hand down his face. His voice was rough. "I can't look across a battlefield a second time and see people I love staring back at me. We cannot afford to fight among ourselves. If you would come speak with us."

"With *us*? And who is us? The generals, the revolutionaries hoping to take over this country?" The object in the king's hand gave back the candlelight.

Zosia recognized it as the small likeness of the tsarina people claimed he always carried with him. She wondered how much his affection for the woman said to have bewitched him affected his decisions, or if his actions were simply the result of his own indecisiveness, his own desire to hold on to power.

"I understand your feelings," said the king. "I do. But we can handle this without bloodshed. You've let those men influence you, draw you into their madness. You cannot trust them. I didn't call you back here so you could join their cause. Starting an uprising against Rusja could very well be a cover-up to hide their true goal to push me, their king, out and claim Lechija for their own."

The prince's brown eyes closed briefly. Helpless dismay pinched his features as he stared at the man who had raised him. "They don't want to take your crown away, Uncle. They don't want to rule Lechija. We only wish to save it." The prince's voice had dropped, enough so that Zosia caught the scuff of soft footfall.

She went deathly still, ears pricking, and spied a second figure watching the scene play out from the shadows. She'd been so occupied eavesdropping that she hadn't noticed the door to the chapel swinging open. For a wild second, an impossible hope bloomed inside her chest.

But it wasn't Marynka rising out of the dark, blazing like the sun. It wasn't the servant of Midday miraculously returned from the snowstorm unscathed, come to challenge her again.

It was only an old monk carrying in a tray, bringing a healing tonic for the prince to drink. The same bent-backed old man with unruly white brows who had tended Zosia's injuries.

The king and prince had lowered their voices at his appearance but were still caught up in their disagreement. The monk paused at a small table to prepare the tonic. Zosia watched him grind herbs with a mortar and pestle. She pushed all thoughts of Marynka from her mind. She needed a clear head now more than ever.

You don't need her, she reminded herself.

But you wanted her, a treacherous voice whispered back. *Otherwise you would not have told her to come with you.*

She wanted freedom, but she'd also wanted an end to her lonely existence. She'd wanted to embark on an adventure into the unknown with someone by her side, someone who would enjoy the challenge of it as much as she did. Someone with whom she dared share all her deepest, darkest thoughts and impulses. Someone who would never be afraid of her. Someone who understood what it was like to be a monster.

Zosia shoved that thought away too. So what if she'd wanted

it? It had been a mistake. One she wouldn't make twice. It had been nothing more than a doomed and childish wish. She should have known better than to indulge in such a fantasy.

A monster didn't need friends. She could do this alone. She didn't need anybody. Black Jaga had warned her time and again that it was a weakness to have to rely on others. She could still remember how ashamed she'd been made to feel when she'd suggested that perhaps she could work with Midday or Morning the way they worked together.

"Are you so weak, Zosia, that you need to beg someone else for help?"

Zosia's tail lashed from side to side. If Marynka didn't want to join forces and share power, then so be it. That was her foolish choice. Zosia would go so far and grow so powerful that she'd never think of her again.

She cast a quick glance at the monk and stifled a feline hiss of pure frustration.

Steam wafted from the cup as the old man, with a quick surreptitious glance at the prince and king, emptied a little vial from the folds of his habit into the tonic and stirred it in. It could have been just another ingredient, but the way the monk's hands were shaking…

Zosia recalled his insistence that Józef's health was worse than it seemed. How was it that every time she attempted to kill this ridiculous prince, she ended up having to save him from someone else who wanted to kill him? How many enemies did Józef have?

When the monk started forward with the tray and opened his mouth to address the prince. Zosia dashed from the shadows and across his ankles—a streak of fur and darkness.

The monk let out a startled cry and tripped. The cup fell from the tray to the floor shattering with an earsplitting crash.

The king and the prince both jumped.

The monk mumbled horrified apologies. His face was ashen gray as he backed out of the room.

Three steps into the deserted and chilly corridor Zosia was on him, shifting from cat to girl to monster.

The monk spun abruptly, retreating until his shoulders smacked the wall. Fear crept fast across his features. But before he could call for help, Zosia had a long, black claw at his throat.

She dug it slowly into his skin. "What did you put in the prince's tonic, Father?"

The man's wrinkled face was white with terror. His pale-blue eyes bulged. Zosia's eyes were black as the shadows she controlled. She lessened the press of her claw enough that he could whisper: "Demon."

"I asked you a question. What did you put in the prince's tonic? Why are you trying to hurt him?"

The monk's gaze darted up and down the corridor, but they were alone and there was no one coming to help him. The fight sagged out of him. "If you're here to eat someone, can't you eat him?"

"Why?" Zosia was honestly curious.

A little fire crept into the man's voice. "Because his foolish hopes for a brighter future will leave this kingdom in ruin. He'll convince the king to go along with this uprising, and hundreds, thousands will pay the price for the risks he and his friends take, just as those lost in the wreckage of the sleigh party did."

"You are not a fighter then, Father? A believer in Lechija's freedom? You would rather us all lie down and accept our shackles?"

"Does it matter who is in power so long as there is peace? We have lived through enough war. There has been enough death. The prince doesn't understand. The tsarina and the King of Prusja know if Lechija rises up the other territories under their control, the rest of the empire's nations will be next. They cannot afford for us to win. Rebellion will spread like wildfire. I have dreamed it, seen it in the candle smoke. They will crush this uprising. They will burn our fields, our castles. They will slaughter our people, rename this land and replace our language with their own, wipe our kingdom from the map. There will be no more Lechija. It will be a catastrophe for us, and the rest of the world will ignore it."

Zosia could see the monk truly believed what he was saying. It made her wonder if this really was what lay ahead for Lechija, if all that ever came of fighting for freedom was death and failure, and if so, was there a point in fighting at all?

A strange anger curled hot through her belly.

"But what would a monster like you understand?" The monk

sighed and changed tactics. "Surely," he coaxed, "there must be more life in the prince's young bones for you to feed on than in mine?"

"Oh I'm sure there is," said Zosia, her resentment rising sharply, "and I do intend to take his life, for I am not always going to be a monster. I am going to consume his heart and make myself into something else. I've come all this way for that sole purpose. But—" Zosia slid her hand from the old man's throat to his chest, watching his expression cycle from relief to confusion to dread. "I think you'll find there are others with rebellion in their hearts. This won't end with him. And just because I'm going to take *his* life doesn't mean I can't also take yours, for I find, Father, that I am really, really starting to hate people who get in my way."

26.

MARYNKA

"HOW MUCH FARTHER?" MARYNKA MOANED, boots stomping dark prints into the crisp, pristine surface of the snow. "We've been walking for hours. I can't feel my fingers. My ears are frozen. My feet are sore. Hey! Are you listening?"

"I've been listening to you complain for hours. Do you ever stop talking?" Three steps ahead, Kajetan stumbled, floundering through a thin crust of snow and into a deep drift with a startled yelp. His heavy boots and robes dragging him down.

Marynka watched him flail with undisguised amusement. They'd left the woodcutter's hut at dawn, Kajetan melting his way through the ice built up against the door with a blast of heavenly fire from his saber. "I could help you up if you loosened these." Marynka waved her bound wrists.

"Why don't I find more cloth to gag you with instead?"

Marynka considered running while his back was turned, which she'd attempted to do twice already, only for Kajetan to drag her back and threaten to cut her head off. So she sat and lay down instead, stretching out lazily on her back. If her hands hadn't been bound, she might've made a snow angel.

Kajetan looked over his shoulder and hissed through his teeth. "Don't you dare! Get up. We're not even close to the city."

"How do you know? You've absolutely no sense of direction. We've walked past that same tree three times. I counted. You're lost. And I'm so hungry and tired I'm about to collapse." Marynka wasn't really. The famished growl of her belly had faded to a sullen grumble as its calls went unanswered, and she'd had more than enough rest. But if she could delay him a little while longer, if she could buy enough time before he handed her off to the prince and his soldiers in Warszów...

Soft tendrils of morning mist curled past her ear, sparkling softly, coiling low across the frozen earth and through the age-old trees surrounding them. In the wintry quiet between Kajetan's curses she could hear the *tock-tock-tock* of a black woodpecker somewhere foraging for food. A frosted spider's web caught the sunlight slanting through the fir branches.

That same light kissed Marynka's cheeks. She could feel her strength returning, a tingling of heat that started at the tips of her fingers. Magic, mercifully, sparking in her blood, a flame coaxed back from embers.

And when the sun reached its zenith, when the hour finally turned to midday...

Marynka flexed her stiff fingers and tugged, feeling the cloth binding her hands together loosen just slightly. She could turn her chafed wrists.

Kajetan's shadow fell over her. "Get up."

When the hour turned to midday, even cloth doused in holy water would not be enough to hold her. She was going to carve this boy who'd dared to bind her into bloody little pieces.

"Why don't you carry me?" she asked sweetly.

Kajetan's hand went to the jeweled hilt of his saber. A breeze ruffled the costly feathers tufting his fur cap. "Do we really have to do this again?"

"That threat's less scary than you think it is. We already agreed you don't plan to kill me. You returned to Warszów to redeem yourself, and you're dragging me back to the city now so you can show off that you caught the monster hunting your precious prince."

Kajetan stared down at her, his expression unreadable, and then his mouth curved into a smile so cruel it would have fit perfectly on Grandmother's face. Despite herself, Marynka shivered.

"I returned to Warszów to redeem myself?" he repeated softly, dangerously. "I think you've gotten the wrong idea. I came back here for the very reason that everyone is saying. My father sent me, or rather, the tsarina did. She doesn't want an uprising, the expense of another war. I came back like the good obedient son I am to make sure Józef doesn't join one, or convince the king to. I was told to use any means necessary."

Something dark flashed in his eyes as he loomed over her. "I am not a good person. I am exactly the things people say I am and worse. And I only need you alive, little monster, so unless you wish me to start cutting small pieces off of you, you'll get up and start walking."

They stared each other down.

"You know," Marynka said slowly, "in another life I feel like you and I could have been friends."

"A pity then that I am most certainly going to murder you in this one." Kajetan hauled her roughly to her feet.

Marynka struggled to catch her balance. She stole glances at him as they trudged on through the snow, following a faint path that wound between the low, drooping pine boughs. Stubble shadowed the sharp angle of his jaw, but he looked younger in the soft morning light. Not so many more years older than her.

She kicked a lump of ice, watched it roll across the snow. "Why not let me kill the prince then? Why try to warn him about us? Why chase me down? We could be working together."

Kajetan let out a derisive snort.

Marynka continued. "Why should we be enemies? I mean we've already shared a bed."

"We did not share—" Kajetan's cheeks turned as bright a red as if she'd caught him naked.

"Set me free," Marynka urged. "I'll take Józef's heart, and then you won't have to worry about him taking part in any uprising."

"Take his *heart*?"

"It's what I do. I'm very good at it. Don't worry."

Kajetan shoved a branch violently aside so they could pass through a gap in the trees. Another chunk of ice fell to the ground and Marynka kicked that too. It smacked the back of Kajetan's legs.

"That was an accident."

In the silence while Kajetan glared at her, Marynka's stomach grumbled audibly.

Kajetan raised his eyes to heaven, beseeching, and then he did something shocking. Reaching into his robes, he came out with a small pouch filled with sesame seed candy.

Marynka gaped.

Kajetan scowled and shoved the candy at her, motioning sharply at her to keep walking. "You said you were so hungry you felt you'd collapse. I'm not carrying you if you faint, and if your mouth is full, perhaps you'll finally shut up."

"You've had this on you all along?" Marynka said, chewing with her mouth full, crunching on the honeyed seeds. "And you didn't share? What about all the times in the hut when I said I was starving?"

"I'm sharing now," Kajetan said, defensive. "Why am I even explaining myself to you? You should be grateful. This is very likely your final meal."

"But not if we work together." Marynka's tone was coaxing. She was taking two strides to keep up with each of his. Curse tall people and their long legs. "We both want the prince dead and—"

"I do not want him dead. I have *never* wanted him dead. I came back because my father told me to, but when I saw you attack him at the costume ball…" He cut off, steps slowing. "I thought my father had sent you after him. I thought he didn't believe me capable of doing what needed to be done. And he would've been right, because my body moved on its own. My first instinct was to draw my saber and defend Józef. In that moment I forgot I had ever raised a blade to him, that we'd ever fought. The only thing I felt was the desire to protect him. When I thought I might lose him forever, I couldn't help myself." He lifted his face to the winter sky. "They say the Karnawał is a time when the world turns upside down. A time when a peasant can be a prince, when a servant might be a master, a sinner—"

"A saint," finished Marynka.

Kajetan shook his head. "I am the furthest thing from a saint. But I realize now that I no longer care what my family wants. I can't go back and undo my mistakes, but I can protect Józef now. From anyone else my father or the tsarina might send, from monsters like you. I want to do something right this time. I want to be able to hate myself a little less. I am not going to let anyone harm him."

"You'll be punished," Marynka said knowingly, "if you go

against your family." Like she would be if she ever turned on the witch she called grandmother, like Zosia would have been for betraying Black Jaga if she hadn't…

The sesame candy turned to ash on Marynka's tongue.

"It would be a far worse punishment," said Kajetan, "knowing that I'd killed my friend. The person I care about most in this world. I thought I had once, and it almost killed me."

Marynka lapsed into quiet. Her boots groaned in the snow.

"And even if I did what they wanted, it would likely not be enough for my father. He'd set me to work at some worse task. There's no pleasing him. Nothing I do is ever good enough. Sometimes I think he likes to set me challenges just so he can watch me fail." Kajetan's jaw clenched. "And so I am done. I am finished proving myself to the person who made me feel worthless in the first place."

Marynka looked away. "Such wise words, Kajtuś. Does your brain instantly fill with wisdom when you grow to be so old?"

"I'm twenty," Kajetan said indignantly. "But it's true this entire experience with you has aged me. I'm surprised my hair hasn't turned white."

Marynka snorted.

"How old are you? Sixteen? Seventeen? You're rather small."

Marynka kicked another chunk of ice at him.

Kajetan kicked it back. "God, I remember being seventeen. What a perfect fool I was. Józef and I were still cadets. We used to talk for hours, dreaming of all the ways we would change the world, how we would change Lechija for the better." He shivered suddenly, and so did Marynka, as clouds crossed the sky, plunging the forest into deep shadow.

Marynka's thoughts drifted and she found herself thinking of the Midnight Forest again. Of Zosia's home. Once, when she and Beata were younger, they had snuck away from their chores with the vague intent of tracking Midnight down so that they could spy on her. It had been Marynka's idea, of course. "We'll learn all her secrets and find out what she really looks like!" And Beata had tagged along simply because she hadn't wanted to be left behind.

They'd crept to the edge of Black Jaga's domain, where their steps had turned hesitant, the air growing rapidly cooler and the light fading swiftly. They'd halted on the very threshold of that forest of death, too nervous to venture past the trees standing sleeping in the starlight, too spooked to break the hostile silence. The Midnight Forest was not a place for the living. Nothing stirred there, not a leaf, not a twig. The gnarled roots of the trees were skeletal claws and the tortured branches bent and twisted. It would have taken a blessed prince on a holy quest to cross that black wilderness to find the house that dwelt at its heart, and the witch as old as the world who lived there.

No wonder, then, that Zosia had wanted so badly to run away, to escape that cold darkness. At least here...

The sun broke through the clouds, setting fire to Marynka's hair.

"I was wrong," Kajetan said, glancing at her sideways. "When you're quiet, it makes me nervous. What wickedness are you plotting now?"

Marynka pressed her bound hands to her heart. "I'm hurt. It's like you don't trust me."

Movement between the trees caught her eye. For an instant, she dismissed the vision as a trick of the morning light. But then a horse, riderless, and pale white as the snow, came trotting through the trees. Its mane gleamed like silk. Its hooves were shod with gold.

Marynka froze in her tracks.

Kajetan too, his face lighting with surprise and wonder. "Oh," he said softly. "She must've been part of the kulig." He took a half step forward, drawn, like a person bewitched. "What a beautiful lady you are." He made a soft clicking sound with his tongue.

A terrible burning hope kindled in Marynka's chest. She dropped to her knees in the snow.

Kajetan whirled at the sound, hissing through his teeth again in exasperation. "How many times must I—"

The instant his back turned, Beata materialized from the mist and morning light. Her hair a golden halo, a large branch gripped in both hands. She brought it down on the back of Kajetan's head with all her strength.

He dropped like a rock, with a single sharp cry that made

Marynka wince. Before she could do anything, Beata was there, throwing her arms around her and clinging to her fiercely, burying her face in Marynka's neck. Marynka let go of every other thought and let Beata hold her, melting into the familiar embrace, savoring it. She wondered briefly if she should let herself get captured more often if it meant Beata was too relieved at the mere sight of her to scold or shout or be angry.

"Thank God. Thank *God.*" Tears sparkled white on Beata's cheeks. "I thought you were dead. I thought I'd *lost* you. I thought the snowslide had killed you both."

There was a horrible knot in Marynka's throat. "I was worried about you too," she whispered hoarsely.

"You were?" Beata said.

"Of *course.*" Marynka was shocked and a little offended her friend would think otherwise. Her fingers clutched at Beata's white kontusik as she pulled back. "I thought you—"

"Oh, your wrists!" Beata exclaimed. Her nails lengthened to claws as she sliced the cloth strips binding Marynka's hands, fury twisting her features as she glanced at Kajetan. "How dare he lay his hands on you! Did he hurt you anywhere else? I'm going to kill him."

Marynka squirmed away from her fussing. Free from the holy-water-soaked bonds, the raw red skin at her wrists was already starting to heal, though far more slowly than she would have liked. "Forget that. Forget him. What about you? Are *you* okay? Zosia's shadows snatched you from the sleigh and—"

Beata's expression darkened at the other girl's name, and she rubbed her shoulder as if to ease some past hurt. "I'm fine. Really. Something like that isn't enough to kill me. And anyway I…" She stopped.

"What?" Marynka said when she didn't continue.

Beata bit her lip, gaze straying beyond Marynka to her horse. The animal flicked its ears. "You can't be angry." Her violet eyes were imploring. "I had to do it. You were lost and I didn't know what else to do."

Marynka's brow furrowed in confusion.

A sudden breeze blew a strand of golden hair across Beata's lips.

The air around them warmed. All Marynka's relief faded away. A cold, creeping dread stole through her veins even as the hot breeze rushed across her skin. "Beata," she whispered, "you didn't."

Beata's expression was a portrait of guilty defiance. "I called for help. I had to."

The wind picked up, blowing wildly now, sweeping away the last of the morning mist, carrying with it the familiar scents of summer: Fresh hay and the heady aroma of sun-warmed earth. Rain-soaked leaves. Red poppy flowers. Snowmelt dripped from black branches as an old woman, her thin back bent with age, her eyes like molten gold and her head wrapped in a bloodred kerchief, strode between the trees.

Marynka's throat was dry as dust. "G-Grandmother."

27.

ZOSIA

THE SUDDEN AND UNFORTUNATE DISAPPEARANCE of Father Mikołaj caused a wave of fresh talk at the monastery.

Admittedly, disposing of the monk in a fit of temper was probably not the best step toward Zosia's goal of acting less like a monster. Black Jaga was also known to devour those who annoyed her. But it was only a *small* setback. She would make up for this later somehow, after she'd taken the prince's heart and killed the witch and gained her freedom. Then she would turn over a new leaf as she'd told Marynka. And anyway, this gave her the perfect excuse to cozy up to Józef.

"It's all so frightening!" Zosia exclaimed breathlessly. "Would you mind terribly if I rode back to the city with you in your sleigh? I'm afraid to be alone now."

"I was about to suggest so myself," he said, raising her hand to his lips and kissing it.

Zosia caught several sly smiles and knowing looks exchanged

among those present. Members of the royal guard looked exasperated, while two old monks frowned openly. She could only pray Józef wasn't about to make her some grand romantic overture because that would really make this next attempt to kill him awkward.

As a procession of sleighs carrying the king and the survivors of the ill-fated kulig left the monastery and sped on ahead, the prince's sleigh set a more leisurely pace, taking a slow, winding route through the forest. Save for the driver, they were very much alone. Hands hidden beneath the sleigh furs, Zosia slid her gloves off. The veins at her wrists darkened from blue to black, shadows climbed her skin. Her fingers tapered to long, lethal claws.

She stole a sideways glance at the boy beside her.

Józef was dressed as magnificently as ever, in a sapphire-blue kontusz and a contrasting underrobe of pale silver. His fur cap was studded with a giant ruby and his saber rested at his side. But his expression was almost grave and he was uncharacteristically quiet.

Zosia wondered if it was because of his recent talk with his uncle.

He caught her staring and smiled slightly. "I feel like I finally have your full attention."

"My full attention?"

"All the other times we've spoken, you've been distracted. It's like you're always thinking of someone else when you're with me. You give these little nods when I talk, even when I say something particularly clever, and then your eyes dart past me, as though you're hoping to see someone more interesting."

"Oh." Zosia was taken aback that he'd been watching *her* so closely.

His black hair curled against his high collar. "Who is it that you're always looking for, Zosieńka? The friend Father Mikołaj said you were worried about or—"

"No," Zosia said quickly. "I told you. She's not my friend."

The prince's brown eyes sparkled with something like mischief. "No, of course not."

The squeak of the runners flying over the snow filled the silence between them. Ancient black trees flitted past, their bare, crooked branches casting cruel shadows over the pale white of the forest floor. The scenery reminded Zosia too much of another monochrome forest that had never seen the light of day.

"If you knew," she said, wanting to change the subject and also because a part of her was curious. She wanted to know before she took his heart. "If you knew you wouldn't win and that fighting might only make things worse for you, would you still fight for Lechija's freedom?"

"Yes," Józef said without hesitation.

"Even if you knew you would die?"

The prince leaned back against the seat and considered her. "You've been talking with Esterka. Did she tell you how her grandfather the Maggid of Koźniewo read my death in the stars?"

Zosia's eyes widened.

"He told me I'd meet my end at the hands of a friend, fighting for freedom on the banks of river far from home."

"So you won't live to see it? Lechija gain freedom?" It didn't make sense, knowing what she was about to do, but saying it aloud made Zosia strangely sad. She didn't feel guilty, but she couldn't make herself feel glad, couldn't summon the happiness knowing he wouldn't see the same freedom she sought.

Józef kneaded the muscles above his knee. "Maybe not. But others might. I'm not fighting alone or for myself or for glory. We're fighting to protect our home and to preserve our way of life. For the freedom to decide our own lives, our own futures. No price is too high to pay for that. I can accept the possibility that I may not be here when the dust settles. It is for those who come after me to make that sacrifice matter. We're outnumbered and our chances may be slim, but I still believe Lechija's best days are ahead of us. They say the Karnawał is a chance to imagine a better world. And, well, better to fall with honor anyway and take as many of the tsarina's soldiers with me when I go, better to die than live as one of her creatures. At least, *I* will not be a slave to that witch."

A chill like lightning ran through Zosia from head to toe.

Józef grinned. "And knowing what's coming gives me an advantage. I think Esterka's grandfather was trying to discourage me from doing anything dangerous, but I feel like it's backfired and made me more reckless. If I know I'm destined to drown, then it can't hurt really to ignore my uncle's warnings or even to ride in this sleigh with you."

Zosia raised an eyebrow. "Is a sleigh ride with a girl so dangerous?"

"Oh, very dangerous," said Józef, leaning in close. "Especially when the girl is so beautiful. Kajtek warned me that I shouldn't be alone with you."

Kajtek. Kajetan. The last time she'd seen him he'd been galloping his horse alongside hers, chasing after Marynka and Józef. Zosia had assumed he'd been lost in the snowslide. He hadn't been among the survivors at the monastery.

She felt the faintest flutter of unease. "I didn't think you were the type to listen to traitors."

Józef leaned away and tilted his head back, staring up as if he could divine some deeper meaning from the path the clouds cut across the sky. "I don't as a rule. But before he was a traitor, Kajetan was my friend. There was a time when I believed he was the one person in this world who truly knew me, a time when I believed he was the other half of my soul. I thought we saw the world through the same eyes. I thought we both wanted to change it for the better. Even now when I'm so angry at him, so angry I could tear him apart with my bare hands…" His voice trailed off. "Even though he almost killed me, I still miss him. I still find myself speaking silently to him in my head. Maybe it was naive, but I really thought, in spite of everything, that he would be on my side."

The words pinched something inside of Zosia.

The sleigh jolted over a rock, and Józef shook his head ruefully. "Selim tells me I'm being a fool, that I'm acting like a girl has left me for somebody else. But I've had my heart broken by girls before, and it's never felt anything close to this. No one warned me it would hurt more to lose a friend than a lover. Lovers I can easily replace. But so much of my life has involved Kajetan, ever since we started at the Royal Cadet School together. He's always been there. A constant presence. I don't know how to move forward without him by my side. I don't know who could ever understand me like he did."

The driver steered the horses deeper into the trees. The sparkling, snow-crusted branches reached for each other, closing like a cage overhead.

"The night of the kulig," said Józef. "Selim said he saw you both chasing after my sleigh. He heard Kajetan shout to him after the snowslide and saw him pursue the monster who'd tried to kidnap me. Esterka would like me to think he was trying to protect me. Selim says he was likely involved, that he's in league with the monster and that they were both sent by the tsarina. Neither have been seen since the snowslide. And I?"

For a second, Józef's princely mask cracked and Zosia caught another glimpse of the haunted young man she'd seen in the monastery chapel. His face was pinched with echoes of old grief.

"I can't decide. I don't know what to think. A part of me knows Kajetan is as trapped in his role as I am in mine. I know he will always be loyal to his father, his family first. And I know what it's like to have to choose between your family and your duty to your country. I can't accept his actions, but I know how he feels better than anyone." He sighed. "Still, maybe you will have the answer for me, Zosieńka."

The sleigh slowed to a stop in the middle of a small clearing where the sunlight streamed down unfettered by the trees.

Zosia's skin prickled. "Me?"

"Yes, what do you think? You were there too, weren't you?" Józef leapt down from the sleigh, boots crunching in the snow. He held out his hand to her.

Zosia hesitated before she took it, before she stood. Her eyes scanned the clearing, the trees black as ink strokes against the silver of the landscape. She let him help her down to stand in front of him in the snow.

Józef didn't let go of her hand. "Selim said he saw you rip a boy from his horse with a strength he couldn't fathom. And then you *stole* said horse, and the things he described you as doing afterward, controlling the shadows, the darkness…"

He knows, a little voice whispered in Zosia's ear. She went very, very still.

"I didn't want to believe it. I couldn't believe it of such a charming and beautiful girl. But then Father Mikołaj commented on how miraculously fast you seemed to have healed, and then he disappeared. Esterka saw you vanish from your bed at night."

He knows.

Zosia swore beneath her breath, cursing herself for her carelessness. The voice in her head sounded like Black Jaga's.

He knows what you are.

She'd given herself away in her fury, in her determination to beat Marynka.

"Who are you really?" Józef finally released her hand, letting his own come to rest on the hilt of his saber. He took a step back. "*What* are you? Who sent you?"

Sturdy horses nosed out of the trees, ridden by the royal guard. The same men who had exchanged knowing looks back at the monastery, only their faces were serious now. Sabers sung out of scabbards. Pistols cocked and aimed. They drew up their mounts and waited, an army of obedient angels standing ready.

Several looked to her with open hostility.

They all *know.*

The realization landed like a blow. Zosia almost staggered from the force of it. Her every instinct shouted at her to hide, to cover her face and vanish. The shadows between the trees whispered her name urgently, calling her back to the dark. Her thoughts were a blind panic.

Who am I?

What am I?

She could see her face reflected in blades of their swords— bone white and her eyes like two dark hollows.

A monstrous reflection. Maybe that was all she could ever be, a monster. Maybe she had no choice even though she'd wanted so badly to be different. After all, she'd been raised for this. She didn't know anything else. There was a wicked part of her that enjoyed it in spite of everything.

And she was so very *good* at it. Black Jaga had made sure of it. She was a tool honed to perfection.

Who am I?

Heart racing and surrounded, Zosia felt something like a weight lift from her shoulders. Darkness crawled over her skin, twined like smoke around her arms. Her fingers tapered sharply as she became Midnight before them, a nightmare in the light of day.

Who am I?

Let me show you.

The grin she gave them was one of Marynka's—wild and full of sharply pointed teeth. The laugh, too, was her rival's, and the very sound of it made the prince and his soldiers flinch. In the end, what did it matter if they knew? This fate that Black Jaga had held over her was not nearly so terrifying. She almost resented the anticlimax. It wasn't as if they could do anything to her. Who were they to make her feel afraid? She was Black Midnight. Why should she be afraid of anyone, ever?

If anything, they should be afraid of her.

But they didn't back away. More than a dozen trembling

sabers pointed at Zosia's chest. The prince's voice rang out clear and calm, and the soldiers' blades steadied.

Zosia scanned the clearing, counting heads and horses. Another young man emerged from the snow-crusted trees carrying golden chains. She kept her back to the sleigh as two more slunk toward her, weapons gleaming.

That made twelve.

A dozen soldiers between her and the prince whose heart she needed.

"This hardly seems like a fair fight."

"Come quietly and we need not fight at all," said Józef.

"Weren't you the one who told me it was better to fall with honor, to go down fighting?"

Józef drew his saber. "If you surrender and cooperate, you'll be granted mercy. Don't make this more difficult than it needs to—"

Zosia didn't wait for him to finish. With a snap of her fingers, she plunged the world into darkness. Day turned to night in a breath. The shadows came to life, writhing shapes leapt over the snow, ripping men from their mounts. Zosia raked her claws through their throats before they could even scream.

To her right, light flared. Flames blazed to life along a trio of blessed blades. The soldiers moved as one.

In the darkness, Zosia smiled.

Three down. Nine to go.

28.

MARYNKA

"I TOLD YOU NOT TO call for her. I told you not to summon her," Marynka said. "I told you, and you promised me that you wouldn't."

"I was worried about you," Beata said softly.

Marynka wanted to strangle her. "Why didn't you call for White Jaga then? Your Jaga?"

"Because White Jaga has no connection with you," Beata said. "She wouldn't have been able to sense where you were. I thought you were lost beneath the snow. I couldn't find you by myself."

Marynka scrambled to her feet as Red Jaga approached.

Beata hovered awkwardly at Marynka's side. She reached for Marynka's hand—their fingers brushed—and then seemed to think better of it when Marynka yanked her hand away like she'd been burned.

"My Red Sun. What trouble have you gotten yourself into this time?"

A little of Marynka's dread ebbed away at the nickname. One of the reasons why she believed Grandmother cared for her was because she always came for Marynka if something went wrong, if her life was in danger. The witch never let anyone lay a finger on her. The only person Grandmother didn't protect Marynka from was Grandmother herself.

The witch gripped Marynka's chin roughly in one skeletal hand. She was radiating heat like a smoldering coal. "What trouble have you managed to cause *me* this time, you tiresome child?"

Marynka did her best not to tremble. She was as tall as the bony old woman now, but staring into those burning eyes, she felt all of twelve years old again. Fear tied her stomach in knots, and it was as though she'd just returned to the house in the Midday Forest with a peasant's heart instead a prince's and been found out.

"Sometimes I think you do these things just to spite me."

"I would never, Grandmother!"

"Would you like to tell me then, why you thought to bury the prince whose heart I sent you to take beneath a mountain of snow? The prince whose pure heart I need. The pure heart you *swore* you could bring me if I only gave you one more chance. I told you what this heart would mean to me. I would finally be more powerful than my sister."

Marynka heard the longing in the witch's voice. She knew exactly what that longing felt like. Excuses spilled from her lips. "It was an accident. I had the prince. Beata will tell you. We had him but Zosia, Midnight, she chased after us. We fought and I—" The words stuck in her throat. "I fought her off. I defeated her. I won. I buried *her* beneath the snow."

Red Jaga narrowed her golden eyes.

"I won," Marynka repeated dully. "I told you I could."

"You buried her, did you? Buried Midnight?"

Marynka swallowed. "Yes."

"Curious then," Red Jaga said, "that when Beata was searching for you, she could not find Midnight either. Not even the smallest trace. I would think if my sister's servant was dead, there would at least be a body left behind."

Marynka's head snapped toward Beata. She was staring grimly at the ground.

"That's impossible. I saw her horse. She couldn't have—" Marynka's heart thundered painfully inside her chest. Zosia, alive. She couldn't name all the ugly emotions burning through her in that instant: fear, denial, and a terrible, intense gut-wrenching relief.

She wanted to sink back to the ground, her legs felt so weak.

"I wasn't able to find the prince either," Beata said. "There's a good chance he's alive too. They were taking the survivors from the sleigh party to the monastery on the hill. Marynka can still bring you his heart, Grandmother."

"And if Midnight is alive," Red Jaga said, "who's to say *she* hasn't already taken it? Beaten Marynka to the prize again, as always. Perhaps even now she's heading back to my sister's dark forest with it tucked inside her pocket." She pinned Marynka with that golden stare, with that fiery gaze that was enough to reduce those who displeased her to ash. "Not a day passes when I don't wish I'd found her instead of you."

The words were a blade driven through Marynka's chest. She felt something tear, not flesh but something deeper, the reopening of a wound at the very center of her core. An ever-present hurt.

I just can't win against her. No matter how hard I try. No matter what I do.

She'd spent years chasing Midnight's shadow. All her hard work, all her efforts to match the other girl. All those grueling hours practicing magic, striving to be better, cleverer, stronger, giving everything she had to beat Zosia. All those wakeless hours, all those defeats, picking herself up again and again.

"If you'd found her," Marynka burst out, Zosia's secret rushing from her lips, "then she'd be stealing hearts from *you*. Trying to run away from *you* and not Black Jaga. At least I'm loyal. At least I always—"

"Oh?" Red Jaga cocked her head. "She's trying to run away, is she?" If the witch was surprised, it didn't show on her wrinkled face. But there was new eagerness in her voice. "Won't my sister be pleased to hear that? She always picks the stubborn ones. You children are so ungrateful."

Marynka's hands balled into fists. "I have done *everything* you ever asked of me."

And it's never, ever enough.

From behind Red Jaga came a low groan. They all turned to watch Kajetan struggle to his hands and knees in the snow. He blinked, looking dazed, his gaze flitting dizzily from Beata to Marynka to the witch.

The blood drained from his face. He seemed to know instinctively who or what she was.

She smiled at him, her rusted iron teeth glinting sharply in the sun. "And then there's this one. The boy you let catch and bind you like some common thief. Have you forgotten everything I've taught you?"

Heat rushed to Marynka's cheeks.

Still on his knees, Kajetan's hand flew to the saber at his hip. He actually managed to unsheathe it, but a glance from Grandmother had the jeweled hilt burning red-hot. The weapon fell from his scorched fingers. The agonized gasp he gave as he clutched his hand to his chest made Marynka's stomach twist.

"All the magic I gifted you when I made you my servant." Red Jaga bent over Kajetan and sniffed the air. "What a waste it was to make you into Midday. Truly, Marynka, I did not think you could disappoint me further, but you always find some new way to outdo yourself. It's like you take it as a challenge." She straightened with a dissatisfied grunt. "He's no prince. His heart is of no use to me. Get rid of him."

Beata immediately, dutifully crossed to Red Jaga's side, her fingers tapering to long, luminescent white claws. Her skeleton seemed to glow through her skin. It had been some time since Marynka had seen her friend become a monster. Morning was a chillingly beautiful creature. A vision bright as the rising sun. She shimmered like a shaft of light. It hurt to look at her. Her smile of gleaming, needlelike teeth was sharp as a knife abruptly unsheathed. "You really should not have hurt Marynka," she told Kajetan.

"Wait!" Marynka grabbed Beata's arm.

Kajetan stared up at her, surprise flashing in his green eyes. A desperate hope pinched his face.

Marynka's mind was racing. If the prince was alive, and Zosia...

She shoved all thoughts of Zosia away. She couldn't think about her right now. She could still turn this around. She hadn't lost yet. Not completely. She could still fix things. She could still get herself back in Grandmother's good graces. "Wait, don't kill him. We can use him."

29.

ZOSIA

THEY THREW ZOSIA INTO A dark cell deep in the depths of Warszów's Golden Castle. A musty room with no windows, empty save for a hard cot and iron cuffs dangling from chains secured to the wall. Torches set in sconces warded off some of the chill, the light they cast falling in long, burning blades through the thick iron bars.

Two of the king's soldiers stood guard on the other side of those bars, a middle-aged man and a woman, wearing matching expressions of wariness. Pain throbbed from a scorched gash along Zosia's ribs, her lip was bloody, and bruises bloomed along one pale cheek. She'd cut down the dozen soldiers who had surrounded her and come within a hairsbreadth of tearing Józef's heart from his chest—but it was the thirteenth soldier who had been her undoing. Selim, riding out from the trees, taking her by surprise.

Holy symbols carved into the walls dampened her magic now, slowing her healing and sapping her strength, stealing her ability to summon darkness, to become Midnight. Pungent incense and blessed herbs burning in a silver brazier clouded her head.

"You have no power here," snarled the taller of the two guards, the man. Zosia wasn't sure if he was saying it to convince himself or because he wanted her more afraid.

She dragged a deliberate finger over the worn brick wall, tracing a sacred symbol, feeling the power of it sting through her skin. Scratching at the line with her nail as if she could wear it away, break a link in the spell work. "For now."

A muscle ticked in the man's jaw and his companion elbowed him in the side. He turned away, but not before making another loud remark about how Zosia's imminent execution would add to the Karnawał fun. The prince should hold a tournament of duels, he suggested, to decide who would have the honor of throwing her onto the fire.

Zosia retreated farther into the shadows of the cell, resentment rising sharply, irritated that these weak fools would dare try to contain her, bind her, lock her up.

She wished she had a weapon. Something like the scythe Marynka carried or a secret knife tucked in her boot, a sharp pin hidden in her long silver braid.

Something.

Anything.

But Zosia had always preferred her own ink-dark claws to the unwieldy heft of a blade. She stared at her scraped palms, at her stubby human fingers. It seemed Black Jaga had been right all along. It *was* safer to stick to the shadows, safer not to let them catch a glimpse of what you were.

She paced the length of the cell and considered her options, blocking out the chatter and soft crunching as the guards snacked on festive crisp-fried ribbons of sugar-powdered faworki, forcing herself to focus. No windows. Only the one passage leading in and out. Black Jaga wouldn't come for her. She had always made it clear that if anything were to happen to Zosia, if she was caught or discovered, she was on her own. And it wasn't as if Zosia had anyone else, family, friends. The closest thing she'd ever had to a friend was Marynka, and Marynka was…

No one is coming to save you.

Zosia gritted her teeth. Could she strike some bargain with the prince? Make him a deal? Offer him something? Information about Black Jaga, about the monk who had tried to assassinate him. He would want to know of that, surely.

Time ticked by. How long had she been in here? Every passing moment felt like an eternity. Each minute dragging as long as an hour. But she should probably savor the minutes, for they might very well be her last.

The two middle-aged guards were eventually replaced with two younger men. One still struggling to grow a mustache, who ogled her through the bars, watching as though any moment now he expected her skin to peel back and reveal something terrible, something monstrous. His partner smacked him on the back of the head.

Zosia sank to the floor with her back against the wall and her knees drawn up to her chest. She pressed her forehead to them, listening vaguely to the men's bickering. It wasn't until much later when someone cleared their throat three times in a row that she even bothered to look up.

She'd expected the prince or a priest come to lay judgment on her and declare her fate. But it was *Beata* of all people who stood before her. Alive and in perfect health. Dressed in a spotless white kontusik and saffron underdress, her golden braids woven into a halo that circled her head. Not a hint that only days ago Zosia's shadows had torn her from her sleigh.

Shock froze Zosia's mouth in an O.

Dark amusement glittered in Beata's violet eyes. "Oh, Midnight, you are in *so much* trouble."

"How?" Zosia tore her eyes away from the other girl. What had happened to the guards? Were they changing shift again? It was only the two of them here alone.

Beata looked around the cell, lips pursing in distaste. "What a state you're in. How do you plan to get out of this?" She brought both hands to the bars, gripping two as if to test their strength. "They're planning to burn you, you know. They're going to make a party of it. With a bonfire and fireworks and masks. What an exciting Karnawał season it's been! They'll be talking about this one for years. They're just waiting for the prince to return before they start arranging things. He's a bit busy right now. I'm afraid I had to bring him some bad news."

Zosia narrowed her eyes.

"A message from a dear friend of ours. Marynka's prepared a little surprise. And Józef was so thrilled that he rushed straight out of the castle to meet her. She has something very precious to him."

Marynka.

Zosia was on her feet. She knew there was definitely something wrong with her then, that she was relieved, even invigorated, to know the person who had tried to kill her was fine. "Marynka's all right?"

And she was nearby. And all set to take the prince's heart.

Zosia's nails dug red crescents into her palms. "And so you came here to gloat?"

Beata moved closer so that she could leer triumphantly down at Zosia in her cage. "Midday's not the only one who's longed to see you lose. Tell me, did you really think she would run away with you?"

Zosia didn't answer.

"She's an idiot," Beata said. "But not *that* much of an idiot." She adjusted her high collar. "And she loves her grandmother."

"If that's all you came here for, then you can—"

"I came"—Beata paused, staring past Zosia at the sacred symbols on the wall—"to offer you our help. Mine and Red Jaga's.

She said if I ran across you whilst delivering my message to the prince that I was to make you an offer. If you agree to become her servant, she'll keep you safe."

The shock was plain on Zosia's face and in her voice. "Red Jaga wants me to be *her* servant?" A long-ago memory drifted back to her, of Black Jaga's saying that Zosia was a prize her sister would envy. But she still didn't understand. "She wants two servants?"

"No." Beata ran the pad of her finger down one of the bars. "Just you."

"But she has Marynka."

"You'll replace Marynka."

Zosia stared. "But Marynka *beat* me. Matched head-to-head, she overpowered me. Her magic was stronger and now she's all set to take the prince's heart, so why—"

"This time," Beata said. "She's beaten you this time, but the rest of the time you win. You always do."

"You underestimate her."

"It doesn't matter. Red Jaga doesn't care. She wants you. It's another point scored against her sister. And this way, she'll release Marynka from her service. I struck my own bargain with her. If I manage to convince you and bring you to her, she's agreed to let Marynka go free. Marynka will come live with me and White Jaga, and she'll never have to be Midday again," Beata finished with a small, grim smile. Her teeth gleamed sharp and white in the gloom of the cell.

Laughter bubbled up Zosia's throat. "And you think she'll thank you for that? Does Marynka *know* about this little bargain you've struck on her behalf?"

Color rose in Beata's cheeks. "It—"

"Do you think that's what she wants? To not be Midday anymore? I don't know what fantasy you've spun inside your head—"

"It doesn't matter what she wants; it's what she needs. Marynka doesn't know what's good for her." Beata's voice had risen in response to Zosia's laughter, rebounding off the walls and ceiling. She cast a quick glance over her shoulder and gripped the bars of the cell. "Well?" she said. "Are you going to accept? I should tell you, Black Jaga knows."

"Knows what?"

"That you lied to her. That you've been taking the hearts you were meant to bring her for yourself. That you blamed it all on Midday."

Dread collected in the pit of Zosia's stomach. Marynka must have told them. Marynka must've told them everything.

Beata nodded. "Red Jaga's already sent word to the Midnight Forest. She said she could *feel* her sister's fury trembling the wind even from this distance. Your grandmother isn't pleased. Not a bit. She's going to make an example of you. So that the Midnight *after* you will remember it's not worth it to fight her."

Zosia prayed the fear turning her blood to ice didn't show on her face. But just the thought of it—Black Jaga knowing what she'd done. And here she was, trapped, injured, and powerless in this tower, with nowhere to run. The walls seemed to press in closer.

"If you're lucky," Beata said. "The prince's soldiers might put an end to you before she arrives."

Zosia barred her teeth.

"Or you can turn yourself over to Red Jaga and let her protect you."

Zosia's stomach knotted. So this was to be her fate, was it? To stay and die engulfed in heavenly fire or let herself be passed from witch to witch like some monstrous prize.

Would she never be free?

Would she always be somebody's pet monster?

Her chest ached. Footsteps broke the tense silence stretching between them, the tread of heavy boots drawing near.

Beata's gaze was intent, her knuckles white where they gripped the iron bars. "So? Do we have a deal?"

30.

MARYNKA

"HE WON'T COME," KAJETAN SAID. "I swear to you he won't. Not to save me."

Marynka sighed. They had returned to the abandoned woodcutter's hut where she and Kajetan had sheltered from the snowstorm. Grandmother was inside, snug and warm and settled in front of the fire that Marynka had built back up, seated on an old stool that Marynka had carefully dusted down. While Marynka was outside, in the bitter, snow-flecked breeze, watching for the prince and standing guard over Kajetan, whose life she was increasingly regretting having saved. And Beata…

Grandmother had sent Beata to deliver their message to the prince because apparently Marynka couldn't be trusted to do so, even though it had been *her* idea to use Kajetan as a hostage.

"Send you? And if you cross paths with Midnight? Will you pick another foolish fight with her, get yourself caught, and let the prince escape a second time?"

The echo of the witch's scornful comments chased themselves round and round her head. Eating at her, the way the sight of Grandmother and Beata with their heads bent close together had. Marynka hadn't managed to catch much of what they were whispering about; when she'd edged closer to eavesdrop, Red Jaga had slapped her.

"What are you doing? Didn't I just tell you to bring more wood for the fire?"

"He won't come," Kajetan repeated, his shoulders straining as he tried to free the wrists Marynka had bound together in front of him. Turnabout was fair play after all. "You don't know the things I've done. How I've hurt him. I helped destroy everything he worked for. Why won't you believe—"

"Why won't you?" Marynka said, stamping her feet and blowing heat on her fingers. When all of this was over, she was never going near snow again. Ever. "He'll come. You can practically taste the goodness dripping off our Prince Józef. He has a heart so pure he'll risk it even to save you." She faced the frosted trees, searching for movement, breathing in the wintry scents of pine and woodsmoke. The golden brilliance of noon had faded. The crimson light of the sinking sun stretched a bloody shadow over the snow.

Kajetan continued to list all his various sins, all the many reasons why the prince wouldn't come for him. Marynka stopped listening.

Soon it would all be over. Over, and she could go home. Home to the Midday Forest. With Grandmother and Beata. Beata who'd avoided her eyes after her little heart-to-heart with Grandmother, who hadn't even bothered to speak to Marynka before she'd set off.

"You'll regret this," Kajetan said.

"No, I don't think I will," Marynka said, distracted, uneasy. With her back turned, she sensed, rather than saw, Kajetan seize on her apparent inattention and make a desperate break for it. She let him get as far as the edge of the clearing, far enough for a tiny spark of hope to ignite inside his chest, before she cruelly snuffed it out.

Marynka lifted a hand, calling to the wind as though it were a pet. It swept Kajetan's feet out from under him, sending him sprawling with a pained gasp. "Do I have to threaten to cut little pieces off of you now? Why are you even running if you think the prince won't come?"

Kajetan lay facedown in the snow, chest heaving. "Because when he *doesn't* come, that witch is going to kill me."

Well, he wasn't wrong. If Józef didn't come, Red Jaga probably would take her anger out on Kajetan and Marynka.

An icy slither of fear pricked her confidence. Prince Józef would come, wouldn't he? He had a pure heart. He was good and kind and brave. Someone like that wouldn't let someone else die for them. Certainly not someone who had once been a friend. And even if they weren't friends now, she'd seen the war of emotions on his face when he'd looked at Kajetan.

He *would* come.

Unless Zosia had already gotten to him, of course. Marynka threw a look of frustration at the woodcutter's hut. Grandmother should have sent her, not Beata.

Zosia wouldn't have given up. Neither of them liked to lose. Zosia was as stubborn as Marynka was, and she couldn't *afford* to give up. She needed the power from that heart in order to escape from Black Jaga. Had Grandmother told the other witch yet what Zosia had planned? Marynka couldn't imagine she would hold back her gloating for long. She savored any chance to one-up her older sister.

She only knows about it all because you told her Zosia was running away.

Well, so what? Marynka squared her shoulders. She had chosen her path. The time for second thoughts was past. There was no turning back. After Black Jaga dealt with Zosia, *she* would be the most powerful servant, just like she'd always dreamed, just like she'd always wanted. There would be no Midnight to compete with. No Midnight standing in her way. No Midnight to make it a challenge. No Midnight to make it *fun*.

No Midnight.

No Zosia.

No…

Marynka imagined a life without the chase, without her rivalry with Midnight that had existed for almost as long as she'd been Midday. The future stretched ahead of her bleak and oh so empty.

Beata had left Kajetan's saber leaning against the side of the hut. Marynka snatched it up, spinning the weapon wildly as she made her way toward him.

Kajetan rolled onto his side, squinting up at her.

Marynka sat on his legs, ignoring his squawked protests and his futile attempts to kick her off. She drew the saber from its sheath, liking the way the curved edge caught the dying sunlight. "How do you make the flames come?"

Kajetan snorted. "You won't be able to summon them. That's a *holy* sword. A saber baptized in blood, forged and consecrated by a priest. Józek and I knelt on the steps of the altar side by side when we asked for the Holy Mother's blessing, when we vowed to give our lives to defend our homeland."

"Hmm," Marynka said. "And then you went and betrayed him *and* your country."

Kajetan stiffened.

Marynka raised the saber, running a fingertip over the delicate floral engravings etched along the steel blade—sunflowers, lilies, and roses. She was so busy admiring the weapon that she barely heard Kajetan speak.

"Back then I believed I was defending Lechija, defending our traditions. My father told me that we were, that if we didn't act, then noble families like ours would lose power, lose our old rights and privileges. He said we had to ally with the tsarina, that doing so was best for Lechija. He said my time at the Cadet School had confused me. And I-I'm loyal to my family. You know how it is, a parent's word is law. I've always assented to his will. I don't think even my father thought the tsarina would go so far, seize so much control."

"You didn't expect the evil tsarina to do something evil?"

Kajetan's eyes were full of bitter memories. "I know the damage we've caused. I know how many people I've hurt. I will spend every breath for the rest of my life regretting my actions and trying to make up for my family's sins." He struggled to sit up. "What if the witch were to take my heart instead of his? What if I offered it to her?"

"If she wanted your heart, she'd already have taken it. There's no power in a heart like yours. That's why she needs Józef's."

"And you want to give that monster more power."

"That monster," Marynka said, throwing her head back proudly, "is my grandmother."

Kajetan gave her a long look, studying her features like he was trying to find the resemblance. Marynka flashed him a grin full of iron teeth, let her eyes glow molten gold. But his expression didn't change and his gaze lingered on other parts of her face. "Does your cheek hurt?"

Marynka's hand rose instantly, defensively, to her face. "No."

"Liar." Now it was Kajetan who grinned. "If you know she's going to hit you, you should clench your teeth. Keep your mouth shut and your chin down and that way you won't bite your tongue."

"You think I don't know that?" Marynka snapped.

"What will she do with it?" Kajetan asked. "The power she gains from eating his heart? What is she planning? What happens afterward?"

Afterward…afterward they would return to the Midday Forest and… Well, it was like at the end of the Karnawał when the world turned upside down turned right side up. Everything would return to as it had been. Everything would return to normal. Masks and costumes would be locked away in chests and closets for another year. Peasants would abandon their disguises, bid farewell to the princes they had danced with. Christians would fast and file solemnly into church to have their foreheads smeared with ash. Musicians would tear the strings from their instruments, and all the glitter and music and madness and firelight would gutter as everyone returned to their everyday roles.

Afterward, Black Jaga would arrive for Zosia and… Marynka shook her head. She didn't want to think beyond this moment, when she was so close to scraping by with a victory, so close to giving Grandmother everything she wanted, so close to proving her worth.

She was so close she could taste it.

"Or is it that she doesn't tell you anything?" Kajetan said, interrupting the stream of her thoughts. "And you just follow her blindly doing whatever she tells you to do."

Anger flared through Marynka. "It's not like that." Though

it was true the witch did not confide in her. But she'd lived with Red Jaga long enough to grasp what she desired. "She tells me what I need to know," she retorted, tone defensive. "We aren't like you. Grandmother has no care for mortal concerns, mortal wars. For the fortunes or misfortunes of normal humans. She only cares about her forest and competing with her sisters. She wants hearts because they grow her power and because those blessed with pure hearts are the only ones who can harm her."

"And you," Kajetan said, "what is it you want?"

Marynka stared at him blankly. "Me?"

"You."

She couldn't answer. All she'd ever wanted was to finally win against Zosia. She'd wanted to prove she was the other girl's equal. She'd wanted to impress Grandmother, wanted the witch to kiss her cheeks and stroke her hair and tell her: *I've never found such a girl as powerful and clever as you. You are like a true granddaughter to me.*

"I—"

But all her hard work, all her efforts had so far earned her only disappointment. The brief moment when she'd thought she'd won had brought her neither satisfaction nor the witch's love.

The words were barely more than a whisper. "I want Grandmother to be proud of me." It sounded so…pathetic. Such a terribly small goal. Such a painfully childish thing to want.

There was an awful understanding in Kajetan's eyes that almost bordered on pity. It made Marynka want to hurt him. Badly. She wanted to take his saber and carve out those eyes, wanted to carve out this awful feeling, this horrible uncertainty suddenly choking her throat. She wanted to lash out, to wound him, to make him hurt the way that she was hurting.

So she leaned in and stroked a hand through his hair. He didn't flinch at the touch, only continued to look at her. "But this is a cruel world, Kajtuś," she said softly. "It is not a fairy tale. And monsters like us don't get happy endings. We don't get what we want. Although your father might, so you shouldn't be too upset. Your family wants Józef out of the picture. Your precious tsarina wants him dead. Now, you can take the credit for it. Think how proud they'll be of *you*."

Fury and despair flashed in his green eyes. Marynka smoothed a lock of hair behind his ear and leaned back, satisfied.

Kajetan set his jaw. "He won't come."

"Who are you trying to convince? Me or yourself?" Color drew her attention to the opposite side of the clearing—a flash of red, sudden as a flame flaring in the darkness. "There," she said, voice sweet with triumph. "Didn't I tell you?"

Kajetan followed her gaze and went very still, a look of utter disbelief, of denial, that quickly turned to fear coursing across his face as a regal figure on horseback rode into the clearing.

31.

ZOSIA

IF ZOSIA HAD DISLIKED BEATA before, now she couldn't stop wishing she'd used her claws of shadow to rip out Morning's throat instead of just ripping her from her sleigh.

Beata was insufferably pleased with herself. A steady stream of smug words poured from her mouth as they paused at a curve in the tower steps, listening for anyone coming. "It wouldn't have made a difference anyway, even if you had managed to take the prince's heart for yourself. Even with the power you gained from consuming it, you wouldn't be a match for Black Jaga. Or Red. Or White. The witches made us. We're their servants. Do you think our magic can even touch them?"

Zosia gave no answer, and when only quiet came from around the curve, she continued up the steps, taking them two at a time with Beata on her heels.

"You wouldn't have been able to kill her. Only those blessed with a pure heart can do them harm. Do you think you've been blessed with a pure heart, Midnight?"

"If you keep talking," Zosia said, "you're going to alert the guards."

The royal dungeons were like a tomb or a crypt, buried deep in the bones of one of the Golden Castle's towers. She'd lost track of the number of steps they'd climbed, the number of rank cells they'd passed.

"Where would you even go if you were free?" Beata continued. "East? West? You have no money. No family. No friends. You think your life would be better anywhere else?"

Again, Zosia didn't answer. It had never been about having a specific place or destination in mind. It was the possibility to choose, to go anywhere, wherever the mood and the wind took her. The freedom to decide her own path no matter where it might lead, the freedom to craft her own destiny.

"The witches take care of us. We never go hungry. They give us a home." Beata's halo of braids gleamed gold as they swept through a pool of guttering torchlight. The stairwell and the twisting corridors leading up to the outside world were as dark and bleak as the cell Zosia had been locked in.

"I know you and Marynka think you're better than me because I'm quiet and don't make trouble, but look who's winning now? You said I underestimate Marynka, but both of you underestimate *me*. There are ways to win if you keep quiet, if you're good and you cooperate and keep your mouth shut. Just do as you're told, say what the witches want to hear, don't stir the pot. Don't take risks. Look how I've survived all this time. Look how I've even managed to free Marynka from Red Jaga's clutches."

"By giving her me instead," Zosia muttered.

"Maybe you should've thought twice before setting your shadows on me."

"Do you hate me that much?"

"It's hard not to. When I've had to watch Marynka be so miserable because of you."

Zosia gritted her teeth. Her anger didn't run hot, but cold, spreading through her veins like ice. Why did *Marynka* get to go free? Why was *she* the one?

Marynka, who swanned about in the sun while Zosia had to claw her way out of the dark. Marynka, who had a friend. Marynka, who didn't even *want* to escape this life.

Zosia regretted having ever wished for freedom. It hurt worse to have wished and dreamed and dared to hope only to have that dream ripped away than to have never dreamed to start. After everything she'd done, all the many months of careful planning, the slow, meticulous accumulation of each heart she'd stolen, all the lies she'd fed Black Jaga, knowing just one slip could get her killed, all of it, had come to nothing.

"You're not the first, you know," Beata said. "I've been a servant longer than you and Marynka. I knew the girl who was Midday before her. I knew the girl who was Midnight before you, and I saw what Black Jaga did to her when *she* tried to run. Why do you think she's tried so hard to keep you separate from us? Night always makes trouble and tries to run away with the sun." She slipped on the next step she took and would have fallen, crashing back down the stairs, if Zosia hadn't caught her wrist and hauled her upright.

For a heartbeat neither of them spoke. The revelation made Zosia wonder what other secrets Black Jaga had been keeping from her.

"You don't know what it's like," Beata said softly, "always being the one left behind, the one left out. I don't want to watch another girl die. It's not a bad life. What's so terrible about following a few orders? Isn't it enough to live like this? Why make such a fuss?"

Zosia dropped Beata's arm. "You like being kept in a cage?"

"You don't notice the bars of the cage," Beata said, "unless you start to throw yourself against them. Surviving is a choice too."

A clamor punctuated her words: shouted orders, panicked footsteps, the crash of doors flinging open. The telltale sound of rooms being searched. Their escape had been discovered. Zosia reached instinctively for her magic, but the holy symbols carved into the tower's walls still sapped her strength. When she called to the shadows lurking in the corners of the stairwell, they swirled, broke apart, swirled, and broke apart again.

She and Beata doubled their pace. Zosia's teeth bit into her lip. She should have fled when she'd had the chance, the second Józef revealed he knew what she was, the second she was cornered. She shouldn't have wasted her time trying to fight. She should have run.

You could still run, whispered a voice in her head that sounded suspiciously like Marynka's.

She could still run, but Black Jaga was already headed this way, summoned by her sister. Black Jaga, who had given Zosia magic and a second chance at life, and all she'd asked in return was Zosia's complete obedience.

"I raised you, clothed you, fed you. You could act a little more grateful."

They'd had a deal of sorts and Zosia was going to pay for breaking it. Unless, of course, she swore herself into the service of another witch and let Red Jaga protect her...

But she *could* still run.

She could still take her chances.

Do you really think you can outrun her?

Zosia's heart jumped as they clambered up the worn stone steps. "Where is Marynka now?"

"Waiting for the prince with Red Jaga," puffed Beata. "There's an abandoned woodcutter's hut in the forest past the outskirts of the city. Near the monastery they took you to."

They reached a landing. The air changed. It was no longer tainted with the scent of incense, the stench of damp and decay. It tasted fresh. Cold.

Beata pushed through a set of double doors, moving swiftly.

Zosia stopped short as steel sang through the air with a flash of silver. A dagger buried itself in the wall inches from her ear. Beata lunged to the side in time to dodge a second blade.

A guard charged them.

But this time they were finally far enough from the dungeon for the dampening spells to lose most of their effect. When Zosia reached for the shadows in the corners of the room, they came alive, drawing themselves up into monstrous, nightmarish shapes. Grotesque faces swelled out of the darkness, their mouths yawning open in silent, agonized screams, their clawed tendrils reaching to wrap around the terrified man's legs and arms and neck.

There wasn't time to relish the victory. More footsteps sounded beyond the doors, the heavy tread of soldiers.

Zosia and Beata fled into the next room and the next. Beata's claws left luminous streaks in the air as they cut through skin and flesh. Together they were a blur of light and dark. It was strange fighting shoulder to shoulder with Morning instead of against her. Their powers were so different, yet somehow meshed together. It didn't feel right exactly, but not entirely wrong either.

It was unnerving.

Perhaps that was the real reason why Black Jaga had kept Zosia locked away from the world and separated from Beata and Marynka. Not to make her stronger, but because it made her *weaker*, and more easy to control. She hadn't wanted Zosia to be able to build connections, to learn things, to have anyone she could go to for help.

"You say our magic isn't enough to harm them," Zosia said, panting. "That I *can't* harm Black Jaga with the magic she's given me. But what if we used other magic? What if the three of us worked together to free ourselves?"

Beata blinked and then laughed outright. "*Us?* Morning, Midday, and Midnight? You're getting desperate. Didn't I just tell you how it worked out for the last girls? And do you really think *we* could work together? After everything?"

She had a point. Look at where trusting and confiding in Marynka had gotten Zosia—captured by a prince, thrown into a dungeon, forced into a bargain with another witch.

Unless...

The words chased each other around her head.

Run. Stay. Run. Stay. Run. Stay.

"Every time I look at you," Beata said, "all I see is Marynka after you've snatched a heart out of her hands. All I see is her thinking she'll never be good enough."

They burst through another set of doors. A line of soldiers stood ready to meet them, their sabers gleaming with holy flame. The dying red light of day speared through a long set of windows. Beyond the glass, the snow-dusted city and a darkening sky beckoned.

Beata's palms glowed incandescent. "Stay back and close your eyes," she ordered in a tone that grated on Zosia's nerves. She was right. They would make terrible allies.

"I'll blind them," Beata said. "You take the ones on the right."

Zosia nodded and moved behind Beata as the men closed in.

Beata raised her hands...and Zosia seized her chance and bolted.

Sprinting for the windows, leaving Beata to deal with *all* the guards and their flaming swords, ignoring her cry of outrage. Zosia didn't stop when she reached the window, but threw herself at the icy glass, crashing through it, plunging down, down, down, the rush of cold air shrieking in her ears.

She felt the full measure of her magic flood back as soon as she was outside the walls, a sensation like shrugging off a too-small, too-tight skin. She could breathe again. Power flooded through her veins.

A breath before she hit the snow at the foot of the tower, Zosia transformed. She was weightless. Formless. Made of nothing but dark wisps of the gathering night and frost-laced air. A whirl-wind of it. The Golden Castle, the city of Warszów, its tree-lined avenues and twining black streets, and its snow-covered rooftops shrank as she let the winter wind carry her away to freedom.

32.

MARYNKA

"THROW DOWN YOUR SWORD," MARYNKA ordered, waving Kajetan's saber at the prince as he dismounted from his horse, the crimson-red of his kontusz burning bright against the white of the winter forest. Marynka cast her senses out, searching for movement among the trees, but the prince truly had come alone. Where was Beata though?

Józef's gait was steady as he crossed the clearing, each of his steps sure. Saffron boots crunched in the snow. But this semblance of poise was undercut by the breathless, angry look on his face.

"Don't be a fool!" Kajetan shouted.

Józef fumbled with his sword belt and cast his saber down. He held up his empty hands.

"And the rest," Marynka said, because *she* wasn't a fool. No matter what Grandmother might claim.

A dagger and a pistol joined the prince's saber on the ground. "You're the girl from the sleigh, from the kulig, from the costume ball."

"Not a girl. A monster. But I'm flattered you recognize me, Your Highness."

"I still don't understand," Józef said. "Who are you? Why are you doing this?"

"They're monsters, Józek," Kajetan cut in. "Witches. They want to take your heart. Flee now while you—"

Marynka kicked Kajetan's long legs out from under him, cutting a look at Józef as he fell. "Run and I'll cut his throat." She raised Kajetan's saber.

Józef smiled tightly. "You say that like you think it would trouble me."

"You came running when you heard we had him, didn't you?"

"Don't misunderstand. Kajetan and I have history. I'm only here because it would pain me greatly to lose out on the chance to drive a sword through him myself. I'm not about to let go of him so easily."

Marynka could tell from Kajetan's expression that he didn't buy Józef's excuse any more than she did. Struggling to his knees in the snow, he stared at the prince like he was both a disaster and a miracle. How nice to know that even in the midst of all this she could still bring a little sunshine, a little romance, into other people's lives. How terribly kind of her. Really, they owed her a thank-you.

Marynka shrugged. "If you say so—" She swung the sword down.

Józef flinched.

Kajetan sucked in air through his teeth as Marynka halted the blade a hairsbreadth from the bump in his throat, and grinned.

"Marynka!" Red Jaga's voice cut across the winter clearing. The door to the woodcutter's hut creaked closed behind her. "Are you finished playing?"

Marynka lowered the saber. "Yes, Grandmother. And look, our guest, the prince, has arrived. My idea worked. I did it. You'll have his pure heart just like you asked. I told you I could do it."

The witch didn't bother to praise her. All her attention was focused on Józef, a look of unmistakable hunger on her wrinkled face, as if she could already scent the goodness wafting off him and couldn't wait to rip her teeth into his flesh. She moved past Marynka as though she wasn't there.

For the briefest second, Marynka could have sworn Zosia was standing beside her, whispering in her ear.

Don't you want more?

Don't you think you deserve more than this?

The air tasted like ash. Before Józef's broad frame, Red Jaga looked almost small, and even more ancient and skeletal than usual. The prince stood strong, his jaw set, his fists clenched, holding his composure. But Marynka saw his eyes grow wide with the kind of instinctual, primal fear you couldn't hide. The color drained from his face.

Red Jaga ran a tongue over her lips, over the sharp points of her iron teeth.

"Run," Kajetan urged, desperate. "Józek."

Józef ignored him, leveling his gaze on the witch. "I'm here. I yield myself up to you. Let Kajetan go."

"If I free him now," said Red Jaga, "what guarantee do I have that you won't fight me? Rest assured, we'll release him once this is over." She brought a hand to the prince's chest as though she meant to lay her palm against his beating heart.

It seemed to glow through his breast like an ember. Light shone through his skin, through the fur-lined silk of his robes.

Yet Red Jaga didn't touch him. She couldn't harm those blessed with pure hearts, not directly, which was why she had Marynka, a servant to do her monstrous work.

Instead she reached a hand into her apron, withdrew it, and before the prince could react, blew a little poppy seed into his face.

Józef's eyelids fluttered, his eyes half closing as drowsiness smothered his mind. He swayed, sinking to his knees in the snow, slumping like a puppet with its strings cut.

Kajetan cried out.

Marynka pressed the saber to his throat. The barest press of that curved edge was enough to draw blood, but Kajetan didn't seem to care. He twisted, looking up at her, begging.

Something squeezed inside Marynka's chest. Thankfully, a gust of frigid air blew her hair into her eyes then, and she tightened her grip on the hilt of the sword as she swiped the strands back.

A wind rose from nowhere and continued to blow fiercely,

dancing the falling snow into whirlwinds. The sudden cold seemed to shake the prince from his stupor. He blinked rapidly. Marynka almost moved toward him but froze, staring wide-eyed as a figure materialized from the gloom on the opposite side of the clearing.

For a breath, her mind went completely silent, hushed as the world after an explosion.

Red Jaga cocked her head and smiled. "So you came, Midnight. I thought you might. You didn't really have a choice, did you? But come, don't stand there in the trees alone. I've been waiting for you."

Zosia came forward, taking one step, then two, then three, something in her seeming almost to protest at the movement. She was only half corporeal. More wind than flesh still. The edges of her body bled into the gathering shadows.

Marynka's heartbeat was raging in her ears. Her thoughts were spinning in every direction at once. She couldn't breathe, couldn't speak. And what would she have said?

Midnight, fancy seeing you here. I almost killed you, but you're looking good?

Her mind was a storm of questions. Had Zosia come to fight? Was this one last desperate attempt to steal the prince's heart? Grandmother was standing right there. Was Zosia mad? Even if she managed to overpower Marynka, she was no match for Grandmother, and if Grandmother fought Zosia... If Grandmother attacked Zosia, what would *she* do?

"What are you doing here?" The words burst from Marynka's lips before she could stop them, choked and breathless. Her grip had gone unsteady on the sword. Vivid in her mind was the last time they'd faced each other. The violent clash of fire and darkness. The chase and the snowslide. The terrible anguish she'd felt afterward.

The agonizing relief she'd felt when she learned Zosia was alive.

Zosia's face was colder and wearier than she'd ever seen it. Her skin was always pale, but now it looked nearly transparent. There was a dull kind of emptiness in her midnight-blue eyes, as though she'd finally given up.

How am I supposed to be happy winning if you look like that?

"I'm here because I was invited." Zosia's eyes darted toward the prince. Józef was still slumped on his knees in the snow. He didn't look up. "Beata found me. She made me a deal. I'm here to take your place."

"I don't—" Marynka didn't understand. She looked from Zosia to Red Jaga in bewilderment, half-convinced she'd heard wrong. She looked around again for Beata but could find no sign of her. None of this made any sense. "I don't understand. What do you *mean?*"

"It's simple," Zosia said, drawing ever closer, steps silent on the snow, leaving behind no footprints.

Marynka had the sudden wild urge to wave the sword at her, to fend off her approach. She fought the urge to retreat. She wanted to scream at her to stay back.

"Black Jaga knows I planned to run away from her," continued Zosia. "Your beloved grandmother told her. After she *somehow* learned that I've been taking the hearts I was supposed to bring her sister for myself."

Cold dread pooled low in Marynka's stomach.

"But Red Jaga has offered to protect me, to spare me from her sister's wrath. In return, I become her servant. I become Midday. She wants *me*."

No, that wasn't…that wasn't possible. Marynka had earned her place at Grandmother's side. She had done everything right. She had proven herself worthy by bringing the witch the prince.

"But, but you don't want to be Midday. You don't even want to be Midnight. You don't want to be a servant. You wanted to be *free*." Her voice cracked on the last word.

Something flickered in Zosia's eyes.

She gave the most delicate shrug. "Maybe it won't be so bad this time. Maybe it will be different. *You* wanted to stay. *You* enjoy it. Being Midday. Maybe your grandmother will treat me better than she does you. Maybe I'll even like it."

You won't. And Grandmother won't and—

"No," Marynka said. It felt as though the very ground was crumbling beneath her feet. It felt like all her nightmares were coming true. "No." She took a shaky step backward, sword lifting from Kajetan's throat to point at Zosia. "No, I won't let you. I won't—"

Don't come any closer.

Don't take this away from me.

Please.

"Don't make a scene," Red Jaga snapped irritably. "Jealousy is unbecoming of you."

Marynka stared at her openmouthed.

"I am fond of you, Marynka." There was a trace of genuine regret in the witch's eyes. "I had such high hopes. But it's meaningless if you're not the best, if you can't help me beat my sister. You're always so quick to burn, but there's no real heat." She turned away. "Well, Zosia, is it? Why are you dragging your steps? Let's see your skill. Open up the prince's chest and carve out his heart. Bring it to me."

Something cracked inside Marynka. All she'd ever wanted was for the witch to be proud of her. All she'd ever wanted was to please her, to be good enough for her.

She was struck with the sudden, terrible understanding that she was never, ever going to be that.

Even after everything she'd done. No matter how hard she pushed herself. It would never be enough and now Zosia—

Marynka wanted to scream. She wanted to cry. She wanted to burn the world down to ash and herself along with it.

"Take it," she said softly. "Take his heart." Her head snapped up. Her eyes found Zosia's. Her voice grew louder. "It's what you wanted, isn't it? You need it. Grandmother can't touch him. He's protected by a blessing. Take it for yourself and run."

The witch let out an outraged hiss as Marynka turned toward her. "After all I've done for you! You ungrateful child!"

Marynka braced for catastrophe, for violence. Yet at the same time it felt like a great weight was falling from her shoulders, like two heavy shackles had dropped from her wrists. As though, with the choice made, the chains that had bound her were falling away.

"I saved you," Red Jaga ranted. "I made you into something to be feared. Years and years I've cared for you, provided you with every comfort, and this is how you treat me?" She took a step forward.

Zosia had frozen.

And Kajetan, in a last-ditch effort, seized on all of their distraction. Surging to his feet he lunged sideways, knocking Marynka to the snow. The fall ripped the air from her lungs. Even with his hands bound, he managed to wrench the saber from her.

Red Jaga came at him with her teeth bared. Ancient. Unkillable. She seized his wrist in one hand as he tried to bring the weapon down with a strength she shouldn't have possessed. Her other hand raked Kajetan across the stomach with her iron claws. Marynka had seen her gut animals in similar fashion, had seen their guts spill steaming onto the grass.

A spray of coppery blood colored the snow, flecking Marynka's cheek.

Kajetan went to his knees with a gasp and it was this that finally broke Prince Józef from his stupor. An animal sound tore from his throat. He stumbled to his feet, rushing forward just in time to catch the other boy as he fell. Together they sank to the ground.

"I have you. I have you. Stay with me." Blood spilled past the fingers the prince pressed to the other boy's stomach. "I swear if you die on me now, I will never forgive you."

Kajetan's hand reached for the prince's face, smearing a streak of red along his jaw, Józef caught his hand, squeezed his fingers, brought them to his lips, pleading.

Before Marynka had even struggled to her feet, before she'd managed to fully process what had happened. Red Jaga snatched Kajetan's fallen saber from the snow and turned the blade, pressing the point to Marynka's throat. "When are you going to stop causing me trouble?"

Cold steel bit into her skin. A thin line of crimson traced the blade's path down her neck. Even with her healing abilities, a blade through the throat, a wound of that magnitude, especially one from a holy blade, would end her instantly.

Zosia, rushing the last distance across the clearing, went deathly still.

Red Jaga smiled. "Ah, let me guess. Midnight and Midday have found one another once again. Do you love her like the last one did, too, I wonder?" The blade's point traveled down Marynka's neck to her chest. "Let me make this clear, Zosia," she called over her shoulder, "I do not wish to hurt our dear Marynka, but if you even think of taking that heart for yourself, you will have forced my hand. The choice is yours."

Zosia didn't move. "Beata said if I do as you say, if I promise to serve you, you'll let her go free."

Marynka's eyes widened.

"Of course," said Red Jaga. "I am known to be very generous to those who serve me well. Now, hurry and bring me Prince Józef's heart."

Józef was still bent over Kajetan. His head snapped up at the sound of his name, features twisted in fury.

Zosia moved forward.

And Marynka, Marynka hated, hated, *hated* losing, and she wasn't going to lose again. She wouldn't let the witch trap Zosia. She wouldn't let her give up her freedom for her sake. She wouldn't let herself be used as a hostage.

She caught the saber with both hands, blood ribboning down her palms, and drove the blade into her own chest.

33.

ZOSIA

ZOSIA FLUNG A HAND OUT reflexively. Futilely. A wordless cry wrenched from her throat. She hadn't known such a sound was in her. This agonizing, tearing sensation—it felt as though she was the one being cut in two.

Marynka's body hunched over the blade. The steel speared through her chest and out her back. Red Jaga caught the hilt of the sword and yanked it free.

It came out with an awful sound, a hideous wet *schlick*, the sharp steel coated vivid red. A stain spread rapidly across Marynka's chest. She coughed blood onto the snow and her legs folded under her, her hair spilling forward to hide her face.

"You foolish, foolish girl." Red Jaga cast the saber aside. Her golden eyes were wide as moons. She went to her knees beside her servant, one gnarled hand pressing to Marynka's chest where the blade had driven in—to hasten her death or heal her, Zosia couldn't tell.

And didn't care.

A fury like no other seized her. "Don't touch her!" She flung herself at the witch.

Red Jaga caught her hand as she raked her claws down, returning the blow with a vicious swipe of her own at Zosia's stomach.

Zosia stumbled back, managed to regain her balance and struck back, sending a squall of wind and shadow at the witch, who didn't so much as flinch. Scorching heat burned the darkness from the air.

"Do you think you can harm me with my sister's magic? Do you think you can even *touch* me with the power we've given you?" All throughout the clearing, winter melted.

The air was almost too hot to breathe. Zosia could feel her cheeks blistering, her body turning to ash beneath that searing gaze. The heat rolled over her in waves. An inferno. Sweat ran down her spine and soaked her clothing. The snow at Red Jaga's feet melted into puddles of steaming water. The shadows writhed.

And then she saw it. Behind the witch, Józef had staggered to his feet and seized the saber Red Jaga had cast aside. He was staring at it like a dreamer, like he did not recognize what he held in his hands. Beyond him, Kajetan lay in the snow very still.

Józef's expression changed. His mouth curled in a furious snarl and heavenly flame blazed forth, licking up the bloodied blade. Zosia's eyes widened, and at that, Red Jaga seemed to finally notice something was amiss and started to turn her head.

Zosia reached for her with tendrils of shadow. The witch let out a grunt as they whipped snake-like around her arms and legs and middle. Burning away almost on touch, but it was enough. In that desperate half-heartbeat of a moment, the prince drove the blade through the witch's throat.

Shock smoothed Red Jaga's wrinkled features. Gold eyes stared at the prince, at Zosia, unseeing. The witch's entire body burst into flame. Her red kerchief, her hair curled and blackened. Her sun-kissed skin flaked away. Her iron teeth and her bones glowed the awful red of embers.

A small sound quavered the air, the softest exhale.

Dazed, it took Zosia a moment to realize it had come from her. There should have been more, she couldn't help thinking—a great crack like lightning or a sound like the world ending. But there was only this, ash and the ancient body before her crumbling, scattering away as dust on the wind, and an absence of heat, as if the witch who had ruled the hours between sunrise and noon was taking all the warmth of day with her.

Silently, softly, fresh snow began to fall. Large, feathery white flakes dusted the prince's heaving shoulders, caught like pale moths in the snarls of Marynka's wildfire hair.

Zosia's heart jolted. Marynka was still slumped over in the snow, but Zosia could tell she was breathing, could make out the faint movement as she sucked air into her lungs.

She started to go to her, but Józef straightened, bloodied saber in hand. Light danced off the flowers carved into the curved blade. He kissed it, raised it to heaven, and then he looked straight at Zosia. "So it comes down to the two of us, does it?"

The monster and the prince.

Shadows stretched across the snow, creeping slowly forward on clawing fingers. "Surrender," Zosia said, echoing what he'd said to her in another winter clearing. "And I'll grant you mercy."

The ghost of a smile crossed Józef's face. "I defeated and captured you once."

"With the help of a dozen soldiers and then only just barely."

An eager wind rose, twirling the falling snow to icy glitter. The forest creaked.

For a breath they stood sizing each other up.

Then they clashed.

Józef struck first and Zosia pivoted on her heel, the deadly curve of his saber slicing past her neck. She cut back at him with ink-black claws, just as fast, just as vicious.

The prince caught the blow with a hiss, baring his teeth in what was almost a grin, bringing his sword up in a sweeping parry.

Shadow attempted to swallow the steel, but a prayer from the prince's lips had holy flame blazing along the blade, throwing sparks across the clearing.

Zosia darted out of reach, circled back. Pulse racing with every lunge and swipe, strike and slash, every time she twisted out of the path of that burning edge. The prince wasn't as fast as Red

Jaga, as Marynka, or as graceful as Kajetan, but his blows had a fierce strength that reverberated up her arms. The sword in his hand was like an extension of his body, the movement so practiced it was as though he'd been born with the hilt gripped in his palm.

Her focus narrowed. Strikes sang like shrieks through the air. There was only the desperate rush of the fight, the burn of her muscles, the blood on her claws. If she faltered even once, it would all be over.

Her claws shredded his shoulder. His blade grazed her torso, ripping through skin and fabric.

Blood warmed Zosia's stomach.

"You know," Józef said with deceptive calm, breathing hard. "Lechija could make use of a power such as yours, terrible as it is. Why not harness it for a worthier cause? Why not use it to do some good? This is your home too." He lunged, feinting left but striking right, bringing his sword down in a blow that would have cut most people in half.

Zosia spun aside, boots sliding in the muddy slush. "Are you asking me to help you fight for freedom? Do you really want someone like me standing by your side? You're forgetting what I am. Look closer. Would you damn your immortal soul, stain your pure heart, allying yourself with a monster?"

The shadows stretching over the snow sharpened to knifepoints that shot toward the prince.

Józef slashed his sword in a sweeping arc, slicing the darkness in half and carving a blazing line of fire between them, divided the clearing in two with Zosia and Marynka on one side, Józef and Kajetan on the other.

"Zosieńka," Józef said, free hand pressing mockingly to his heart. "I would partner with the devil himself if it meant seeing my people free. I am not like the priests. I do not care from what unholy source your magic comes. We cannot afford to have our strength divided. We are not strangers." His expression turned serious. "We're all in this together. We share a common fate. We need every man and every creature if we're to win this."

For a split second, Zosia did genuinely consider it. The Kingdom of Lechija with the power of Midnight at its beck and call. And, if she could convince Marynka, if they both lived through this, Midday, also. Day and night wearing Lechija's colors, fighting side by side, back to back. Unbeatable. Unstoppable. She couldn't truthfully say the vision wasn't tempting.

Józef held her gaze. "Will Lechija's monsters fight with us?"

If they did, would it be enough to turn the tide, to drive the invading forces out of the kingdom? If they fought at the prince's bequest, under his command?

And therein lay the problem.

"Fight with you or *for* you?" Zosia said softly. "I have no love for those who've invaded our home, but I won't take orders. I won't shackle myself to another master, to anyone, whether it's this kingdom or you." She was going to live as *she* wanted, answerable to no one. She wouldn't settle for anything less than complete freedom. "I am not going to be someone's pet monster summoned to cut down their enemies, someone's weapon. I'm going to serve no one's ambitions, no one's desires but my own from here on out. I am going to decide my own fate."

There was a flicker of understanding in Józef's brown eyes. His tone was almost rueful. "I had to ask, for Lechija's sake. If you ever change your mind, the offer stands. For now, it seems we're at a stalemate. However"—he twirled his saber, irritatingly confident—"I see no river before us. I know that *I* at least am not destined to die here."

"But what of your friend?" Zosia said, gaze flicking past the prince to where, behind him, impossibly, Kajetan was staggering to his feet.

"I told you not to move," Józef said sharply, worry raising his voice a half octave.

"How much longer," Zosia continued, "do you think he'll last if I drag this out? How long can he go without a doctor or a priest with healing magic?"

"And your friend?" Józef shot back.

Behind Zosia, a terrible crunch of snow told her Marynka was making an equally ridiculous attempt to join the fight.

"I'm fine," Marynka rasped out. "We can take them."

Zosia resisted the urge to glance behind her, to curse at the other girl furiously.

"Don't listen to her," Kajetan was telling Józef, a hand

pressed to his wounds. Red leaked past his fingers. "I'm fine. I can fight. Get behind me, Józek." He swayed a little, his face ghostly pale.

Józef's gaze slid from Zosia to Marynka and back. His expression was grim, but the corners of his mouth twitched. "What do you say, Zosia? A truce? Why don't we each retrieve our fool and go our way."

Zosia was silent. She didn't look away from the fight before her, couldn't afford to, but unease knotted inside her stomach. Vivid in her mind's eye was the sword driving through Marynka's chest. She could hear the other girl's breathing was ragged. "My fool's a monster. She doesn't die so easily."

"And mine's a stubborn traitor," Józef said. "Believe me, he'll cling to life just to spite you."

They stared each other down. The blessed flames blooming from the prince's saber burned bright and steady despite the eager wind and writhing shadows. It was a battle of will to see who would break first.

Zosia let her hands slowly start to fall to her sides, as if considering the offer, as if pondering the possibility. "Very well," she said carefully. "After you then, Your Highness."

"Oh no," Józef said, smiling with all his teeth. He tightened his grip on the eagle-headed hilt of his sword. "Ladies first."

Fresh tension pulled the air tight. Zosia's boots shifted minutely in the mud. Her focus narrowed to the rivulet of sweat running from the prince's temple, tracing a line down his stubbled cheek, catching on the sharp line of his jaw.

A snowflake grazed her cheek. A sliver of ice brushed her claws.

They moved at the same moment.

Marynka let out a cry of outrage as the darkness receded from Zosia's skin, as her claws shortened to the length of normal human fingernails.

Kajetan collapsed to one knee as Józef sheathed his saber. The prince rushed to his side, turning his back.

Zosia turned too. "I hope you know this is only a temporary truce." She roped one of Marynka's arms over her shoulders, supporting the other girl's weight and ignoring her protests. Marynka's face was bloodless. Her freckles bright against the alarmingly gray pallor of her tanned skin. "I'll be back for your heart. I hope you'll try not to lose it before then."

She couldn't see Józef, but she heard the smile in his voice. "Ah but, Zosieńka, who said you have not stolen my heart already?"

There was a loud objection from Kajetan. The crunching of labored steps in the snow. The prince whistled for his horse.

Zosia bit back a smile of her own as she dragged a still-protesting Marynka in the opposite direction, across the clearing and into the ice-white trees. She did not look back.

"Until next time then, Your Highness."

34.

MARYNKA

"OW! THAT *HURTS!*" MARYNKA HISSED, breath short with pain. "Are you trying to make me die faster?"

"Maybe if you stopped squirming, maybe if you hadn't *stabbed* yourself, you wouldn't be dying," Zosia snapped back.

Marynka glared, watching, as Zosia made a frankly poor attempt to bandage her wounds with makeshift strips torn from the sash that had circled Marynka's waist. "We could have taken them."

Zosia snorted.

"I even let you have his heart."

"You *let* me, did you?"

A loud flapping of wings silenced them both. Shadow flashed as an owl flew overhead, across the crescent of the moon. Zosia's head jerked up, but she didn't take her hands from Marynka's chest.

The touch sent a rush of cold through Marynka and she shivered, tensing, as those icy fingers drifted over her skin, over her rib cage, skirting the place where the blade had driven in. She could still recall how it had felt, the cold steel scraping like teeth over bone, the horrible sear of tearing flesh. Such a wound from a sacred blade should have been lethal. If it wasn't for the flare of magic Grandmother had pushed into her chest, it would have been.

Marynka leaned her back against the tree trunk, legs splayed out in front of her. Zosia was practically sitting in her lap, with a knee on either side of her hips. They'd walked—or in Marynka's case limped, Zosia's arm around her waist the only thing keeping her upright—until the sun had vanished. The sky fading from hazy red to vivid black. The world growing darker, colder by the heartbeat. A deep winter wind was blowing, the kind that froze the breath before it left your lungs. How they'd managed to make it even this far...

They'd stopped in the densest part of the forest, sheltering beneath the snow-hung boughs of an ancient fir. Neither of them dared light a fire. With Black Jaga likely tracking them, it wasn't worth the risk. Instead, Zosia had dug the snow away from the trunk right down to the bare earth, burrowing out a little cave for them beneath the evergreen's lowest branches, laying a few boughs on the ground for insulation.

Zosia was growing increasingly jumpy. Dark lashes cast half circles on her ghost-pale cheeks. Her mouth formed a grim line.

Marynka dropped her gaze. "Why did you accept Beata's deal?" she asked quietly. "Why—" She couldn't finish. *Why were you willing to give up your freedom, the freedom you want so badly, to save me?*

Zosia was silent before she spoke. "I don't know."

Marynka's brow furrowed.

"I wasn't going to accept. I left Beata behind and started to run, but when I was flying over the forest..." Zosia looked up, holding Marynka's gaze. "Maybe I wanted to see what you would do when you thought I would take your place. Or maybe I thought it worth the cost if at least one of us would go free. But mostly, I think, I just wanted to make you angry."

Marynka blinked twice, and then she threw her head back and laughed. A truly unwise decision that made her gasp. "Oh God, that *hurts.*"

"You did try to kill me, burying me in that snowslide," Zosia said.

"I didn't try to *kill* you. I had complete faith in your ability to survive my attacks. I knew an avalanche wouldn't be enough to get rid of you. I wasn't worried about you at all."

Zosia shot her a disbelieving glance.

Marynka gestured at her wounded chest. "Does this make us even then?"

"Not even close."

A sudden, bone-achingly cold gust of wind rushed through the black trees, stripping snow from the branches. The forest creaked in the darkness like an old wooden house.

Marynka continued to watch Zosia, her expression serious. "You need to leave me here."

Zosia buttoned Marynka's kontusz closed over the makeshift bandages, ignoring her.

Marynka tried to push her hands away. "Stop. You don't have time for this."

"There's time," Zosia said, putting her hands right back where they'd been.

"There *isn't*," Marynka insisted.

Zosia sat back on her heels, weight resting on Marynka's thighs. In that moment they didn't need words. Their matching expressions spoke for them.

Let me save you.

No, you *let me save you.*

Even with their lives balanced on a knife's edge, they couldn't stop trying to outdo each other. Marynka stifled the urge to laugh.

The cold sharpened, nipping at her cheeks; even the shadows were shivering. The night itself trembling in anticipation. There was a growing pressure in the air, like a storm was brewing.

"You can feel it too. Black Jaga's coming and I'm too weak to fly on the wind like this, but you can still get away." They had to split up. Even if Marynka didn't want to, even if it was the last thing she wanted to do right now.

But she was slowing Zosia down and that was unacceptable.

She tried to sit up more. "We're wasting time arguing." Each second that passed was another second wasted. Zosia had to get moving. On a night this dark, the witch would be stronger than anything either of them could throw at her. "Go as fast as you can. She knows you betrayed her." A heavy weight, shame, settled in the pit of Marynka's stomach. "I shouldn't have told Grandmother you were running away, that you'd been taking the hearts for yourself. If I hadn't—"

"Even if you hadn't," Zosia said, "they would have realized eventually. Black Jaga was already suspicious that I lost to you four times in a row because we both know how very unlikely that is."

"You say that like I didn't *just* beat you. I had the prince in the palm of my hand."

"And she would have realized if I'd taken his heart," Zosia continued, ignoring the interruption. "At least now…" She glanced up at the trees, watching the uneasy stirring of the branches.

"I told you," Marynka said. "We could have taken them. You could've taken his heart, absorbed its magic. You'd be—"

Zosia shook her head.

Marynka was suddenly suspicious. "You didn't want to take his heart, is that it? You're not getting *soft* on me, are you?"

"Don't be ridiculous."

"He's very handsome. I saw him kissing your fingers at the frozen lake."

Zosia rolled her eyes. "I promise you it isn't like that." She brushed a strand of silver hair behind her ear. "He's trying to stop his country from being devoured by an evil witch. I can appreciate the sentiment. And I told him—until next time. For now, let Józef attempt to free Lechija. After he succeeds, I'll return then and take his heart."

"Do you think he will free Lechija?" Marynka asked. "Do you think he can win against Rusja's tsarina? He's naive if he's hoping everyone will fight together. He can't really believe that everyone shares the same thoughts and feelings just because we've grown up on the same land."

"Maybe he is naive," Zosia said. "But you could say the same about me and my hopes to ally with you. He might succeed. He did survive us."

It was Marynka's turn to snort. "You *do* have a soft spot for him. What was it he said to you?" She pressed a mocking hand to her chest, putting on a deep voice. "'*Oh, Zosieńka, but you've already stolen my heart!*'"

Zosia punched Marynka's thigh.

"You seemed to like dancing with that boy at the costume ball too, and—"

"You seem to pay a lot of attention to what I do with boys. Are you jealous?"

Heat rushed to Marynka's cheeks. "You wish!"

Zosia leaned closer, a wicked smile spreading across her face.

Marynka leaned back, flustered, her head knocking against the tree trunk.

"Maybe I do wish."

Marynka's eyes widened. Zosia closed the space between them, pressing her cold lips to Marynka's startled mouth.

Marynka froze, inhaling sharply. And then she reached, fingers grasping at Zosia's collar the moment Zosia started to pull away. Their mouths met so forcefully it was almost painful. All teeth and hot breath and bruising touch, the rough bark of the tree trunk scraping against Marynka's back, the taste of blood on her tongue. A part of her wasn't even truly surprised. Maybe this was where they had always been headed. Maybe this was always going to happen. This thing between them had been simmering away for years, fueled by every confrontation, every clash. Maybe this was what she'd been trying to deny all along. Because she'd known deep down that once she gave in, if she let whatever this was start, it would be over for her. She wouldn't stand a chance.

"Don't…" she managed to get out, trying to catch her breath. "Don't think this means I like you."

There was a dark gleam in Zosia's eyes, the faintest hint of what might have been laughter in the curve of her mouth. Marynka would've been incandescently furious, wouldn't have been able to stifle the urge to shove her away if she hadn't been able to feel Zosia's pulse racing equally fast, frantic and thundering beneath her fingertips.

"I would never think *that*." The tip of Zosia's nose, ice-cold, brushed Marynka's cheek.

She kissed Marynka desperately, like they were never going to get another chance, like she thought Marynka might never let her do this again, like she couldn't bear to let go. Her hands fisted so tightly in Marynka's hair that it hurt, dragging her closer, not letting her escape.

Marynka sank her teeth into Zosia's bottom lip in retaliation, and Zosia made a sound that could have been pain or something else, kissing her harder in response, digging her nails into Marynka's scalp, shooting shivers of lightning across her skin. Her chest burned from lack of breath. It was as though even this was a competition, as though neither of them could bear to be outdone, undone, by the other, as if Zosia were trying to prove she was so much better at this, too.

She pressed Marynka back against the tree, pressed so close they cast a single shadow on the snow.

Marynka winced at the weight pressing on her injured chest.

Zosia broke away immediately and Marynka, embarrassingly, found herself trying to chase her lips. A bitter wind blew as they stared at each other, ruffling their hair, racing through the trees, sending snow dancing in eddies over the frozen earth. A chilly reminder of reality.

"You need to leave," Marynka repeated hoarsely.

Zosia's eyes closed tight as she scraped herself together. Marynka could almost hear her thinking up counterarguments, weighing the words before she gave in. "Tell me where to find you. I'll lie low, and then I'll come back for you once she's stopped searching for me."

"Can't she track you? Grandmother always knew where to

find me if she needed to." They were—had been—connected by the magic she'd gifted Marynka. No matter the distance, day or night, the wind would bring Red Jaga to wherever she was.

"I can hide my presence from her. I didn't eat all those princes' hearts for nothing."

Marynka bit the inside of her cheek. She hadn't really given any thought yet as to what *she* would do now, where she'd go. "The Midday Forest," she said finally. What would she find there? Would the old wooden house still grant her entrance?

Zosia nodded. "Wait for me."

"Don't get yourself killed before then."

Zosia smiled. "Only because you ask so nicely." And then she was standing, drawing the shadows around herself like a cloak. She took a moment to cover the mouth of the shallow cave Marynka was sheltering in with more branches ripped from the tree to keep the snow out, ignoring the face Marynka made in response.

She looked back once, looking like she wanted to say something more, but at that moment the wind leapt and then she was gone, carried away with the frosty air. The flash of a silver braid dissolved into the dark. The night stretched into stillness.

A strange panic choked Marynka's throat, and she fought the irrational urge to call after her, chase after her. Just how far would Zosia have to run? How fast?

With no one to see, she curled in on herself and squeezed her eyes shut. Truthfully, she was afraid, and not only for Zosia.

She didn't know what would happen to *her* now that Red Jaga was gone—a fact she was not ready to think about, refused to think about. Even just prodding at the memory made her feel ill. Grandmother was dead and she honestly didn't know what to feel. Should she be crying, mourning for the witch who had taken her in? Or should she be dancing with relief that she was finally free? She'd never see her again. Ever.

Grief seized Marynka's heart in a fist.

Questions chased each other round and round her head. Would the fire in her veins gutter and burn out? Would the magic she'd been gifted die with Grandmother? If so, it really was better that Zosia had left. Marynka didn't want Zosia seeing her like that, as someone weak, defanged, and ordinary.

She reached for the flame inside herself and imagined cupping her hands around it to keep it burning. She imagined blowing breath to kindle the dying embers of her power to new life. The air surrounding her warmed slightly. She thought of the wound in her chest and willed the flesh to knit back together. Eventually, exhaustion dragged her into an uneasy, sleepy oblivion.

When she woke, night had left and morning arrived. A white horse was nosing at the branches that covered Marynka's shelter. A girl stood by its side, her twin braids glowing like gold in the soft dawn light.

"So," Marynka said, licking cold-cracked lips, "when were you going to tell me you bargained with Grandmother for my freedom?"

Beata didn't bother to look innocent or sorry. There was a vicious tear in her sleeve. Dried blood stained the white fur trim at her collar. She looked tired and annoyed and also a little like she was going to cry.

Despite knowing there would be no one, Marynka found herself searching the clearing. She wondered how far away Zosia was now.

"What happened?" Beata asked, reaching a gloved hand down to help Marynka climb out of the snow cave. Her body still ached, but she felt stronger than before.

She took a deep breath, leaning her weight against the horse, watching the east flame red through the trees. She told Beata everything—how Zosia had appeared just as Grandmother was about to take the prince's heart, how she'd learned Red Jaga intended to replace her, how she'd turned on the witch knowing her life was basically forfeit. She told Beata about driving the blade into her own chest and the prince killing Grandmother, about Zosia and the prince's truce, and Zosia fleeing from Black Jaga.

Through it all, Beata stood silent and then she shuffled closer to wrap an arm around Marynka's waist. Marynka pressed her face into the crook of Beata's neck. She could feel Beata's sigh, her breath in her hair.

"Do you think she'll get away?"

"She has a head start. And she's Midnight." The thought gave Marynka comfort. She *would* get away. When she'd kissed Zosia, it hadn't felt like something ending; it had felt like something was just beginning. "I—" She lifted her head. "I might not hate her as much as I thought I did."

Beata didn't even pretend to look surprised. "I wondered when you were going to figure that out."

Marynka scowled.

"What will you do now?" Beata asked quietly. "You're free. There's no witch to tell you what to do. You can come home with me. I won't tell White Jaga everything that happened, only that things went wrong and the prince killed her sister, which isn't a lie. Or—" Her voice grew even softer. "Will you go after Zosia? The last girls, the Midnight and Midday before you, left without me. I think they didn't trust me or maybe they didn't like me enough to want me with them. So I just... Will you promise you won't go anywhere without saying goodbye?"

"Beata," Marynka said slowly, in the tone of someone explaining something to a small child. "If I go anywhere, you're coming with me."

Beata's head snapped up. "What?" The horse pressed its nose into her chest.

"With *us*."

"I'm not tagging along pathetically while you and Zosia are all—" Beata made an incomprehensible gesture with both hands.

Marynka raised an amused eyebrow.

Beata huffed, her breath smoking the air. Her cheeks had

turned pink. "Anyway, you're still recovering. You should let yourself heal completely first."

Marynka brushed a sprinkling of snow off her shoulder. She tipped her face up to the sun, letting its growing heat reach down into her bones and soothe away the cold. Some of the tightness in her muscles unwound. "Let's go then."

"Where?"

"To begin with, someplace warm."

Epilogue

Marynka

THE FIRST TIME MARYNKA SET out to take a heart for herself, she had just turned eighteen. The world had thawed to summer and the Kingdom of Lechija was in the midst of a violent uprising. Blood stained the earth and fed the crops, as deep a red as the tiny wild strawberries that grew beside the old house in the Midday Forest. Lindens were blooming alongside the battlefields and the hot sky trembled with the thunder of cannon fire as the country fought tooth and claw for freedom from its foreign oppressors.

A contingent of Rusja's troops was making camp at the edge of Marynka's domain, and the soldiers were wandering into the trees, seeking shade and solace from the sun. All day long it had plagued them, leaving them dizzy and sweating, white-lipped and wild-eyed. It had parched and peeled their skins. Tempers had flared. Fights broken out. At times men whispered that they were seeing things—a glowing pair of golden eyes, something that might have been a girl, a strange shimmer in the heat haze.

But when they spun toward it the unforgiving breeze would whirl and the vision would vanish.

Marynka smiled as they clutched talismans meant to turn away bullets, as they tried to distract themselves with gossip. With talk of a Lechijan prince rumored to have joined the ranks as a common soldier, who was even now fighting side by side with peasants and the son of a famous magnate while his uncle the king, keen to have a say in things now that the rest of the kingdom had risen up, whined that he wasn't allowed to address the Lechijan army, seemingly unaware of how unpopular he was.

The foreign soldiers' own prince, a general in Rusja's imperial forces, was sheltering inside his tent having complained of a racing heart and a headache.

"I know that look," said Beata, materializing suddenly at Marynka's elbow. They stood in the trees on the edge of the makeshift camp, two silhouettes against the backdrop of the setting sun. Marynka hadn't even heard her friend sneak up on her. "It's the one you wear when you're about to do something ridiculous."

Marynka grinned.

"You left all the other soldiers alone."

"That's because they were *our* soldiers."

"Since when does that make a difference to you?"

It didn't, really. Marynka was acting more out of the itching need to do something, go somewhere, fight someone, than out of any kindness of heart or patriotic feeling. She was restless. Impatient.

She'd more than healed from her injuries all those long months ago, and she was tired of doing nothing but waiting at the house that had once belonged to Red Jaga but now belonged to her.

She reached up and adjusted the red kerchief she'd taken to tying over her curls. It too, had once belonged to Grandmother, and Marynka's pulse jumped as she pinched the embroidered cloth. It was as though some part of her still wasn't fully convinced the witch was truly gone. She still jumped at odd creaks the house made when it settled, still sometimes woke to the echo of Grandmother's scoldings and whirled when a twig snapped suddenly.

The witch's death had freed her, but she didn't think she'd ever be free of the memories. Even annoying Beata or picking through all the treasures left behind in the house by long dead princes wasn't enough to quiet her thoughts, to distract her. It wasn't enough to wear her out. Her mind wouldn't stop spinning. She was too full of the energy she would once have devoted to completing the witch's impossible tasks and obsessing over Midnight.

She still did obsess over Zosia. She'd replayed their kiss a thousand times over until her lips heated just from the memory of Zosia's mouth. She imagined Zosia in hiding as she polished the bone wreathes and the skull lanterns. She imagined her running, imagined her as she'd looked when she crossed the winter clearing. She imagined her with hearts clasped in her hands, held between her pale fingers like crisp red apples. She'd started to wonder what a prince's heart actually tasted like. Metal? Magic? Freedom?

Traipsing through the sun-drenched trees as far as the light fell before it softened to ordinary daylight, she'd thought about just how many hearts Zosia had already taken for herself. That was what she'd been doing when she first spied Rusja's prince-general and his soldiers, when she'd thought, *Well, why not?*

What was life without some kind of challenge? Marynka craved that thrill, that rush of adrenaline. She didn't know what to do with herself when there wasn't something to panic over or prepare for. "I'm going to eat his heart," she declared.

Beata groaned.

"What's the matter? Think about it, Beatka, Zosia consumed four hearts and she was fine. Her magic grew. Imagine how power-ful *I* could become if I even the score. I bet I'll finally be able to grow claws."

"Why do you even want claws?"

"You say that because you already have them. You don't understand my pain. Why are you even here, anyway? Aren't you still running errands for White Jaga?" Marynka turned to face her friend, finally catching sight of the figure hovering behind her.

She stopped breathing.

The first thing she took in was the birch branch gripped in the boy's hand, then his black embroidered vest. His black felt hat. Their edges seemed to melt into the lengthening shadows. His eyes, which were staring back at her with open awe, were dark as a winter night's sky.

Beata shifted. "He says he's—"

"Midnight," the boy piped in a lilting voice. His straight silky hair was the color of ebony, his skin a rich brown. He was long-limbed, gangly, and couldn't have been more than eleven or twelve years old. Around the same age Marynka had been when she'd become a servant. A cold chill of fear whispered through her.

"Companion and servant to Black Jaga," he continued. "Are you the witch of the Midday Forest? I wanted to ask you a question."

Marynka took an unconscious step back. A twig snapped beneath her heel. A strange pressure was building within her. If Black Jaga had laid a finger on Zosia, Marynka was going to—

No. This didn't mean anything. What did it matter if the witch had taken a new servant? It didn't mean anything bad had happened. Zosia's moon-bleached bones were most definitely *not* being used as posts to fence in the house in the Midnight Forest. There was no way that anything had happened to her. The honor of taking Zosia apart was reserved solely for Marynka. This meant nothing. Zosia had escaped. She was in hiding. She was *fine*.

If Marynka repeated the thought enough times she could force it to be true. Zosia was fine and Marynka would wake from this awful nightmare and Beata would say something annoying and then the *real* Midnight would appear and all three of them would deal with this fake impostor.

The boy opened his mouth. "The servant before me, she—"

"If you don't shut up," Marynka said, "I am going to burn you to ash where you stand."

The boy swallowed audibly, the bump in his throat bobbing up and down.

"Marynka," Beata snapped. "It's not his fault. Just listen to him."

Marynka did not want to listen. She'd stopped listening almost as soon as Beata said her name. Her body was on fire. Cinders and sparks danced through her veins. The gleeful thrill of teasing the soldiers was gone. The air shimmered with heat as the afternoon breeze started to rage.

Beata caught her forearm and gripped it hard. "*Listen*, idiot."

"Black Jaga sent him here to ask if you'd seen Zosia because he's been tasked with tracking her down."

"We're connected," the boy cut in. "We're made from the same magic so I can sense her presence even when she tries to hide it. Black Jaga promised me a gift if I could catch her. I've been searching for ages. But every time I get close, she disappears again. I managed to follow her here this time—"

"Here?" Marynka interrupted. Beata relaxed the grip she had on her forearm. The wind died down.

"I know this is the edge of the Midday Forest," the boy said breathlessly. "I ran into Morning and she told me. She said it belonged to you now. Is it really true you used to be a servant?"

Marynka didn't answer. Her eyes had strayed back to the soldiers' camp. There was some commotion among all the tents and wagons. Something had spooked the already spooked troops and the horses in their picket lines.

"Oh, oh, she wouldn't *dare*."

Deepening shadows were swallowing the faint gleam of cook fires.

"I wonder if she thinks you lured them here on purpose," said Beata. "As a kind of present. A prince-general waiting right on the doorstep of the place where you're supposed to meet. It's like you've prepared her a meal."

"That's my heart, Beatka! *I* was going to take that one."

"I didn't realize you were still competing."

"Stop enjoying this." Marynka stabbed a finger at the boy. "Look after the brat. Don't let him escape."

"I'm not a brat—"

"Wait, where are you—"

"You don't think I'm going to stand here and let her take it, do you?" The wind was already stirring back into a wild, dust-filled whirlwind. There was an equally wild grin on Marynka's face. Sparks flew from her curls. "I told you, I have to even the score. Watch me; this time I'm going to win."

Author's Note

The Midnight Girls is a work of fantasy set in a kingdom heavily inspired by the Kingdom of Poland at the end of the eighteenth century—a tumultuous time in Polish history when the lands of the Polish-Lithuanian Commonwealth were invaded and divided between Russia, Prussia, and Austria. For 123 years, Poland was erased from the maps of Europe and its people deprived of their identity, although its people never stopped fighting for freedom.

While I've included many Easter eggs and hinted at references to true events, people, and places, this story is not meant to be an accurate representation of history (though I like to think I captured a little of the spirit of the times). I took considerable creative liberties and of course, added in a whole lot of fairy-tale magic. If you would like to learn more about Polish history and culture, I recommend making use of your local library and librarians.

ACKNOWLEDGMENTS

Where do I even begin? I was told book two would be a challenge, but wow... I drafted this story in our year of 2020 in the middle of a global pandemic, during my stressful debut year, in the midst of a mental health spiral. Honestly, I'm amazed I finished it. I'm even more amazed that the plot makes sense and that soon readers will be able to meet my chaotic monster girls. All of which would not be possible without the help of so many incredible people.

First and foremost, a massive thank-you to Annie Berger and Amy Thomas (my amazing U.S. and Australian editors) and to Rena Rossner (my magical agent). Thank you for believing in me and putting up with all my missed deadlines and panicked emails. Thank you for giving me the time and advice to get this story right.

Endless thanks, too, to the wildly talented and hardworking teams at Sourcebooks Fire and Penguin Random House Australia. To fabulous copyeditors Cassie Gutman and Diane Dannenfeldt. To Nicole Hower and Charlie Bowater, for designing and illustrating the cover of my dreams!

To all the readers of *The Dark Tide*, who were kind enough

to say they wanted to read more of my work—your enthusiasm means more to me than you'll ever know.

To Anna Didenkow, for all your feedback and for catching my typos! I'm so grateful for all your excitement for this story.

To my friends and family, for your never-ending support. I love you all so much. You keep me going.

And to every reader who's made it to this page. I hope you enjoyed Marynka's and Zosia's story. Thank you for supporting sapphic villains!

About the Author

Alicia Jasinska is a fantasy writer hailing from Sydney, Australia. A library technician by day, she spends her nights writing and hanging upside down from the trapeze and aerial hoop. She is also the author of *The Dark Tide*. Visit her online at aliciajasinska.com.

FIREreads

⑤ #getbooklit

Your hub for the hottest young adult books!

Visit us online and sign up for our
newsletter at FIREreads.com

 @sourcebooksfire

sourcebooksfire

firereads.tumblr.com